I0760874

WARRIOR OF BLADE AND DUSK

THE ZHENINGHAI CHRONICLES

FOR MY OWN YE YE
AND THE WONDERFUL YEARS WE HAD TOGETHER.
THE WORLD LOST ONE OF ITS BEST MEN ON
NOVEMBER 5TH, 2022.

CHAPTER 1

KISSING ARANYA HAD definitely not been on the list of things Kai planned to do today.

His plans had involved running as far away from his family and Gebei as he could, finding a way to free Aranya from the spelled vines that bound her wrists and ankles, and then collapsing onto a bed and sleeping until the Festival of New Lights.

Of course, his comrades likely had plans to discuss *important* things like what in the seven valleys was a princess doing in his family's dungeon, who this rebel leader Fang Zedong was, and how his mother and brother had gotten entangled with him.

Delan probably wasn't finished scolding him for various things, so that was likely on the agenda, too.

But kissing Aranya? Nope. That wasn't to say he had never thought about kissing her—because he had. More times than he'd like to admit. But thinking about kissing her and planning on kissing her were two entirely separate things.

It was a knee-jerk reaction. He was standing there with Aranya, with her poor swollen and discolored hands, while she tried not to give into discouragement when the curse breaker was unable to help her. He teased her, trying to get her mind off how miserable she must be. It seemed to be working, too, when he returned from fetching her food with only a single rice cake and earned a particularly vicious glare from her.

But then he looked beyond her, across the street, and the recognition slapped him harder than a blow. Those brown eyes, the short-cropped hair she'd always worn, the perpetual downward tilt of her mouth and the line between her eyebrows.

Jie.

Jie had always wanted him to take his place with his family. When they had been together, she had pushed him, nagged him, refused to understand why he wanted nothing to do with his rich parentage, why he wanted none of the prestige. He'd tried to explain, had nearly shared everything with her once, before he discovered that she'd snitched on him to his brother Yong. That was the final straw. He cut ties with her and was desperately relieved he hadn't divulged his secrets to her in a faulty attempt to make her understand.

Jie stood across the street. Her jaw dropped at the sight of him—and then she was *smiling*. As if they were long-lost lovers finally reunited.

Kai's face must have shown something, because Aranya said, "What's wrong? *Please* don't tell me your brother is behind me."

"Oh, no, definitely not," he said quickly. But running into Jie was the next worst thing after running into Yong or Mother. Aranya's brow went taut with a question she didn't want to ask. She started to turn, and that movement was enough to send a flash of panic down his spine.

Not again. Not again.

He couldn't open Aranya up to his family's schemes and abuse again. He couldn't let them hurt her. And he refused to let Jie be the means through which Yong got his hands on Aranya for a second time.

He grabbed her shoulders, forcing her to not move, and the instant her confused and concerned gaze met his, the idea assaulted him.

One kiss. Right here, right now, in front of Jie. Maybe then Jie would leave them alone, maybe she would see that when he had said it was over, he meant it. Maybe she would finally move on and leave him alone.

Jie looked each way, checking for carts, before she stepped into the street, coming straight for him with a broad smile on her face. The words were spewing out of Kai's mouth before he could think of anything else.

"Remember that fine your grandfather accrued that you couldn't pay in Zushui?"

"How do you know about that? I didn't tell—"

"I paid it. Now—"

"You *what*?"

Jie was almost halfway across the street. "—I'm calling in my debt."

"You're—"

"Just forgive me in advance, alright?"

"Kai, what in the seven—"

"Please don't hate me," he breathed too quietly for her to hear as he pulled her into his arms and ducked his head to press his mouth to hers.

She grabbed his shirt with both of her fists, and for a second, he thought she was going to push him away. Which was definitely better than her skewering him with her talons. But if she rebuffed him, Jie wouldn't get the message.

So he caught her face in his hands and deepened the kiss.

That time in the woods that Aranya had called a kiss, when their lips had barely brushed for one second? Not a kiss. *This* was a kiss. He'd show her the difference.

I'll show you a real kiss.

Her grip on his shirt loosened, the resistance flowing out of her like water poured from a glass—so much that she stumbled, and Kai's arm shot out instinctively to catch her, his fingers looping around her knife belt to keep her steady.

His heart, which had just been hammering a frantic, erratic rhythm, now soared in the sunset stained clouds above them. *She wanted this.* The realization was intoxicating, turning him lightheaded and dizzy as he kissed her. His thoughts raced ahead, voicing things in his mind he would never dare to speak aloud. *I'd kiss you like this every day for the rest of your life if you wanted.*

A sudden fear stabbed his chest. What if he was misreading her? What if she didn't want this? What if—

He pulled back and opened his eyes. Hers stayed closed for a heartbeat longer, her lips parted, her throat bobbing as she swallowed. Then her eyes opened, and there were unshed tears glimmering on her lower lashes.

Tears? What did this mean?

Nothing could cut him to the quick like the sight of her tears. But what did they *mean*? He wanted to ask her what was wrong, if he should stop, if . . . if he should keep kissing her. His throat clogged, preventing him from getting words out.

Instead, he leaned down again, nuzzling his nose into hers. *Are you alright? Have I upset you?*

A tiny sound escaped her as she closed her eyes and lifted her lips to his. Shock turned his ears red-hot, but he wasn't about to hesitate and ruin everything. Not when his soul had just come alive. He kissed her again, gently, as one of her tears escaped and slid over his knuckles.

Oh Aranya.

If Yong even dreamed of lifting a finger against her again, Kai was going to rip him to shreds—and anyone else who meant her harm.

Jie.

The name was like an unwelcome guest showing up at the door and expecting supper. He'd forgotten all about her, even though she was the reason he was kissing Aranya. But before he had a chance to pull away, she suddenly shoved back against his chest, breaking their kiss and nearly toppling herself over.

"What was *that*?" She dashed away her tears with the side of her swollen thumb.

Oh no. She was angry. But she hadn't been angry a moment ago! She'd very clearly asked for the second kiss, and—and—

His mind scrabbled to understand what just happened, like he was falling off a cliff and clawing for any purchase on crumbling rocks. Had he misread her so grievously? He must have—which meant he couldn't let her see the way her lips had just imprinted themselves on his soul.

The only reliable shield now was a smirk. He donned one the bare instant before she looked up at him and glared.

It wasn't just anger on her face. It was hurt, embarrassment—if the color of her cheeks was any testament—and plenty of other things. She sniffled. His gut dropped straight to the earth.

Dragons blast it. He'd screwed up. Badly.

But then her bonds fell off like he'd just sliced his knife through them. Like they hadn't been uncuttable mere seconds ago. It took several more seconds for his brain to catch up with what he was seeing.

The Yanzhao Technique. A kiss to break the spell. Of course. Seven valleys. He should have kissed her ages ago! Why hadn't he thought of it?

They *had* been rather preoccupied.

"Fathers," he breathed as she rotated her wrists. They needed to get her medical attention as soon as possible to restore the function and vitality to her hands and feet. She'd probably have scars where those bonds bit into her skin.

Her head snapped up, her gaze locking on his. "*Why* did you kiss me, Shi Kai? What is wrong with you? I'm not one of your dalliances! Seven valleys, I'm your *colleague*!"

She was mad because he'd crossed a professional line? It seemed like it was something else. But now that they were done kissing, there was nothing to distract him from the frozen Jie in the street behind Aranya.

He leveled a look at Jie. A look that was probably colder than it needed to be. One that told her very clearly that when he'd broken things off two years ago with her, he'd meant it, and she'd better move on.

Jie's gaze shifted from him to Aranya as she turned to follow his gaze. Aranya's mouth fell open.

This was getting far too messy, far too quickly.

Kai snatched her elbow and dragged her toward their horses. "Come on," he growled. *Here come the questions.* It wasn't even like he could claim to have been performing the Yanzhao Technique. Both of them knew that hadn't been his intention.

"Who was that? Do you know her? Why was she—why did you—"

He didn't want to tell her. But if he didn't tell her, she would keep pestering him, and he'd drive the wedge of distrust between them even deeper than it already was. He exhaled between gritted teeth and yanked the buckle tighter on his saddle. "She and I . . ." How could he describe it? She was going to hate him. "We were involved. Back at the Academy. I didn't . . . She thought . . . I guess she thought it was serious—"

"Wait, you *courted* at the Academy?"

"I didn't court! At least, *I* didn't think it was—"

"And you just used me to get back at her? You used us *both*—"

This was going even worse than he'd imagined. "She's been insistent. Years later! I've told her *no* a thousand times and she won't listen, and she knows my family and—look, you saw my family—*Spitfire.*" He spat out the curse under his breath. "I'm sorry, Aranya. I shouldn't . . . It was all I could think of. She's gone behind my back more than once to tell my mother—"

This wasn't working. It sounded worse saying it than just staying quiet. Kai shut his mouth and focused his gaze on untethering their horses, the weight of her stare heavy on the back of his head. When he couldn't keep avoiding it, he brought his eyes to meet hers.

"At least . . . you're free now," he said, and hated himself for how lame the words sounded.

She turned away from him, facing down the street where Jie disappeared. Her hands clenched and unclenched like she was fighting the instinct to shapeshift. He ground his jaw. Why was he being so defensive? He'd kissed her without her consent; for that and that alone, he owed her an apology. But obliging her request for a second kiss? That was different, and it wasn't *his* fault she was embarrassed. Besides, he kissed her to protect her, and the result was that her bonds had fallen off.

She couldn't blame him for everything.

He crossed his arms over his chest and leveled a glare at the back of her head. Fine. If she wanted to argue, to be angry, then very well. He'd be angry back.

She whirled to face him again, lifted her chin, and said, "This isn't over, evanescer."

"Who said it was, Partial?" he said, his mouth spreading in a dark smile. "Catch this." He tossed her the lead of her horse. She snatched it out of the air. "We've got to get out of here."

CHAPTER 2

THEY WALKED DOWN the darkening street in the direction Delan had disappeared. Aranya stormed ahead, leaving Kai to trail behind her. She wouldn't look. She *wouldn't*. She would focus on finding Delan, on searching for him between donkey-hitched carts and milling people in long robes and laughing children running underfoot.

Her eyes betrayed her. She glanced back once.

Cool hazel eyes met hers, bright in the golden glow of evening. "Yes?"

Her mouth opened, something knotting tightly in her chest and warmth crawling up her neck. Then, slamming her jaw shut with a click, she whirled on her heel and marched forward. It didn't matter what he thought of their kiss. In fact, it was stupid if he thought anything at all. Even stupider if *she* thought about it.

"If it's another kiss you're wanting, you just have to ask."

Her face flamed, but she wouldn't give him the satisfaction of even a glare.

"If you asked, I'd say yes, eventually. Now, I might say no a few times, just to be *sure* you mean it when you ask. But if you keep asking, eventually I'll say yes. Especially if you throw in a little begging."

"Shi Kai," Aranya growled, stopping in the middle of the street so his horse almost bumped into hers. She looked over her shoulder at him so fast her braid swung and slapped her neck. He blinked innocently at her. She lifted one of her tingling hands in a fist and flashed a brief glimpse of her talons. "One more word, and I'll kill you."

Nearby, a chicken squawked and a few heads turned. Aranya ignored them.

Kai lifted an eyebrow. "In broad daylight? I'm afraid that's illegal, love."

That last word did strange things to her stomach. Before she could do anything embarrassing, she whirled back around and marched forward, redetermined to ignore him no matter how he goaded her.

Finding Delan didn't take long. He was easily recognizable atop his horse, despite the shadowed streets of the city. He looked even more exhausted than Aranya felt. His hair stood out in frazzled angles, his robes torn at the shoulders, and his eyes the color of weary storm clouds. The moment he saw them and her free limbs, his eyebrows shot skyward.

"How?" he gasped. "How'd you get them off?"

Heat flared in her cheeks, but her explosion of frustration immediately covered it. She pointed back at Kai. "He *kissed* me!"

Kai shrugged. "Yes, I kissed her to break them off."

"Liar! That was *not* the reason! He was trying to get back at a girl he saw whom *apparently* he made out with a bunch at the Academy—"

"That is *not* what I said," Kai snapped.

She wouldn't stop. Not even for the anger in his tone. "And he decided he was calling in some sort of debt that I didn't know he'd paid. Lights above, Kai, but you couldn't have told me? I'll pay you back—"

"You already paid it," he said matter-of-factly.

She stared, her jaw dropping open. Delan sat on his horse in shocked stillness. She found her hands fidgeting, not caring how the movement brought pain. The ground was suddenly the most compelling thing she'd ever seen. It was one matter to have this happen; it was another *entirely* to relay it all to Delan and let his staunch displeasure roll over them like the waves over Suguan's shore.

The silence stretched out. Finally, Aranya peeked a glance at Kai.

He was smirking at her.

Heat flooded her face, her neck, even as dread sank into her gut. Whatever he was about to say—

"You enjoyed it," he drawled.

That snide retort hit her like a punch to her gut. He looked away from her, his face composed nonchalance. *This* was the infamous Academy flirt. The one who used girls and dumped them on the wayside.

Aranya was a fool for ever thinking . . . She shook her head, gritting her teeth.

Delan groaned, running a square hand down his face. He sounded oddly like Qigang, their Zushui supervisor, as he muttered, "What a mess. Kai, what were you *thinking*?"

A muscle in Kai's jaw clenched. "I agree it's a mess. But her bonds are off and now we can go back to our mission. Since our relationships are merely professional, this will change nothing." He stalked forward with his horse in tow and swept his cloak behind him.

He didn't look at Aranya.

Fury mounted like the pounding of horse hooves in her chest.

Oh, this changed *everything,* but not in the way Kai was thinking. He could attempt to fluster her all he wanted, calling her *love* and whatnot. But she wasn't going to be just another girl in line for his heart, especially when he described their relationship as *merely professional.*

Delan fixed him with an icy glare. "Take care that it doesn't change anything."

Kai met his gaze evenly. Was that protectiveness flashing in Delan's face? A tiny bit of the tension in Aranya's chest eased.

"It's late; we'd better decide where we're staying tonight," Delan said.

Kai's heart hammered. He hoped his sweaty hands weren't obvious.

For a few minutes, they stood around their horses and exchanged curt, tense suggestions, the air hanging heavy over their party. It gave him time to recoup his fractured composure, to pretend he didn't notice the bubbling hurt and fury in Aranya's eyes.

Then two wielders slinked out of the shadows of an alleyway, and nearly ruined his composure all over again. He recognized the gait of one immediately.

Things had just gone from bad to worse.

A quick glance at Aranya revealed that she recognized the girl, too. Kai drew a deep breath, trying to bolster his courage as they turned to acknowledge the newcomers.

This is really, really bad.

Jie was the first to step out of the shadows, her face hard and firm. She looked down her pointed nose, one large freckle above her upper lip, with an upturned sharp chin. Before she'd ratted him out to his family, he'd found her pretty. Next to her, a male warden casually rested his hands on the hilts of the knives in his belt, adjusting his stance like a posturing peacock.

Jie didn't look at Kai or Aranya, but addressed herself to Delan. "We are here to arrest you three for disturbing the peace by causing a scene outside the curse breaker's hut."

Delan scoffed, waving a hand through the air. "It's only a misunderstanding. I apologize for the earlier ruckus, but we're wielders too and we're in a predicament—"

"You can explain yourself before a judge. If you're lucky, they'll have hearings tomorrow."

Kai wanted to groan. Why had he ever thought kissing Aranya would fix things with Jie? He should have known she would turn around and do something like this.

Now both of them hated him. Well, he hated them, too.

At Jie's statement, Aranya's eyes went wide, her hands fisting by her side. Her poor wrists looked horrid and painful, but she almost didn't seem to notice them. Delan's face hardened, his jaw flexing.

Kai willed Jie to look at him. Willed her to stop being an idiot, to stop being so driven by whatever whim of intense emotion overcame her moment by moment. But that had always been Jie—always letting emotion get in the way of *everything*. There had been a time when he wasn't sure a rational thought had ever entered her mind.

He knew better now. She was half psychopath.

He'd been a fool to think he could use her to convince his family of his wayward nature. He'd been a fool to ever think his father would believe the reputation he'd created for himself at the Academy was a proper reflection of his character. He would have been better off ignoring girls like Yong had.

He'd been a fool then, and he was a fool now.

"We're on business from the capital," Delan tried again, gruffer this time. "These two here are wardens from Zushui. You ought not delay us."

Kai's gut sank into his boots. *Fathers.*

"Both from Zushui?" Jie said, blinking her eyes and letting them rove in a long assessment over Aranya. They flicked briefly to Kai, and though they didn't look directly into his, the strength of her attention on him was palpable.

Kai wished he dared step forward in front of Aranya, to take away that malicious gaze from her. But such an action would only make things worse. Besides, Aranya was busy meeting Jie's stare with her own.

After a second, Aranya grinned and stepped forward, putting out a hand. "Hi! I'm Sun Aranya. This is Lian Delan, and Shi Kai."

He barely kept himself from shaking his head at how obviously out of place her chipper greeting was. Unlike most people, she faced her enemies with bright smiles. *Usually*. An image flashed in his mind—of a knife flicking beneath her eye, the wicked grin of his older brother dancing behind her, the panic in her face. His stomach twisted, and he blinked it away.

Jie eyed Aranya's proffered hand with obvious disdain. The male warden's eyes darted between them, as though waiting for an explosion to happen. Surely, he realized something of what his comrade was.

Jie sniffed and stepped aside, gesturing down the road. "Come with us, *wardens* of Zushui, and Lian Delan, from the capital. Let us clear up this misunderstanding at the wardpost."

"You may bring your horses," the other warden said.

Kai and Delan shared a look of thick annoyance over Aranya's head. Hopefully that concealed the terror flooding his veins. With a sigh that rattled through his body, he made to follow.

"What are you doing?" Aranya hissed, grabbing his arm.

He jerked free from her touch, just in time, before Jie turned a suspicious eye toward them. Aranya scratched her temple, then gave a quick nod as realization hit. Since the kiss had backfired, more touching would only make things worse.

She didn't speak again, though the question filled her eyes: *Why?*

Before Delan could answer and claim her attention, Kai muttered, "This is their jurisdiction."

"I *know* that," she growled back, her and Delan falling into step beside him with their horses. "I know they have a right to take us in, but why aren't we protesting more? We're on a—"

Kai silenced her with a sudden, frantic look. His attention darted forward to Jie. She hadn't turned. *"Feral,"* he mouthed to Aranya and Delan.

Both of them looked alarmed, realizing that she could probably hear every word they spoke. The last thing they needed was Jie knowing they were on a Secret Services mission. Not only would it compromise their secrecy having a low-level person like her know, but she could relay that information on to his family.

Jie would do anything to get him to comply with his family's wishes. She wanted him to take his *"rightful place"* at his brother's side because that would have afforded Kai's wife a higher position in society. No matter that Jie was never, ever, *ever* going to be that; she seemed to believe it remained her destined fate.

The look Delan gave the back of Jie's head told Kai he had some *very* choice words for her supervisor. But then Delan glanced at Kai, clearly having just made the connection. His eyes widened, and he pointed subtly between Kai and Jie, raising his eyebrows in question.

If only Kai hadn't had to tell them Jie was feral, he might have gotten away without Delan realizing who this girl was.

Too late. Delan's glare was like icicles, silently demanding why he'd dragged this drama into their mission. As if it was Kai's fault or choice that they'd run into her. *Her, of all people.* As if it was his fault she was the vengeful girl she was. As if it was his fault his family was . . . his family.

The wardpost loomed before them, bigger than Zushui Wardpost, with lanterns lit along the outside against the advancing evening. Kai tried to shove away the twisting of his stomach. If he couldn't get Jie to be silent, his family would find out exactly where he had fled this time.

Vanishing again would be so much more difficult.

CHAPTER 3

HER HORSE IN tow, Aranya trudged behind the girl—Kai's former *something*—and tried not to think about how much her wrists and ankles still hurt, how exhausted she was, and how much she only wanted to flop in a comfortable bed and *rest*. Instead, she eyed the colorful robes of a wealthy lord as he stepped out of his litter and entered what seemed to be an exclusive drinking establishment.

Anything to distract her from how furious she was at Kai. Had it been only an hour or two ago that she'd been asleep against his chest while they shared a saddle?

She was so stupid.

Instead of a break after a *very* long day, this girl and her fellow warden were talking of incarcerating them because Delan yelled outside the curse breaker's house. Except . . . Aranya knew better. It was because of Kai and their history. It was plain in the girl's eyes whenever she looked at Aranya, whenever she *didn't* look at Kai.

Unconsciously, for probably the twelfth time in the last hour, she swiped her arm across her lips. As if to wipe away the memory of that kiss. It was the last thing she wanted to think about.

She would pretend it hadn't happened.

The girl and the other warden herded the three of them up the wardpost steps but not through the main entrance where the supervisor would be waiting and where warm light spilled out onto the wooden slats of the porch. They started to lead them away—toward the barred incarceration unit between the warden's side of the complex and the judiciary side.

Were they truly intending to lock an evanescer in a cell?

Delan planted his feet firmly and growled, "We must speak with the supervisor."

"Not tonight, I'm afraid," the girl said without turning her head. "Tomorrow morning, perhaps. We can request an audience for you if you'd like."

At this, she *did* twist enough to look back at them. Her eyes landed not on Delan, nor on Kai, but on Aranya. Her gaze pierced hard, loaded with an emotion that Aranya couldn't distinguish. She could tell, however, that this girl had no intention whatsoever of telling their supervisor.

"Warden," Delan said, his voice full of warning. "You do not want to delay us."

"If there has been a misunderstanding, it will be cleared up before the courts. Like everything else."

Kai's face went quite pale. He blinked, catching Aranya's look. Just as quickly, his gaze darted away, over her head.

Delan crossed his arms over his chest. "I'm afraid this arrangement isn't going to work. I have official summons from Suguan that I can show your supervisor. We can have this cleared up in but a few minutes—"

"Like I said, you can explain to the courts."

So Kai had been involved with an idiot. Aranya wasn't sure if this made her feel better or worse about him kissing her.

Probably worse.

Delan's gaze snapped to Kai's, and he jerked his head backward. Silently telling him to evanesce away to the supervisor's office. Aranya expected him to immediately vanish and save them from this mess. Instead, he stayed where he was, face going even paler. Delan shot him a look, gesturing with his hands to hurry.

Kai's eyes darted to the girl leading them. *He is afraid of her.* He was not simply avoiding awkwardness because of their history. No, Shi Kai, for whatever reason, was actually scared of her. Like she held some power over him. Memory of the fragments he'd sputtered after their kiss floated through her mind. He'd said something about his family. She'd been too flustered to listen to what he was saying, but now pieces came back, making her blood run cold.

Were they on the verge of *another* confrontation with Yong and Lady Shi? Oh fathers, Aranya didn't think she could do that again for a while. Or ever.

Kai drew a deep breath, and with a final glance ahead at the girl, vanished.

The moment he did, both the girl and her fellow warden whirled. Delan put his hands up, arching one eyebrow. "You put us in an awkward position. What could you expect? Even you should know that there's no containing an evanescer."

Aranya winced at the insult.

The girl lifted her chin. Her comrade straightening his shoulders and his hands slid conspicuously to the weapons on his belt.

"This is how things are going to be, then?" the girl growled.

Delan shrugged. "I'm afraid so."

A new light entered the girl's eye, nearly manic and full of hatred. They landed on Aranya. "I am going to murder that Shi Kai."

At least they could agree there.

"Murder is illegal, I'm afraid," said Delan, unperturbed.

Aranya's hand drifted to the knife at her belt. She could shift, of course, but they didn't know she was a shifter. It was probably better to wait before revealing that. She widened her stance, mirroring the two wardens' aggressive postures.

Delan alone remained cool, one leg crossed over the other. His arms were folded across his chest. Only his face, however, was furious.

"Forward," the girl barked, jerking her head.

Delan sniffed. "No."

Aranya braced herself, readying for a fight. Waiting for the moment Kai would bring the supervisor out to rescue them. The girl seemed to realize they only had moments. She drew her knife and leapt at Aranya.

"Come. *Now*," she snarled.

Aranya whipped out her own knife in time to deflect the blow. She almost hadn't been quick enough; she wasn't expecting the girl to actually try to injure her. While Aranya forced her knife up, the girl withdrew a second in her other hand and stabbed toward her exposed stomach.

Aranya let out a cry, shifting her left hand just soon enough to swipe the second blow aside. Fury roared in her blood, driving her knee up to hit the girl sharply in the thigh. Thankfully, though the girl was feral, her abilities did not include unnatural strength. She was still strong, but so was Aranya.

In her periphery, the second warden attacked Delan. She wondered at their idiocy. Did they want to be dismissed? Or would feigning innocence be enough to get them free without punishment?

The girl surprised Aranya with a quick maneuver, knocking the knife out of her hand. In the process, she hit her raw wrist hard. Aranya cried out at the sudden pain, but she swallowed it with a growl, shifting her other hand and leaping to catch the girl's wrists. She was quick to evade one of Aranya's snatching hands, but Aranya's adrenaline surged, nearly overcoming her rational thought. She snarled like a wildcat, jumping sidelong and using her grip on the girl's one wrist to wheel her around and slam her into the wardpost wall. The girl landed hard, barely catching herself with a fist around the hilt of her knife before she crashed her nose into stone.

Aranya twisted the girl's arm behind her, avoiding the knifepoint. She pinned her other wrist to the wall, leaning her weight against the girl. She gasped when the girl tried to twist the knife she gripped behind her to plunge it into her stomach, but with a burst of strength that made sweat break out on her forehead, she forced the girl's wrist to twist and let go of the knife. It clattered to the ground.

They stood there, panting for air, as the sound of hurrying footsteps echoed around them. The girl sagged in Aranya's restraining grip, but Aranya didn't fall for the girl's trick. She tightened her hold, pressing her weight more firmly against her.

Only then did she look around.

Delan had pinned the other warden beneath him on the ground, holding him at knifepoint beside one of the porch's supporting pillars. More wardens ran toward them, led by Kai and another man, one with a topknot and a receding hairline, who must be the supervisor. Kai's eyes rounded when he saw them, his gaze flicking from where Aranya had his former darling love pinned against the wall to her sidekick incapacitated by Delan.

The supervisor barked angrily, "What is happening?"

Carefully, so she wasn't stabbed, Aranya eased away from the girl and backed up a few steps. She kept a wary eye on her, but at Kai's quick look, she obliged his unspoken request and shifted her talons away.

"Ah, what a relief," Delan growled, picking himself up off the ground and offering a hand to the warden. "We need to speak with you, supervisor. Away from these incompetent lackeys."

Kai visibly stiffened, and Aranya tensed at the insult.

But the supervisor pursed his lips and nodded tensely. "I shall speak to them later. Go back to west patrol, you two."

"It was a misunderstanding!" the girl cried, picking up her knives. "They were disturbing the peace, and I wasn't sure if I could believe their story, so we thought it would be best to bring them in, and then they attacked us—"

"You are dismissed," the supervisor barked, waving his hand. His long sleeves cast shadows on the wall behind them. "We will discuss this later."

"May I . . ." Kai stopped himself, swallowing. He tried again. "May I speak to her first, good sir?"

"About what? If you're going to cause another altercation—"

"No, sir," Kai hastened to say. "She was a friend of mine from the Academy. It's a personal matter."

The girl finally looked at him fully, staring unabashedly. Was that hope Aranya saw in her eyes? Or merely gladness for the acknowledgement?

"If she will speak to you, very well. But I will not wait around."

"Of course not," Delan said, taking Aranya's elbow and guiding her toward the supervisor. "We will discuss what happened with you and request safe passage while we're in your city."

Aranya didn't look back at the dissipating wardens, or at Kai, and followed mutely after the supervisor into the wardpost. The door shut behind them.

"What is this that you have done, misleading my good wardens—which you call my incompetent lackeys—and causing multiple scenes?" the supervisor asked sourly, positioning himself on his mat behind his desk.

Despite how these walls weren't whitewashed like in Zushui, but instead a natural wood, buffed and stained to shine, it was eerily close to standing before Qigang and defending herself with silent Kai. Aranya tensed up. Thankfully, Delan took the lead and explained the situation, from her getting kidnapped and bound with magical vines, how they were trying to get them off, to their unfruitful visit to the curse breaker's hut.

"She's not bound anymore," the supervisor observed with lowered eyebrows. The flickering candlelight made his eye sockets seem unusually deep and his brow especially prominent.

Aranya's face heated. She lowered her gaze slightly, wishing she could close her ears too when Delan said, "Well, the young man who retrieved you thought to try a different approach and used the Yanzhao Technique to break the bonds. It worked."

At this, the supervisor snorted. "Never underestimate the power of the Yanzhao Technique, I always say."

Delan chuckled. Her cheeks burned. He continued the tale, explaining the confusion with the wardens. Aranya expected him to berate the wardens' performance, call them incompetent lackeys again, but instead he blamed it on a misunderstanding.

He was trying to not offend the supervisor a second time, she realized.

Faster than she anticipated, the supervisor waved his hand. "I apologize for this misunderstanding. My wardens meant well; I assure you. Sometimes the newer ones can be a little overenthusiastic, which I will address with them. You may be on your way. Fathers bless your journey."

Delan and Aranya bowed before hastening to slip out of his office. Once outside again, surrounded by the darkness and coolness of late evening, voices carried from nearby. Charged, angry, somewhat hushed, but increasing in volume. Two shadows stood near the edge of the wardpost. Kai and the girl.

Aranya sighed, rolling her eyes.

"That boy needs a lesson on keeping his professional and personal lives separate," Delan muttered.

Aranya said nothing.

One voice rose to a shrilling peak, contrasting the opposing low tones. A sharp slap punctuated the exchange. Aranya jumped at the sound, at the sudden silence that followed. Delan went quiet, not moving a muscle. The girl's following words were clear in the night.

"I hate you."

CHAPTER 4

They tromped in silence to an inn, their horses in tow. Aranya and Delan took the front, Kai trailing behind them. The girl had run off, leaving him standing in the darkness. When he'd emerged from the shadows a minute later, he grabbed his horse's reins and started walking. He didn't look at either of them.

"I'm going to talk to him." said Delan.

"Not tonight," Aranya said quickly. "He seems pretty down already." Why was she defending him? She was still mad. It served him right to take a verbal thrashing from Delan after what he'd done.

"He's down because of this mess he's created. More reason to discuss these things while they're fresh. I don't like having conversations hanging over our heads."

"What about tomorrow morning?" she said, and immediately hated herself again for how quickly the defenses leapt to her lips.

"Kai is not a sniveling little boy to be coddled. He's a grown man and can take it. If he can't, then perhaps he shouldn't be here."

Aranya bit her lip. How long had she been wishing for a supervisor to take her side against Kai? She didn't feel as triumphant as she expected, nor did it satisfy her fury. Not when she glanced back and saw the dejected stoop of his shoulders.

Did he still have feelings for that girl? She didn't think so; the sudden kiss and the fear seemed to indicate he didn't love her anymore. Yet, if not, what had they been talking about? She had the odd inclination to slow her pace, match it to Kai's, and ask him what was going on. Maybe he'd want to talk about it.

As soon as she had the thought, she shook her head. *Unlikely.*

Kai loved his secrets.

The inn was busy after dark, but even though it was still full of the roughened drinking crowd, it was tamer than the first inn they'd stayed at. Delan marched up to the counter, Aranya at his heels—Kai had taken the horses for stabling—and said with a big sigh, "Two rooms, please."

"Welcome! Two rooms, yes. Let me pull your keys for you."

Aranya managed to withhold her gasp of relief that they would not have to repeat the last time, except this time with three people crammed into one room instead of two. Delan completed the transaction and ordered two steaming bowls of meaty stew and rice with a few side dishes.

"What about Kai?" she asked.

"He can get his own."

Kai entered the inn just as she and Delan were settling down at one of the low tables in the back of the inn. Aranya winced as she knelt on the mat, her whole body protesting with the movement. Especially her ankles, which didn't burn as bad as her wrists, but still hurt nonetheless.

She waved Kai over and held up her bowl. "You can order one," she told him, taking a sip.

He turned to Delan and held out his hand. "Key. I'm going straight up."

Delan regarded him through lowered brows. Kai met his gaze steadily. The older man sighed, pulling one key out of his robes. "This one is yours and mine." He pulled the second key out and slid it across the table to Aranya. "This one is yours."

Kai accepted the key and turned to leave, but Delan caught his wrist. "Don't go to sleep immediately; we'll be speaking once I finish supper."

A muscle jerked in Kai's jaw, but he nodded and left. Once he was gone, Delan pulled a few coppers off his cord and slid them across the table to Aranya.

"Get yourself some salve for your wrists if there isn't enough in the saddlebags."

"I'm pretty sure we have enough," Aranya said, pushing them back.

"Keep them anyway. Separate from your personal funds, of course. But you ought to have some of your own. In case we're separated again."

She met Delan's eye, nearly cocking her head. Did he . . . trust her? Respect her as a comrade? Was this him proving himself protective of her? Or did he simply doubt her ability to avoid getting kidnapped again?

She accepted the coins and slid them onto her cord. Then, quickly, she slurped up the rest of her stew and picked the key off the table. "I'll head upstairs, too. Goodnight." There were still the saddlebags to rifle through for some salve and bandages, but she wanted to deposit her satchel in her room first.

The hallway was darkened, and the loudness of the downstairs lobby dimmed to a background buzz. Despite the dark, she could not miss the shadow outside one room. The quietness only emphasized the key jiggling in the lock.

"Forget how to use a key?" Aranya said.

Kai looked up, blinked, and yanked the key out of the lock. "I think they gave us the wrong key."

His hands shook. Her eyes flitted back up to his face. She forced a small smile onto her own. "I've never known a locked door to keep Shi Kai out."

Pretend the kiss never happened.

He glared at her, holding out his hand. "Give me your key. Maybe he got the rooms mixed up."

When she obliged, he stuck that key in the lock and it immediately turned. The door swung open into an even darker room, revealing that the innkeeper hadn't even bothered to leave embers glowing in the hearth or light a single candle.

"The first rule of evanescing," Kai muttered, "is always knowing where you're going and what's waiting for you there."

"I suppose it's not your habit, then, to evanesce into random rooms? Unless they're mine, of course."

She expected him to ignore her and keep pouting. Instead, a lopsided grin split his face, white teeth flashing in the darkness as he moved to the next door and tried his key. It worked. "It wouldn't be a random room if I knew you were in it."

She cocked her head, not sure if this was some sort of veiled compliment. Instead of puzzling that out, her curiosity got the better of her. Though Kai's grin was smooth, it couldn't hide everything. She blurted, "What was that girl's name?"

His head lifted, his back tensing as his hand froze on the doorknob. "I prefer not to talk about her."

"What is her name?"

"Jie." He swung open Aranya's door and went back to his.

"Why were you so . . ." Did she dare say it? "Why were you so scared of her?"

He flinched, halting in the doorway of his and Delan's room. It was too dark to tell for certain, but it looked like he chewed the inside of his cheek. Then he turned, leaned his back against the doorframe, and crossed his arms over his chest. He hid his shaking hands in the folds of his robes.

"I'll tell you if you tell me what happened to your family," he said.

"My family?" Aranya repeated, blinking. "What about them?"

"Why is it just you and your grandfather? Where are your parents? Siblings? Aunts, uncles, cousins?"

For a strange reason, she found herself flushing. It took her a moment to gather a coherent response. "Why do you want to know?" she managed, eventually.

"Why do you care about that girl?"

"Because you kissed me to spite her."

So much for pretending that it never happened. In the space between their words, jeering laughter floated up from the floor below them, wrapping around them and then vanishing into the darkness.

"It was not for spite," he said, so quietly she almost missed it.

"Not for spite? Then why?"

She felt his glare more than she saw it. "If you won't tell me about your family, then I won't tell you about Jie."

"Why do you care about my family?"

Kai pushed off the doorframe and stepped into his room. "This conversation," he said, already closing the door, "is going in circles. Goodnight, Partial."

He shut it in her face.

She stared for several seconds at the closed door. Then, after releasing a huff, she made her way to her own room, dumped her satchel on the floor, and set about lighting a small fire with the provided wood and tinder. While she was working, more footsteps stomped up the stairs and down the hallway. *Delan*. The door next to hers opened and shut.

Voices.

Aranya paused her work as Delan's irate tone drifted through the thin walls. The conversation started too quiet for her to hear, but it quickly grew loud enough that she could make out some words.

"What were you *thinking*?"

A muffled response.

"There is a code of conduct for comrades of the opposite gender that you've blatantly disregarded. As our partner, Aranya deserves your respect. And for that matter, that other girl deserves your respect, too. You could have landed us in jail, boy!"

A louder, but still muffled, response.

"This *does* have to do with her! She's not a pretty girl to flirt with at the Academy!"

This time, Kai's response was clear. "I wasn't flirting with her!"

"Kissing isn't flirting?"

"That wasn't *why* I kissed her—seven valleys!"

Kai sounded mad. Madder than she'd nearly ever seen him. She certainly hadn't ever heard him talk back to Qigang.

"Professional and personal relationships stay *separate*, boy. Never court someone you work with. They taught you that at the Academy, right? Or have they gone lax on that, too?"

Silence.

When Delan began speaking again, his voice was lower and harder to distinguish. She could only catch snatches of it. ". . . fun to tease; I tease her, too. But you're a handsome young man . . . extra careful . . . your actions are *clearly* only . . . This mission is turning out to be far more dangerous than any of us . . . I need you and her to both . . . heads screwed on straight to your shoulders . . . done with this mission and back at Zushui, you can have all the . . . but not here, while we're trying to prevent someone from *conquering* our *people*.."

Whatever Kai said in response was not discernable, but it was obviously exasperated. Aranya didn't blame him, even as she blushed furiously that *this* was what Delan was berating him for. Did he think her so stupid as to be won over by flirting and a single kiss?

Perhaps he didn't respect her as much as she'd earlier thought.

Did he also truly think that Kai would ever think of her that way? She might have believed it for a split second when he kissed her, but definitely not anymore. Whatever Yong had been talking about regarding Kai's feelings had been nonsense. She had seen the look on Kai's face when they'd pulled away from their kiss. That hard coldness. She'd heard his taunts, of making her beg for another kiss.

In Kai's mind, she was just another girl to be toyed with.

The voices grew more muffled. She waited, her hand still gripping the tinderbox, but there was no more to hear. She finished up lighting the fire, glad to finally have something to blame for the warmth of her cheeks.

Then she stood up, drew her cloak around her shoulders, and swept downstairs to find the salve for her wrists.

CHAPTER 5

KAI TRIED NOT to growl himself to sleep, what with Delan being so near and so incredibly *nosy.* He lay on the dragon-eaten floor because Delan had pulled rank for the bed.

Despite how frustrated he was, it paled in comparison to his relief. It was hesitant, uncertain relief. It was relief mingled with humiliation. But it was still relief, like water through his sore limbs.

His face stung. Not truly, but the memory of that slap would always make him feel less of a man. He wasn't going to pretend he'd treated Jie well, but he could say for certain that she had treated him *worse.* Far worse. At least for now, she wouldn't tell his family where he was. Not just yet. Her delay might be all he needed to finish this mission and submit a request for a transfer. If things went well here, he could have a wider range of options for where he would go next.

Perhaps he would even try to find an open position in the Secret Services. It was risky, but it was probably the last place his family would think to look for him. It was too obvious, too close to home, too good a fit for his magic.

Out of nowhere, an image flashed before his mind.

Aranya's eyes fluttering closed, her lips parted and, for a minute there, very willing. The way she'd leaned into him, tilting her head back. It didn't matter that her face was a mottled collection of bruises and scrapes.

He dragged a hand down over his own face, pulling his skin and lips into a frown, and gnawed on the inside of his cheek, his anxiety rising like an unquenchable storm. If Jie broke her word to him, it wouldn't just be Kai who paid the price.

Aranya would pay it, too.

His fists clenched around the thin blanket atop him. He nearly groaned. This disaster just kept snowballing, and even if he hadn't kissed Aranya, it still would have been a disaster. Perhaps just a slightly smaller disaster.

Delan shifted in the bed, making Kai's ears perk up, and he glanced around in the darkness. Delan gave a few sniffs, grunted, and settled back to sleep. Kai tilted his head to one side, propping himself up on his elbow. Just as he expected, light footsteps sounded close outside their door. Aranya was leaving her room.

Her footsteps were soft, getting quieter the further down the hallway she got.

Kai waited, his breath held, for the sound to disappear completely, and for Delan's snores to resume. It didn't take long, to his relief. Slowly, without making a sound, he got to his feet, caught up his tunic—debated for a wicked moment going without—and shot another look to make sure Delan was still sound asleep.

Just when he was about to evanesce, he paused, tunic in hand. Was this a good idea? Or was he being an idiot? He *was* losing his head, just as Delan had warned. It was stupid, dumb, and so utterly enthralling.

He never should have kissed Aranya. Nothing in his mind made sense anymore.

He evanesced out of the room, into the hallway, snarling under his breath, "This is a dragon-flaming basket of *garbage*."

He had to be careful. Treacherous, gaping chasms awaiting him on either side of the line he walked. If he stumbled only barely, he would plunge headlong into disaster. Him, Aranya, and Delan together. He must be careful, or his family would destroy everything they hadn't destroyed already.

He marched toward the stairs, anyway.

Aranya eventually located the salve in Kai's saddlebags after what felt like half an hour of muttering, "Where in the seven valleys is that phoenix-scorched thing?" but was probably only a few minutes. It was too dark in the stables to apply it, so she took the container to the door, where a pair of lanterns poured light inside to illuminate her work, and sat on a half-eaten hay bale.

When she unstoppered it, a sharp medicinal smell assaulted her nostrils. The familiar scent immediately took her back to being a small child, seated on the table in their old Suguan tenement, sniffling over a scraped knee. She remembered the crinkles around his eyes as Ye Ye smiled gently at her, told her in a voice much stronger than the one he possessed now, "Deep breath, little sunflower. Look how brave you're being!"

She remembered the way the evening light cast through the lattice windows, turning the whole room orange, the way it caught on his graying hair. It was always hard to remember what he looked like years ago, but she distinctly remembered a time when his hair wasn't completely white. A time when he'd been the one taking care of her, not the other way around.

Pinching her lips together too tightly, she swiped a dollop of the cool, smooth ointment. The first press of it to her raw wrists dragged a hiss from her mouth.

"Let me do it."

Aranya leapt up, wheeling back her arm to throw the salve at the intruder. She stopped as the voice registered in her mind. "Seven valleys, Kai!"

She saw a pair of upturned hands first, as though in surrender. Then Kai emerged from the shadows of the stables and gestured to the salve, a slight smirk playing on his lips.

"It's easier if someone else does it," he said, holding out a hand for the container.

She immediately bristled, sitting back down even though her muscles tensed for flight. "Does Delan know you're here?" The moment the question was past her lips, she wanted to take it back. Of course Delan didn't know.

Kai only raised an eyebrow.

"You're devious," she said.

He gave her a lopsided grin and then, without another word, evanesced to her side, snatched the salve out of her grip, and sat next to her. "If we hurry, I might even be able to bandage them for you before Delan realizes I've gone."

She frowned, biting her lip, unsure whether she should protest further. "You should be sleeping."

"Can't."

"So you're just going to keep evanescing and making your insomnia worse?"

He smirked at her words, even though he didn't look up. His gaze was focused downward as he gently took her left hand and swiped more of the salve with two fingers. "Ready? Three, two, one—"

Aranya sucked a breath in through her teeth, gripping the prickly straw with her other hand. "It stings."

"I know."

She grimaced as he began carefully rubbing it in. Her fingers curled at the pain. She glared at the top of his downward tilting head. To what could she attribute this sudden shift in behavior? The Kai she'd known up until now would have flung the salve in her face and told her to deal with the application on her own. He probably would have even called her a dragon runt for how she reacted to the pain. Was this his way of apologizing for earlier?

It wasn't until he reached for her other hand that a memory resurfaced.

She had just stomped through the forest underbrush to a clearing where a girl was mounted up on a horse, hands bound and eyes teary. The girl had stared as Kai gently consoled her, pressing his hand comfortingly to her knee.

He held Aranya's hand so carefully now, mumbling soft reassurances whenever she flinched.

"Almost done," he said.

The realization was like a slap in the face. He was treating her like he had treated Lord Meng's daughter, the kidnapped girl they'd rescued in Zushui—like some damsel in distress to be wooed and added to his collection of admirers.

She yanked her wrist back, snatched the salve out of his hand, and stood. "Thank you," she said curtly. "I'll finish the rest."

Kai stood too, confusion flashing across his face. "What's wrong, Aranya?"

Not Partial.

She marched back to him, glaring up at his bewilderment and not caring that she barely reached his shoulder. "I'm not Jie, Shi Kai."

"I never—"

"I've *seen* how you behave around girls, but you've always treated me differently. Until now. One kiss, and suddenly you're pulling the charm out of your pocket like I'm another one of your Academy dalliances!"

His brow lowered, his eyes darkening even as his mouth curved up in an unamused smile. He tilted his head closer to hers, modulating his tone deeper. "Flattering ourselves, are we, Partial?"

There it was. She flashed a grin, disregarding the curling doubt in her stomach. Perhaps she had jumped to conclusions—perhaps he didn't think of her that way, but she couldn't back down now. Especially not if she was *right*.

"See how quickly this dissolves?" she said slowly. "One minute, you're crooning over my injuries, and the next you're insulting me. I've seen how you manipulate situations to get what you want, how you portray the version of yourself that people want to see. I'm not claiming to be the smartest person ever, but I can tell when you're giving me a load of false kindness."

He tilted his chin upward, his eyes narrowing with each accusation. She met his glare evenly, challenging him with every breath puffing out of her nostrils.

His hand slid up to cup the back of her head. She stiffened, inhaling sharply.

"False kindness?" he said, eyes flashing as his gaze roved over her face. His thumb swept across the apple of her cheek. "Have you not considered that perhaps I care about you? And not like one of my so-called *Academy dalliances*?"

Her lips burned; the memory of their earlier kiss seared there forever. But though his face was so close to hers, close enough that she could tiptoe and press her lips to his, and even though her eyes wanted to flutter shut, she swallowed and fought to clear her mind.

"Does it matter?" she growled. "Does it matter when I cannot trust anything you do or say? Proclaim your undying love for me, Shi Kai, but I will not be moved. Not when I've seen your patterns of behavior." She abandoned her smile entirely, reaching up to place one hand on his chest—a threat, as she let her claws lengthen just slightly. Just enough for him to see them, to feel them if she pressed. "Take your hand off my face. I'm not about to be another girl you string along for fun. You may think it's fine to steal kisses whenever you like, but it's not fine by me."

"Proclaim my undying love!" Kai scoffed, anger and other things smoldering in his eyes. "I didn't have to pay that fine your grandfather had accrued with the landlord in Zushui. You think I did that because I hate you and just want to take advantage of you?"

"You didn't exactly give me a chance to be grateful! Will you now hold this over my head? Keep reminding me how good you are because you, the rich boy in town, decided to have mercy on a poor soul like me? I *am* grateful, Kai—" She stopped, her voice breaking only slightly. "I don't know what I would have done. But you've gone and taken a good deed and made it ugly! Instead of being thankful, I'm . . . I'm furious!"

And so very confused.

He broke their gaze, his jaw working as he stared toward the inn.

She wasn't done. Not until he fully understood how serious she was. "I'm your comrade, not a girl to be wooed. And if you ever try to kiss me again without my permission, don't think I won't take steps to protect myself." She should have stopped there. Should have left her threat unspoken, but suddenly she was voicing the one thing she knew without a doubt would elicit a strong reaction from him. "Your brother wanted the name of Zushui—"

He vanished so quickly she couldn't brace herself as he reappeared behind her and pinned her hard face first against the coarse wood of the stables. She gasped, his full weight pressing against her back. She immediately shifted her hands and tried to angle them for attack.

The cold, cruel tip of a knife pressed against her neck.

Aranya stilled.

Her blood went cold for only an instant, then it burst into a boiling rage. How dare he? How *dare* he! Strong reaction, indeed.

"Since we are apparently threatening one another," Kai said smoothly, his mouth just above her ear. His voice took on an edge she'd never heard, harsh and potent. "You will *never* contact any member of my family, for any reason, under any circumstance, and you *certainly* will not use them as blackmail over me. After what they did to you, I didn't think I'd have to say this, but here we are. Do I make myself clear, love?"

She growled low in her throat.

He pressed into her harder, the blade tickling that place just below her jaw where her pulse throbbed. "That wasn't an answer."

"You wouldn't hurt me," she snarled.

"Wouldn't I?"

"It's illegal."

He snorted, as if that was not the answer he expected. Then he whispered wickedly, "I have quite extensive experience getting away with doing things I shouldn't."

She struggled, trying to elbow him in the ribs, but he held her fast. He had one of her hands pinned against the wall, the other he gripped tightly.

He didn't touch her chafed wrists.

"I'm proposing a mutually beneficial agreement," Kai said, not able to see how her realization sent a feral smile spreading across her face. "You will avoid my family at all costs, and I won't kiss you." He paused, then added devilishly, "Unless you want me to, in which case we can renegotiate the terms of our agreement."

"Qilin-spawn!"

"Agree?" He pressed the knife harder into her skin, but not enough to make her bleed. For all his posturing, he wouldn't hurt her.

She growled again, but let her body go limp. "Fine. Agreed."

The pressure against her vanished. She whirled, yanking up her claws by instinct.

But Kai was gone.

CHAPTER 6

"THIS MAP THAT you saw in Gebei," said Delan over breakfast the next morning. "Tell me more about it."

They'd risen early and found themselves the first to be seated on colored mats, with bowls of congee in front of them. Candles flickered, illuminating the quiet lobby before the light of dawn streamed through the windows.

Aranya had just taken a rather large mouthful. She set down her chopsticks, pressed the back of her hand to her mouth, and swallowed swiftly. Then she shoved aside her bowl, laying her palms flat on the table. "This is the ocean," she said, gesturing to the air off the edge of the table. "This is Suguan." She poked her finger on the table's lip. Then she circled the bottom half of the table. "This is Zheninghai. And this upper half of the table is Butagin."

Delan nodded, watching carefully. Kai, on the other hand, seemed much more interested in the contents of his bowl than her words, and she wasn't sure if he was tired or purposefully ignoring her after last night.

"This is Shaanet." Another poke at the table where the city would be roughly on her imaginary map. She listed several more cities she'd seen on the map, designating each one. "There were routes from each of these cities, and several more that I can't remember, and they all converged *here* at Gebei." Her finger pressed into the wood, she dared a glance up at Kai to find his attention firmly fixed on his breakfast. Her jaw clenched. "Then it went from Gebei up to Khaiduk, which apparently is a fortress on Butagin's side of the border."

"You also saw the eldest princess, Princess Meiling, held captive at the Shi residence," said Delan.

"Escorted by three brigands that I recognized," said Aranya. "One of them was the illusionist Kai and I fought on the way to Suguan. Yong said something about them staying too long in Shaanet, and one of them was a fire-wielder. I can't help but wonder if it was the same fire-wielder that destroyed the body we found outside of Shaanet while we were investigating Zuan Wan's disappearance."

"It's possible," said Delan, ignoring the way Kai set to eating more vigorously, as if the taste of food could block out the sound of his brother's name. "There is a strong likelihood, based on this information, that the princess is being taken to the fortress."

"To Fang Zedong," said Aranya.

Delan dropped his chopsticks into his bowl and rubbed the bridge of his nose, letting out a great sigh. "I'd really hoped this wouldn't involve him."

"Who is he?" she pressed. "I know he defected from the Academy many years ago, that he's trying to muster Butagin troops, right?"

"We don't know much. He was apparently good friends with the queen while they were at the Academy. I believe I heard a rumor of a conflict he had with His Imperial Majesty, who was the Crown Prince at the time. At some point, he defected. No one knew where he went until rumors and intelligence were leaked from Butagin that he'd become an influence there and was mustering the strength to broach an attack on the empire."

"Seems foolhardy to me," said Aranya. "An Academy drop-out trying to take over the largest empire in the world."

Delan's eyes snapped to hers, arresting her with sudden force. "Thinking like that will get yourself killed and others with you. Never underestimate your enemies."

He was right, she knew, but that didn't stop the bolt of embarrassment to her stomach. She lowered her gaze and nodded, dragging her bowl back in front of her and continuing to eat. Her congee was suddenly tasteless and hard to swallow.

Kai's eyes were heavy on the side of her face, but she refused to look at him.

Delan let out a long exhale. "It looks like we're operating under the rough assumption that our main enemy is Fang Zedong, and he has successfully convinced powerful Zheninghai wielders to defect with him, based on the traps left on the trail, and the spelled vines that Yong used to bind Aranya."

The mention of those bindings made her wrists and ankles ache even more, despite the salve taking the edge off the pain last night. Now, they were bandaged somewhat sloppily, since she'd done it herself. It would be awhile before they fully healed.

"The princess was a captive," said Kai, breaking his silence. "What if the others were too?"

"Evidence suggests otherwise, but we cannot rule out the possibility."

"It would make more sense if Zuan Wan, Kang Lei, and possibly others left of their own volition," said Aranya. "What use would someone like Fang have with them otherwise?"

"If Fang could subjugate ones as powerful as these wielders, especially Zuan Wan, then he would be a worthy foe indeed." Delan turned to Kai, eyebrows lowering. "Are you *certain* you know nothing about your family's involvement?"

Kai glared at him, took a deliberate mouthful, swallowed. "I know nothing. I have no idea why they would be in contact with Fang, or why the princess would be in their dungeon."

"No matter how they're involved, they're full-blooded traitors who must be stopped. What about the brigands?" Delan demanded. "Why did your family have brigands around?"

Kai's jaw twitched. Subtly. But all he said was, "Every rich family uses brigands to do their dirty work."

He'd said something like that before, when they had rescued Lord Meng's daughter back in Zushui. Aranya frowned, glancing between the two men, her breakfast long forgotten. A silent battle seemed to wage before her, between Delan's narrowed gaze and Kai's lifted chin. The former no doubt looked for a shred of falsehood in the latter, but apparently, he couldn't find any more than Aranya did.

For all that Kai loved secrets, silence, and evasion, he was an honest person.

"Our only option at this point seems to be to send a message to Suguan, informing them of the lead on the princess, and track them ourselves. She is our only lead now, so we recover the ground we lost getting Aranya's bonds off, head toward Khaiduk, and see if we can overtake those brigands before they reach Fang." Delan set down his chopsticks, grabbed the bowl with both of his hands, and poured the rest of his congee into his mouth. Then he stood, groaning like an old man, slapped a few coins down onto the table, nodded at the innkeeper, and winced into the rising sun shining through the windows.

"Time to ride," he said.

If there was ever a blight on mankind, it was travel on horseback. Kai considered once or twice amputating a limb to disqualify himself from this mission, but despite how wonderful it would be to turn his horse around and ride back to Zushui, it seemed like it might be more hassle than it was worth. *Probably.*

Trying *not* to let his eyes follow Aranya's movements as she dumped her saddlebags by the campfire was its own kind of torture. She was determined to ignore him, all while she engaged Delan in conversation every chance she had.

He focused on brushing down his horse and hobbling its front legs. Horse hair was much coarser and dirtier than it looked from afar, when it shone like a polished stone. His horse stomped and twitched its head, flicking its mane, and putting its ears back when he bent to hobble it. Irritable thing.

"Wei-chi during supper, anyone?" called Delan from where he was roasting rabbit over the fire. It turned out that having a feral-wielder who could smell rabbits from what seemed several li away came in handy. Kai was tired of rice cakes and fish jerky.

"Me!" chirped Aranya. "Give me a minute to get these bandages retied. They keep coming loose."

Of course they did, because she hadn't wanted to accept his help. Kai finished with his horse, giving it one last pat, and settled down by the fire opposite Aranya and Delan. He picked up one of the rabbit meat skewers Delan had made and held it over the fire. The juice dripped into the flames, sizzling and popping loudly.

He stole a glance at Aranya. Her face bunched into knots as she fought with the bandages on her wrists. She'd mostly gotten the one on her left hand bound—though it looked like it might come undone during the night with all the thrashing she did while she slept.

He was *not* going to offer to help.

She scowled as the bandage on her right wrist came unraveled for the third time in the last thirty seconds. "Qilins," she cursed, and made to try again.

Kai focused on the meat he was roasting. Not too much longer . . .

"I give up!"

He sighed, putting down his skewer. *Fine.* He'd offer—

"Delan, would you help me?"

Kai picked his skewer back up, trying not to scowl at the fire. In his periphery, Delan got up and knelt beside Aranya as she held out her wrist to him.

"Every time I go to fasten it, it comes undone!"

"Quit your fidgeting and be still," said Delan in that gruff sort of tone that Kai would imagine an affectionate father using to instruct his favorite child. "You didn't apply more salve!"

"I applied it last night!"

"Every day, shifter. Morning *and* evening. Otherwise it'll take you forever to heal, and we can't afford you to be disadvantaged."

Kai propped up the skewer, then leaned over to rummage through his saddlebags. Aranya was still protesting when he pulled out the container of salve. "Catch," he said, and threw it before she turned to look.

"Hey!" she said, even as her hand flew out instinctively to catch it. She glared at him—the first time their eyes had met since breakfast. He only cocked one eyebrow and then focused on grabbing another skewer and roasting it.

"How many children do you have?" asked Aranya, rubbing the salve into her ankles haphazardly. The pain must have gone down since yesterday.

"Three." Delan set to bandaging her ankles while she slathered salve onto her wrists.

"Boys or girls?"

"All girls."

"*All* girls?" Aranya laughed, eyes sparkling in the campfire. "How old are they?"

"Eleven, six, and three." Delan couldn't seem to help but crack a smile as he worked.

"Aww, how adorable! Are they wielders?"

"The eldest is. She's a feral like I am, and she's in her fifth year at the Academy. We're still waiting to know about the younger two."

"But you said you don't live in Suguan, right?"

"That is correct." Delan let out a deep sigh, a line appearing between his eyes. "We do not get to be together as a family very often. Between her being at the Academy and me traveling so much, it's difficult. But we make sure we're all in Suguan for the main festivals." He moved to her wrists, working slower now.

At first, the thought of Delan with a passel of little girls clinging to him didn't seem to quite suit, but the more Kai thought about it, the more it suited perfectly. And Kai couldn't help but smile a little. It quickly faded.

He didn't have to see Delan with his daughters to know he was a better father than Shi Mu had ever been to Kai.

"That's my least favorite thing about the Academy," said Aranya, fiddling with the salve stopper while Delan worked. "It takes you away from your family. It's hard being there alone, and I'm sure it's difficult for you as a father to send your daughter off by herself."

"It's why I make sure to visit her every time I'm in Suguan. And then each time, I get a heart attack because she's grown up so much while I was gone. I'm afraid that if I don't visit often enough, I'll come by and I won't be able to recognize her anymore." Delan tied off the last bandage, returning to his spot by the fire. He picked up the skewer he'd cooked, handed it to Aranya, and grabbed another to roast. "But then she crinkles her nose when she smiles, and I know I'd recognize her in the thickest festival crowd."

Aranya's gaze was fixed on Delan, warmth and understanding shining in her expression. "I'm sure she loves having such a devoted father."

Delan's nose twitched—probably from the strong smell of the cooking rabbit—and he said dryly, "She'd better. If not for me, she wouldn't even be alive."

Aranya grinned. Kai looked down at his lap while he blew to cool off a bite of rabbit.

"Ready for wei-chi?" she asked suddenly, waving her skewer around and drawing Kai's gaze back up. "I think I've figured out the secret strategy to demolishing you." Then she took a bite of rabbit, gasped at the heat, and set to fanning her open mouth.

Delan's lips quirked. "Come on, then, shifter. Show me this secret strategy."

Kai was glad *they* were friends. He was fine being ignored. Very, very fine. Finishing his supper, he grabbed his bedroll and laid down, setting his back to the sound of stones being placed on boards and Aranya's lighthearted chatter.

CHAPTER 7

THEY SPENT SEVERAL days riding hard, stopping only after the sun was fully set. They were off again before it rose. This sort of endurance was what Aranya had trained her whole life for, but every morning when she dragged herself back to her horse, it wasn't the toning of her body that made it easier, but the strength of will she'd learned at the Academy.

"Pain is in the mind," they'd told her.

So she didn't complain despite the lack of sleep, the ache of her muscles and wounds, and Kai's cold silence.

"Have you not considered that perhaps I care about you?" The words echoed in her mind as she determinedly ignored Kai as much as he ignored her. He was sure doing a fabulous job proving that he cared about her.

Delan caught a scent.

It was on the third day, after taking a rather treacherous pass to shorten their journey. Aranya had been too busy being glad her horse hadn't taken a wrong step and sent them hurtling into a deep ravine to listen carefully to what Delan was saying. It took her a second to tune in and find him describing one of the scent "flavors" as being similar to the blackening fire they'd encountered in Shaanet, and the other flavors could easily belong to the rest of their quarry.

A thrill shot through Aranya. It was soon followed by restlessness, and then boredom, when still several more days passed with no sign of the princess. The only good thing between all the grudges, irritation, and silence was when she got to take off the bandages on her wrists and ankles.

Then, one day—*finally*—Delan's nose suddenly shot up in the air. Aranya perked in her saddle and demanded, "What? What do you smell? Are we close?"

He ignored her, his pupils focusing like pinpoints on the forest ahead of them. He kicked his horse faster, and she followed in suit. Kai took up the rear, not increasing his speed.

"What?" she hissed as they proceeded. "What do you smell?"

"I think it's those brigands," Delan muttered, pulling his horse to a halt. He swung down from the saddle, hands automatically going to the weapons buckled on his belt. "They're close. Aranya, you follow me for a better look. Kai, stay back in case things go wrong."

Kai said nothing.

Aranya leapt out of the saddle, an insuppressible grin spreading across her face. Finally—something interesting! She drew her *jiaun* out of its holster, nocking a pair of arrows into the slots. No talons just yet.

Delan kept sniffing the air, motioning for her to follow as he ducked under a low-hanging branch. Silently, she crept behind him. They moved swiftly, following his nose. Her blood thrummed with excitement.

Would they be able to recover the princess?

Delan glanced back at her, warning that they were close. She steadied her breathing, bringing her *jiaun* up to firing position. He reached back, placing a hand on the top of the weapon and lowering it. He gave a quick shake of his head, and they kept moving.

She swallowed her huff and followed him.

Only a minute later, he held up his hand again. But this time, Aranya had already stopped. The sound of talking, of impatient huffing horses, drifted toward them. Moving with painstaking care now, they inched closer until she could make out swatches of color and movement through the foliage.

She parted the branches a fraction of an inch—just enough to get a clear view.

Immediately, she recognized the three brigands. There was a woman, her face and square form shrouded by a gray cloak. On the opposite side of the clearing stood that same tall illusionist she'd fought in the rain weeks ago. A third brigand with a jagged beard wrapped his meaty hands around the slight upper arm of a cloaked girl atop one of the horses.

Princess Meiling?

She wore no royal garments, only the drab, nondescript garb of a commoner. But there was no mistaking the grace with which she moved, the subtle elegance. Aranya was not a girl of refined taste by any means, but even she could tell the difference.

Careless of hands bound behind her, the bearded brigand dragged the princess off her saddle and onto the ground. She landed hard, unable to catch herself. Delan winced, but Aranya's talons were already lengthening. Eyes widening, he reached out and gripped her arm. He shook his head, warning her. She barely caught herself from growling as she shifted away her claws and returned her gaze to the clearing.

There were others. A few dressed similarly to the three brigands with the princess. But two more stood out to Aranya. They wore animal pelts—as though used to a much colder climate than Zheninghai—with their hair tied in tight braids down their scalps. One had an ax strapped to his back, and both wore swords much longer and broader than the ones Kai and Delan carried.

Aranya's throat went dry.

They were from Butagin. *Barbarians.*

The eight warriors watched the girl on the ground as she struggled to her knees, no one bothering to help her. She said nothing, only spat out dirt and grass. But though she did not fight or protest, her eyes burned with passion. With anger.

"Shuren will catch up in a few days," the woman said to one of the unfamiliar brigands and the barbarians gesturing at the silent illusionist. "He's got to tie up some loose ends. This is the last captive. She shouldn't give you trouble like the healer or that plant-wielder. Tell the other groups that this is it, and we can head back to the fortress now."

One of the other brigands, a short and stocky man, nodded and reached down to wrench the princess to her feet. "Very well. Tie up those ends quickly; Fang will want you to return with us."

The illusionist nodded, a blank expression on his face.

"Just some trackers," said the bearded one. "He'll take care of them."

He meant . . . *them*. Aranya's insides clenched. Delan's face was like flint beside her. *Captives*—they'd just confirmed that Zuan Wan and the healer were captives, not defectors.

But *why*? And *how*?

A few more words were exchanged, but Aranya was too focused on deciding which one to shoot first. As one of the brigands yanked the girl to another horse and hoisted her up roughly into the saddle, Aranya lifted her *jiaun.*

Delan shook his head, giving her a look of hot warning. She glared back at him, as if to demand why. He only shook his head again and began backing out the way they'd come. She stayed, eyes wide with disbelief.

They were just going to *let* them take the princess? They weren't going to intervene?

She clenched her fist tightly around her weapon, fighting the urge to shift, fighting the urge to ignore Delan and shoot, anyway. But she drew her impulses under control and eased out of the brush after her comrade.

When they were finally out of earshot, she whirled on him.

"We *need* to intervene! That was the princess—I'm sure of it!"

"And then what happens when we're outmatched eight to three—assuming Kai came along in the nick of time—and they kill us all? No one will know where the princess is. Part of being a good wielder in the Secret Services is knowing when to pick your battles. We weren't going to win that one, and I don't know about you, but I have youngsters I want to go home to."

She paused, the knowledge of his correctness warring with her instinct to fight and save the princess. Reason warring with passion.

They broke through a denser part of the forest, retracing their steps, until the horses were visible again.

"This changes everything," Aranya said.

"Keep your voice down; we don't know how close they are."

She lowered her voice but kept talking. "If Zuan Wan and the healer were as captive as the princess, then . . . doesn't it stand to reason that the rest of them likely were too? They didn't defect—they were captured. It would explain why it appears the same set of brigands performed many kidnappings in a short amount of time while still managing to get them back to this fortress. They had meeting points, essentially forming a bucket brigade of captives."

Delan grunted in agreement.

"Meeting points with *barbarians*."

"A very serious development, indeed."

When they reached the horses, Kai was leaning against a tree, picking at his fingernails. Nearby, the horses grazed absently, tails swishing at flies.

"Anything interesting?" he asked without looking up.

Suddenly, out of nowhere, a pair of hands darted around the tree and grabbed Kai by the throat. His eyes bugged with shock—and then he vanished.

They were moving in an instant.

She and Delan both snapped up their *jiauns* into firing mode, but she didn't have a chance to shoot before a hooded figure burst out from the trees, leaping on all fours like he was more beast than human.

He pounced on Aranya.

Her *jiaun* went flying, knocked out of her grasp. She shifted her hands into claws. *Scrape, slash, rip.* Her talons tore into flesh, but the man only let out a cackling laugh, foam spewing out of his mouth onto her face.

His weight wasn't what landed her on her back. He weighed so little she could have lifted him up in her arms. But his *strength* was so inhuman, so strange, so vicious. She could hardly fight when he slammed her into a tree trunk.

Stars danced across her vision.

A bony, gnarly hand clenched around her neck. She gasped, choked, as she was lifted off the ground, her feet kicking in midair.

Can't breathe. Can't breathe.

She sputtered, swiping with her claws uselessly at thin air as the brigand cackled through a snow-white beard. She kicked, fumbled to unsheathe a knife. Her vision started to go black. But not before she saw the face under the hood.

An ancient, decrepit man with maniacal eyes smiled at her.

He wheeled back his arm—the one that held her—and she realized with sickening clarity that he intended to bash her head into the tree. She choked.

An arrow landed straight in the old man's bicep. He let out a feral snarl, leaping to grab hold of Delan as his grip clenched tighter around Aranya's throat. He caught Delan by the front of his shirt and dragged his face close.

The brigand let out a foam-gushing yell. Delan twisted his head away, reaching for a knife. Kai appeared on the brigand's back, his arm looping around his leathery throat. His other hand plunged a knife with lightning speed straight into the man's back.

The brigand shrieked.

Delan landed a powerful blow to his jaw. His grip loosened, and he dropped Aranya.

She landed, rolling to her feet as her vision spun. The instant she was upright, she stumbled backward, but her foot knocked into something on the ground. With more instinct than clarity, she swept up her *jiaun* and nocked an arrow.

No time for two arrows.

Kai stabbed the brigand again, his face a twisted grimace of strain. The brigand reached back, caught him by the leg, and ripped him forward. Kai let out a cry, only barely vanishing before the brigand slammed him into the ground.

Then the brigand, bleeding from his multiple wounds, leapt for Aranya again.

She gasped as she let her arrow fly. It hit his shoulder, but that didn't stop him from pouncing on her and knocking her clean to the dirt. He roared in her face. She screamed, throwing up a hand as spittle and blood landed on her skin.

"Don't you *dare* touch her!" came Kai's vicious snarl.

She didn't see much—only his swinging broadsword glinting in the sunlight, coming straight for the brigand's neck. Then the brigand let out another roar, snatching the blade, utterly heedless of how it sliced into his palm. He stopped the blow before it reached his neck. Instead, he redirected that momentum and shoved it down toward Aranya's throat.

Kai let out a cry, which was abruptly cut off as he and his sword vanished. The sword came down again, on the opposite side, aiming for the back of his neck.

The old brigand, still pinning her, gave her a wild grin through his beard. He pushed off her, launching into the forest, blood trailing in his wake. The sword sliced empty air.

All was suddenly quiet.

Kai crouched beside her. "Aranya!" he gasped, reaching for her as she tried to prop herself up. His arm slid under her back, hoisting her up and against his chest.

Her breaths came easier now, but her blood thrummed with adrenaline, with the need to fight, to chase. Delan was already leaping around them in pursuit, his *jiaun* loaded. Aranya gasped, struggling to make her trembling limbs obey her.

Then she realized her face was pressed against Kai's sweaty, heaving chest and her forehead rested against the column of his neck. His arms were around her, shaking almost as much as her own.

Something about it . . . A bolt of fear more terrifying than facing an insane brigand with feral strength hit her in the gut. She couldn't—she wasn't—this was too . . .

Frantically, she pushed away from him, scrambling to her feet. His eyes were round, his mouth open, and his voice broke when he said, "*Please*, Aranya, don't—"

She was already stumbling after Delan, her cheeks burning as her neck swelled with more bruises. Her legs buckled beneath her, but she kept moving, following the trail of blood. Kept running until she ran straight into Delan's face full of terror.

"Run!" he cried, grabbing her arm and dragging her in the opposite direction, back to Kai.

"What?" she cried back, trying to fight him.

"The whole lot of them are chasing us!"

"We ought to fight them!"

"Don't be an idiot!"

Kai, who had already come after them, evanesced straight to the horses at the sight of their faces. He untethered all three with quick yanks on their leads, just in time for Aranya and Delan to leap into the saddles.

Together, the three of them tore off into the wilderness.

They didn't slow their pace until Delan was certain they had lost their pursuit. Their horses were panting—they were panting themselves—and they were forced to stop. Despite this, Delan kept his nose in the air, his shoulders tense, as they dismounted.

"We need to get water for the horses," he said. "I smell some this way; follow me."

On foot, they guided their heaving horses after him. Aranya wasn't sure if she dared glance back at Kai, not after . . . She wrinkled her nose at herself. It was only her adrenaline, only the panic of that moment, that had made her think there was something in Kai's eyes earlier that she hadn't seen before.

To prove to herself that everything was normal between them, she *did* glance back at him. He was already looking at her, eyes glowing too brightly.

She swallowed quickly and hurried after Delan.

The fire crackled before them, the darkness so thick it almost hid the ridge of the bluff they camped near. Aranya had her chin propped up on her hands, her elbows resting on the knees of her crossed legs, trying to ignore how sore she was from head to toe. Kai stared emptily into the fire, and Delan wasn't much better, at least until he started talking.

"We can't jump to conclusions," he said, then cleared his throat. "But today we've confirmed that Lord Zuan Wan and the healer Li Feiyan were captives, not defectors, and evidence seems to indicate they weren't the only ones to be kidnapped. At this point, it's a matter of *why*. Why kidnap these wielders?"

Aranya yawned, then shrugged. "The healer is easy. She's the only person alive right now who can heal any ailment with a touch. Fang probably wants to use her for that."

"And if he can use her, then maybe he has a means of using the others," said Delan grimly. "Using our own against us."

Aranya nodded mutely, munching on a rice cake.

"The barbarians . . . change things," continued Delan. "We're not just tracking brigands anymore, or even Fang Zedong. This is confirmation that Butagin means war. Which means we are in a *situation*."

"A situation?"

"We are three wielders. That crew heading north—presumably to Butagin and that fortress—is more than twice our size. Additionally, we have confirmation at least one of them was sent to throw us off the trail. So—"

"So we need to watch our backs and never let our guards down," said Aranya. She picked up a small stone and tossed it toward the edge of the bluff.

Delan cast her a look. "You . . . *should* be doing that already. What I'm saying is that one might make the case we ought to find the nearest city, send a missive to Suguan, and wait for further instructions."

Right then, the wind shifted and blew the smoke of the campfire straight into Aranya's face. She set into a fit of coughing, scooting away from the eye-watering fumes as her mind spun.

They couldn't wait for instructions from Suguan! Absolutely not. "That would set us back at least a week! We're in the middle of nowhere, and to wait for our message to arrive in Suguan and *then* wait for their response to reach us . . . it might even take several weeks!"

"It would."

"But what about the princess?" Aranya couldn't bear the thought of abandoning the princess to the heavy hand of her captors, regardless of her curse.

"The princess makes this situation much more complicated."

"We can't just leave her. If we go wait for instructions from the capital, we'll have let our only lead go. We're the only ones who have seen the princess since she was captured. We *have* to go after her."

"We're outmatched," said Kai, speaking for the first time in hours. Both Aranya and Delan turned to him in surprise. "What happens if we go after her and get killed because we're outnumbered and then *no one* knows where the princess was?"

Of course Kai would take this opportunity to argue with her. She fixed her gaze firmly on Delan and let the flickering fire take up her periphery.

"Both options are risky. Neither is preferred, and as far as I'm concerned, there's no clear right answer. We're justified in choosing to halt pursuit, send word to Suguan, and wait for further instructions. That would be the *smart* choice, considering the barbarians."

"But it's the *princess*," said Aranya.

"But it's the princess," agreed Delan. "Outnumbered as we are, there is still a chance we could save her."

Kai looked up from beneath a lowered brow. "You're saying we should still go after her? Despite the risks."

Delan cracked his knuckles. "I like myself a little risk here and there. Gets the blood pumping. And it makes me feel like I'm not nearly forty."

"Oh fathers, I was so afraid you'd say we couldn't go after the princess!" Aranya beamed, relief settling the weight in her chest. "Besides, if worse came to worse, we probably wouldn't do *that* badly against those brigands and barbarians."

"Keep underestimating your enemies and I'll leave you behind," said Delan sternly.

Kai actually snorted at that, and when she shot a glare his way, he smiled at her. She blinked and quickly looked away.

"I'll take first watch," she said.

Apparently, no one was in the mood for wei-chi tonight.

CHAPTER 8

ARANYA NUDGED KAI awake with her boot. His sleep-softened face puckered, and a soft groan escaped his lips.

"Your watch," she whispered to avoid waking Delan.

He nodded mutely, sitting up and wiping the sleep from his eyes. He stared blankly into the fire for a long minute, then glanced at her. For a second, she hesitated, as though she had something to say. But she didn't, right? She turned away before anything stupid came out of her mouth. "Goodnight," she whispered, laying down on her bedroll and curling up into a ball.

The exhaustion was so heavy, her body so sore, that the thick dullness of sleep quickly descended upon her. *So tired . . .*

She was on the brink of oblivion when whispered words wove into her mind.

"I'm sorry, Aranya. I'm sorry I kissed you. Truly sorry."

Something about that voice, so near, so low—her brow pinched in confusion. But she was too close to sleep to process any of it. The speaker, the meaning, the implications. It was the one thing keeping her from drifting beyond awareness, that voice.

Then something warm touched her face.

Aranya was suddenly wide awake. Wide awake and in motion.

Instinct made her slam her arm against her assailant, rolling her weight into him. Caught off guard, he fell backward. She continued her momentum, moving and shapeshifting her hands until she straddled his waist, claws around his neck.

It was Kai.

Her sleep-fogged mind cleared, her eyes widening. He held up both hands in surrender.

Aranya snarled, tightening her claws around his neck. He didn't resist. "What are you doing?" she spat, keeping her voice low to not wake Delan. "Seven valleys. You scared the daylights out of me!"

He grinned.

Belatedly, his words registered in her mind. *His apology for kissing her.* A real apology. But instead of making her soften, it made her even more furious.

"Apologize to my *face*, Shi Kai. Not when I'm asleep!"

"Apparently you weren't asleep," he said, one eyebrow cocked.

She stared at him as she held her claws against his vulnerable skin. Then realization hit her like a bolt of lightning, and it must have been written across her face, because his grin went lopsided.

He wasn't evanescing away from her.

"Qilin-spawn," she growled, climbing off him.

Kai only grinned wider, and the sight made her angrier and . . . strangely *happier* at once. She hated watching him brood all the time, and he'd been nothing if not brooding ever since they'd escaped his family's house. Still growling under her breath, she moved back to her bedroll and yanked her cloak around her. "Let me sleep."

"I'm sorry," he blurted.

She paused, twisting to look at him over her shoulder. His smirk was gone, replaced by something much more honest. More vulnerable.

"You're right," he said. "I should have apologized to your face. I'm sorry, Aranya. I shouldn't have used your situation with your grandfather like that. I'm sorry, and I hope you'll forgive me."

Her mouth opened, but this time, no words came out. Instead, she stared at him, hardly believing Shi Kai was *actually* apologizing to her. He stared back, his gaze unflinching. Probably reading all her thoughts.

She stuttered, opening and closing her mouth. Then, finally, one cohesive thought formed enough in her mind for her to speak. "Why did you pay the fine?"

He sat up, hooking his elbow around his propped knee. With his other hand, he tore up bits of grass. "I overheard the conversation you had with our landlord. I saw you two talking, evanesced behind the door, and listened. Then I left before either of you could find me. I . . . You couldn't pay it. The fine wasn't your fault. I had the money, so . . . It wasn't all that much."

"Not much for you." She laughed ruefully.

He pursed his lips. "Wealth can be a curse as easily as a blessing."

"You mean to say that, when I went to talk to Lim, the landlord, the next morning, you'd already paid it?"

He nodded, not looking at her. "But I thought you would perhaps be offended. That's why I asked Lim to tell you the deadline was extended."

There was a long pause, filled only with the crackle of the fire and the crickets of the forest. Kai stood, stepping away to his post.

"I'll let you sleep," he said quietly.

She bit her lip, blinking, watching him. If he had apologized to her face, she could thank him to his. Drawing a deep breath, she said softly, "Thank you for paying that fine, Kai. I honestly had no idea what I was going to do."

Kai stopped, his back to her. After the silence lasted a few breaths, he turned enough that the profile of his smirk was visible. His dry voice carried across the fire. "I'd say *any time,* but you sure rack up the fines quickly. I'd be bankrupt before the Festival of New Lights."

"Why do I bother?" she muttered, rolling over and pulling the blanket over her head.

His quiet chuckles drifted over to her.

CHAPTER 9

KAI WAS LIGHTER than he'd been in days. Having Aranya accept his apology was like a sack of rice off his chest, despite the constant worry about his family, and the ever-present guilt over what had happened in Gebei.

The long travel days were grueling. Despite their earlier spotting of the princess, Delan had yet to catch the brigands' scents. They kept their pursuit north toward the Butagin fortress in hopes that they would come across her again or possibly even reach the fortress before the princess did—if that was even possible.

There was always the chance they might stumble across the other Secret Service wielders who pursued the trails of the rest of the missing wielders. If that happened, then they'd be more equipped to launch an attack on the brigands, should they discover them again.

But so far, it was just the three of them and the endless Zheninghai wilderness.

Kai tried not to sneak glances at Aranya that were too obvious. Currently, she was looking at Delan, her lips parted like she wanted to say something, before her eyes darted to Kai's. He met her gaze evenly. She flushed and looked away.

He couldn't help the curl of satisfaction in his stomach.

She chewed her lip, looking again to Delan, who lifted his eyebrows and sighed loudly.

"If I've told you once, I've told you a *dozen* times," he said. "Traveling isn't a social event."

Kai smirked, though he remained silent.

"But that makes traveling so *boring*!" Aranya cried. "You shun me all day, and then when we camp, I'm not supposed to talk? When am I supposed to have regular human interaction?"

Kai's smile was less smirk and more amusement. If only Delan was somewhere else right now, then he could more openly tease her. Maybe rile her into a tizzy of feigned outrage. Scowls shouldn't elicit delight, but . . . well, here they were.

He wanted to kiss her again.

No, no, no. He couldn't think those thoughts. He gritted his teeth and reached up to scratch the back of his neck.

Delan rolled his eyes. "The idea is that we're professionals, and we don't need regular human interaction. We're able to thrive under harsh, strenuous circumstances while on a mission."

Aranya scowled. "We're not required to starve ourselves while on a mission to prove we're so rugged. Is it so terrible that I want to have a five-minute conversation once in a while?"

"Once in a while." Kai snorted.

She glared at him.

He lifted both hands, palms up. "I'll talk to you, if you want."

Delan shot him a sidelong glance, a warning potent in every line of his face. Kai merely shrugged, stuffing one hand into the pocket of his robes, and failed at wiping the smirk off his face.

Aranya looked between them both, as though trying to read Delan's silent admonishment.

"My offer stands," Kai said dryly.

She flushed red and looked away. Which was definitely not the reaction he'd expected. He stared at the back of her head, confused. Until he remembered the last time he'd said something similar—when they were staying at that inn and he was offering to share that cramped bed with her.

He ducked his head and clamped his mouth shut so he didn't laugh aloud.

Delan straightened suddenly, nose stuck sharply into the air, to their left.

"What?" Aranya sat up in her saddle, tightening her grip on her reins.

Delan's face was grim. "Kai, I'm going to need you to check on something—"

But before he could finish, the shrieking of bells cut through all thought, all conversation, all except the sudden, terrifying realization. Kai turned horrified eyes to Aranya, finding hers the size of saucers in her pretty face.

In a flash, they dismounted, the unspoken agreement about their responsibility as magic-wielders of Zheninghai. Aranya and Delan had their *jiauns* loaded, Kai had his broadsword drawn.

With one last glance toward each other, they broke into a run. Kai evanesced ahead, wary of the trees. In a few short leaps, he reached the source of those bell-like brays.

And very nearly evanesced right back at the sight of a full qilin herd.

When Aranya reached the clearing, she could hardly process what she saw.

Everywhere—cacophony. Fire sizzled in every direction, color flashing like jewels and precious metals each way she turned. *So many.* She lifted her *jiaun* and fired. Her aim was wide, and though she hit the beast, it was not a killing blow.

The qilin roared, rearing back on cloven hindquarters and billowing fire from its maw. Enormous antlers struck low hanging tree branches. Its glasslike eyes focused on her as she whipped out more arrows, reloading them as fast as her hands could move.

But before she could fire again at the beast before her, another came charging for her, one she hadn't been watching. The gleam of its scale-like hide reflected sunlight so bright it was nearly blinding. She didn't have time to throw up her hands to protect her eyes; she lifted her weapon and shot into the whiteness flooding her vision. Screams told her she'd hit her target, but there was no earth-shuddering thud of one falling.

The reflected light shifted as the qilin reared back, and it was just enough for her to see that the other one was charging for her. Her breath lodged in a knot. She leapt to the side, rolling up to her feet again as it skidded past her.

Another charged at her, its beard burning and dripping fire.

So many. How could they ever—

Then a different *jiaun* pointed over her shoulder, and the charging qilin fell.

"I've got your back!" Delan called. "Watch mine!"

Relief flooded her, followed by a burst of determination like fire in her blood. She squared her shoulders, bumping into Delan's back as they each took up firing stances and aimed at the beasts opposing them. They shot, reloaded, and shot again. Sweat poured down Aranya's forehead, stinging her eyes as she aimed.

"How many?" Delan called.

"There's too many to count!"

"No—how many have you killed?" he shouted.

"Uh . . . four, so far."

"I'm beating you! Seven down!"

She couldn't help the grin that split her face as she reloaded and fired to her left, hitting another. "That's five!" she called.

A new noise filled the deafening discord. This one was deeper, rumbling through the ground—a bell that sounded bigger than the forest surrounding them. It rattled her ribcage, sending fear dousing through her blood. Stomping hooves shook the world, unsteadying her knees. Aranya lowered her *jiaun,* eyes painfully wide, as she lifted them to the opposite side of the clearing.

At first, all she could see was shadow. Where there had once been light and sun, there was nothing but dark and night. Snorting breaths filled the clearing, and the brightly colored, fearsome qilins backed away, their own bell-like cries damping from a roar to a whine.

Delan's presence at her back vanished. She jerked her head toward him as he stepped to his side, his face iron-hard and eyes blazing. "This," he growled, reaching out and snatching her elbow, "is when we *run*."

"Where's Kai?"

Delan's eyes darkened. "I don't know."

"We can't leave until we know he's safe!"

"He's fine. He's an evanescer."

"That does *not* mean he's fine—it means he's *probably* fine! We must be sure!"

Delan ignored this comment, turning on his heel as fire sparked in the depths beyond the trees, where a huge presence lumbered closer. He dragged Aranya after him. "Run!" he cried. "We'll worry about Kai later!"

But the moment they broke into a run, they skittered to a halt. Not ten paces away, three qilins stared at them, gold, emerald green, and iridescent white. Their eyes were emotionless pools of black glass, lethal and shimmering.

Aranya took a step back, glanced over her shoulder. More qilins waited there, also staring.

The breath fled her chest in a soft gasp. They weren't attacking, but they certainly were threatening. Waiting—for their alpha.

"Wherever Kai is," Delan growled, "he's in a better position than we are."

The heavy breathing from the approaching shadows was louder than the shrieks of the qilins. It billowed like a gust of wind over the glittering bodies they'd already slaughtered.

As one, the qilins surrounding them took a step closer.

Then, Aranya could do naught but stare, her head tilting backward, as the alpha emerged from the forest. Her hand holding her *jiaun* drifted down to her side, only the barest instincts maintaining her grip on the weapon.

He was the color of deep night. His beard, his hide, the tree-sized antlers protruding from his brow were like polished ebony stone, sharpened to deadly points. His eyes were gleaming ink, so pigmented they would stain anything they looked upon. Even the fire that billowed from its gaping maw was black. Burning smoke.

He was majestic, his mane sucking the sunlight out of the world.

He was death.

Aranya's mouth gaped open, her neck craned, her feet like stumps rooted several li deep into the earth. She had no mind for the qilins surrounding them, nor for Delan at her side.

It was only her and this monster.

Her—and her death.

The beast snorted, blasting air into her face. It stomped one hoof, but she couldn't drag her gaze down from its terrifying face to see that its hooves were the size of small boulders. It snorted again, this time spattering black fire droplets.

One landed on her cheek, the other on her arm, burning through her sleeves instantaneously. The searing pain scorched her skin down to her very soul, and the scream that burst from her rent the air in two.

It broke the spell.

Aranya stumbled back, nearly dropping her *jiaun* as pain lanced through her. Her scream turned to a hiss, snapping her gaze from the monster to her burned arm.

Delan cried out, too. The sound made her blood turn to fire, her fear to rage.

This was *not* how they were going to die. Not from a mere breath from a fire-dripping *mó guǐ*. No, she wasn't leaving Ye Ye for this. She didn't care if it was a thousand feet tall, or whether it was a nightmare incarnate.

This was not her death.

She yanked her *jiaun* up and shot straight at the beast. Her tiny arrows couldn't miss; he was so huge. They hit his throat, and the blood that spurted from the wound was not black, but glittering molten gold. The alpha reared back, its thunderous roaring knocking them to the ground. Black fire billowed into the sky.

She vaguely heard Delan scream her name, but was already loading another pair of arrows.

The beast landed back on all fours, and the impact of its front hooves hitting the ground sent Aranya flying. She landed hard in the dirt, looking up in time to see the monster drawing in a deep breath—she felt the rush of air pulling her toward its mouth—readying to spew decimating fire at them.

Then there was a new sound.

One of tiny, tinkling bells. A whole chorus of whimpering, whining chimes cutting through the rumbling, earsplitting roars around her.

She rolled over, pushing up on her elbows. Her talons dug into earth—when had she shifted? Her *jiaun* had landed just out of reach. She bit back a snarl as the high-pitched bells grew louder, more insistent. Crawling forward, she strained to reach her weapon. The surrounding herd of qilins' ears perked, and even the alpha swung its giant head to the side.

Before she had time to prepare herself, a small herd of qilin calves stampeded through the clearing. Aranya screeched in surprise, rolling several times until she dragged herself up behind a tree to avoid being flattened. She saw a flash of a tall figure she recognized, wielding a hefty branch and shouting, "Hi-ya!" at the calves.

The noise that erupted around her from the entire herd sent her curling up in a ball, pressing hands over her ears. In a not completely rational moment, she let her own screams join the uproar, as if it would keep her ears from splitting in half.

The ground rumbled, shaking under the pounding of hooves. Aranya scrambled further against the tree she hid behind, pressing her head between her knees as she felt how near the qilins stampeded past her. She was a pebble falling over the edge of a waterfall, drowning in the roar as the world fell to pieces.

Then—*quiet*.

Around her, the air whined with silence. The ringing of bells slipped into something that was either memory or confusion, and she had only enough strength to melt against the tree.

Then someone was gripping her shoulders, shaking her. "Aranya? Aranya! Are you alive?"

Her eyes fluttered open, her vision clearing at the sight of beautiful, light-brown eyes staring back at her, ringed in white. The lines of Kai's face were drawn so tightly, so frantically, that she smiled at him kneeling before her.

"I'm alive," she croaked.

Kai's head sagged between his shoulders, his grip on her going lax with relief. It was only a brief moment, for the next he was reaching for her face.

Aranya yelped and tried to scoot backward more, only succeeding in bumping into the tree. "No kisses!" she shrieked, scrambling away.

"You're burned!" he said, knocking her hand away and gingerly touching her cheek near the wound.

She scowled and pushed him back, stumbling to unsteady feet. "It's better than being dead. Where *were* you?"

"In case anyone's wondering, I'm alive too!" Delan's voice called from the clearing. "Not that I would want anyone to worry too much about *me*."

"Delan!" Aranya cried, leaping away from Kai.

Delan grunted, shifting himself against a tree. He scowled, sweat dripping off his brow. "I never, ever, *ever* want to see one of those things again."

"Are you hurt?" she asked. She winced at her own pain as she crouched next to him, half reaching out a hand. "Where did it burn you?"

"It's no big deal," he snapped. His dark eyes darted from Aranya to Kai, standing behind her. "Glad you decided to stop by for a spot of tea."

Kai closed his eyes, drawing in a deep breath. She waited for him to growl something about saving their lives, but instead, he swallowed and said in a surprisingly earnest tone, "I'm so sorry. It was harder than I expected to herd the calves this way. Had I known, I would have stayed and fought with you."

"And died with us," Delan grumbled. He released a great sigh, his shoulders sagging as he covered his eyes with his hand. "As mad as I am, your thinking was quick. I want to be furious, but . . . well done. We both owe you our lives. But next time, for the fathers' sakes, communicate with us before you vanish without a trace!"

Kai's eyes dropped to the ground. "We ought to tend wounds before heading out. I'll evanesce to the horses and bring them back with the medical supplies."

He vanished, leaving Aranya to turn her attention back to Delan. "You look like you're in a lot of pain."

"Oh, I'm mostly banged up and bruised. I only collected a handful of burns and a nick on the arm from the horns. What about you?"

"I think I fared a little better," she said as she began rolling back his sleeve to expose the trickling wound.

"Shocking, considering the idiotic move you pulled at the end."

She looked up and couldn't help her grin. "I wonder how many people have landed shots at qilin alphas and lived to tell the tale?"

"I can assure you, you're probably the sharpest one of the few who have," he growled.

She paused, tilting her head. "Is that an insult or a compliment?"

She hadn't realized how tense she was, how worried she was, until Delan smirked. Relief washed down her spine, making her answering smile the most genuine she'd smiled in a while.

"You decide, little shifter."

CHAPTER 10

KAI'S HEART NEARLY beat out of his chest. He fought to keep his face neutral, but that could not hide his slick palms or the sweat running down his back and making his clothes stick to his skin.

He looked back at Aranya, propped up against a tree, opening the container of salve. Her brow was furrowed, her eyes flashing with alertness, and her face looked . . . horrible. The new burn was red and blistering under the sweep of her cheekbone. It would certainly scar. The rest of her bruises and scrapes from their recent altercations with the brigands and his family hadn't fully healed.

He looked away, swiping up a damaged *jiaun* from the ground. It might have been hers or Delan's, but it needed restringing and balancing. This would be a good thing for him to focus on—something to calm his nerves.

"If you'll excuse me," Delan said, groaning as he hauled himself to his feet. "My britches very narrowly escaped soiling during that episode with the qilins. I will be back in a dragon's sneeze."

Aranya wrinkled her nose. "I didn't need to know that."

Kai glanced at Delan, who was smirking at him. He returned it, glad for the slight assurance that he was tentatively back in Delan's good graces, but his mouth wobbled. Aranya glanced between them, glaring at being left out.

She ought to just be glad that she was Delan's favorite.

Delan tromped into the forest, but his turned back couldn't disguise how his hands trembled.

They were all shaken up.

Though Aranya acted as if new wounds and nearly facing death were a mere inconvenience. She grimaced as she rubbed the salve onto her cheek, but her working hands remained steady and brusque. He remembered the terror on her face when Yong had held her at knifepoint. Was she just trying to rush past the terror before it fully settled in?

Her eyes snapped up to his, the ire plainly evident in her tone. "That *jiaun* isn't going to restring itself."

Kai exhaled through his nostrils, forcing himself to turn around and rummage through the saddlebags for string. Behind him, Aranya hissed in pain. His shoulders tightened, his hands fumbling in the bags.

Finally, he found the string and, without glancing toward her, settled himself down onto the ground with the *jiaun*. His legs shuddered with his movement. Even when he was seated, and his limbs should relax, they remained tense and wobbly.

He allowed himself a quick look at her. She was nearly scowling, not exactly like she was in pain, but rather that she was very annoyed at the pain.

He wouldn't offer to help. If she wanted help, she would ask.

Well—probably not.

Words slipped unbidden through his lips. He tried to stop them, to clamp his lips shut, nearly resorted to clapping a hand over his mouth. But they came out anyway.

"I'm glad you're mostly unharmed," he said. The instant he said them, his face flamed and he ducked his head lower like he was focused on his task. Even though he was only unwinding and rewinding the string around his fingers.

She snorted, rolling her eyes. "Me, too."

Only Sun Aranya would brush past a scrape with death. Only she would be nothing more than a little irritable after facing a qilin alpha. Only she would miss that his terror was not for them as a group, but for *her*.

Thankfully, the task of restringing a *jiaun* was rote and routine for him. His vision didn't focus, but he measured the proper length, snipped it with his knife, and threaded the end through the contraption.

Bit by bit, his limbs stopped quaking. Doing things with his hands cleared his mind and helped him regain control over his composure. He couldn't shut out the sharp intakes of breath as Aranya continued treating her burns, but better she suffered a little pain than be dead.

Delan returned, sighing in relief and making Aranya wrinkle her nose in disgust again. His hands had stopped shaking, his face cleared, and Kai wondered if relieving himself hadn't been the primary reason he stepped away.

"Let's get back on the road," Delan said. "If we want any hope of catching up with the brigands, we ought to increase our pace."

"Sounds like a plan," Aranya said, failing to hide a wince as she scrambled to her feet.

Catching up with the brigands and the princess was beginning to seem hopeless. Could they even make it to Butagin? Or would they be shredded to pieces along the way?

CHAPTER 11

ALL THIS TRAVEL was slowly suffocating Kai. When they stopped for camp that night, everyone moved decidedly slower than yesterday at fetching kindling for a fire, brushing down and hobbling the horses, and removing saddles and saddlebags from the poor beasts. Melancholy settled over the group, as if everyone knew, but no one was willing to voice that it had been days since they'd seen the princess. By now, it didn't make sense to switch plans and detour to a city to send a message to Suguan. What use was the location of the princess a week ago, when she could be anywhere by now?

The trail was cold, but there was always the chance they could come across it once again. There were only so many travelable routes to Butagin that the brigands and barbarians could have taken the girl.

Kai, the bridles of his horse and Delan's hanging from his elbow, approached Aranya's while she brushed it down with uncharacteristically long, slow strokes. Today had taken a toll on her, no matter how much she pretended otherwise.

Keeping his voice low, he said, "Next time we stop for supplies, I'm going to buy some cheese."

Aranya glanced at him, confusion drawing a line above her nose. "Delan won't let you."

"And *then*," Kai continued as if she hadn't spoken, "I'm going to crumble it into little pieces. Some of it will go in your bags, some in mine."

Aranya's jaw dropped. "Shi Kai!"

He leaned a little closer to her as he pulled the horse's bridle over its ears and slid it off. "One tiny piece is going to go in Delan's lavender pouch."

"You are evil!"

Kai grinned. "Just imagine the *face* he'll make."

"He'll be furious," said Aranya crossly. But despite her best attempts at control, a tiny smile slipped free.

Triumph thrilled in Kai's belly.

"What are you two giggling about over there? I smell mischief," called Delan from the pot of rice he was cooking over the fire.

Aranya coughed, face flushing. "We're not giggling!"

Kai smirked at her, then strode past to hang the bridles on a branch until tomorrow. He kept his back turned as Aranya's footsteps tromped back to the campfire. Stones rattled in a wooden box—Delan must be getting out his game.

"It's been a while since I've played the Academy wei-chi champion," said Delan, and Kai didn't need to turn around to know exactly what smug expression currently played across the older wielder's features.

"The champion is tired," replied Kai.

"He's afraid you'll beat him again," said Aranya to Delan.

Kai swiveled his head over his shoulder to glare at her. She grinned in response. And for just a moment, he forgot everything except the sight of her smile. Then he blinked quickly, shifted his gaze to the ground, and marched to where Delan was setting up the game. He sat cross-legged across from him and studied the blank board and the two boxes of colored stones. Delan had given him black again, as usual.

He made his move.

They took turns placing and capturing stones. Once or twice, Delan's lips quirked, but he said nothing. Kai kept his face blank, trying to ignore Aranya eating her rice and peering over their shoulders.

The end came quite suddenly. Kai sat with his chin propped on his fist, staring down at the white and black pattern before him, hunting for moves. But as he played each move out in his head, with Delan's subsequent moves, it was suddenly clear. He'd lost again.

"Pass."

Delan's gaze flicked from the stones between them to him. "Pass? Look again, evanescer. Don't give up too soon."

"I'm not giving up," growled Kai. But he looked again. "I'm not seeing what you're seeing."

"What about this?" Delan took one of Kai's stones and set it down on the board.

Kai shook his head. "But you'll place yours here." He took one of Delan's stones and set it down next to his. "One more turn and you'll capture these of mine. Even if I place mine here, it still won't protect them."

"So go on the offensive." Delan plucked up another black stone and set it on the board.

Kai stared. Blinked. *Oh.*

"If you're always defending yourself, you'll never take territory. You'll never *win*."

When Kai glanced up, Delan wasn't looking at the board, but at him. They held each other's gazes. Kai could almost hear his parents' voices in his head.

"You'll be the death of us," his mother had often said.

"Take this knife, son," his father had once said. *"And kill him."*

He'd chosen not to listen to them. Everything about the way they'd addressed him, forced him, guilted him, and coerced him had grated on his soul until he rejected them outright. Something about how Delan spoke to him, however, made Kai want to listen and learn.

"See?" Delan said, playing out a few more turns on the board and drawing him back to the present. He smiled at Kai. "You would've won."

Kai stared down at the board, understanding dawning.

"I'm so lost," said Aranya, around a mouthful of rice. "It's my turn, anyway. Move aside, evanescer."

Kai relinquished his spot on the grass. He tried to occupy himself with his supper, but no matter how famished he was, he couldn't stop watching Aranya and Delan play. The dim light somehow made her eyes brighter as she oscillated between giggles, saucy retorts, and confused frowns.

He needed to be alone, even if it was just a few spare moments.

Getting to his feet, he said briskly, "I'll get more wood, so we have enough for the night."

"Don't die!" Aranya said brightly as she placed her next stone.

It was only a few steps before he'd passed the ring of firelight. The cooling wind and all-encompassing darkness swallowed him whole. What a relief to be *alone* for a few minutes. It was only him, the chorus of chirping crickets, and the wild forest. He had to stay on his guard anywhere in the wilderness, as always, but for a few minutes he could *breathe.*

So breathe he did.

He was busy collecting wood, smelling strains of vanilla mingled with earth, when something made the hairs on the back of his neck straighten. Immediately, he set down his bundle of sticks, whipped out a knife, and evanesced a few feet away, behind a tree.

"Kai? Kai!" came Aranya's distinctive call.

His shoulders loosened. *Just Aranya.* "I'm here," he called back.

"Oh, good! Delan sent me to find you. He was concerned that you were taking so long."

"I've only been gone a few minutes."

"He's a little paranoid after today."

Kai sheathed his knife, stepped out from behind the tree to scoop up the sticks he'd dropped. From here, he could make out Aranya's shadowed form picking her way through the forest toward him. When she saw him, she smiled. A real, happy smile.

He stopped, hesitating.

Her smile turned sheepish, and she halted a few paces away. She looked down, and though it was dark and hard to tell . . . was she flushed? Kai's heart quickened. He swallowed.

"Kai . . . I'm sorry. I'm sorry about earlier. I know I can be cold with you sometimes, and I don't mean it. I think I just have had a hard time understanding everything since . . . since . . ."

Since their kiss. His neck could have blistered from the sudden heat flooding his skin.

But why was she saying this *now*? Why not the other night when they'd talked after Delan had gone to sleep? Did it have anything to do with what happened today?

He wasn't sure. Wasn't sure of anything. He swallowed again.

"It's alright," he said, his throat dry. "Things have been confusing for me, too."

Her smile was tentative. He tightened his jaw, trying to fight the sudden rush of heady emotion through his limbs. When had he last been this uncertain, this uncomfortable, this *bumbling* around a girl? Probably not since he was twelve years old.

He took a step closer. Then another, wishing he had Delan's night vision so he could see her face more clearly, so he could better determine what she was thinking, feeling. With the night around them, he could see little more than the brightness of her eyes. They caught and reflected every shred of light, like animal eyes, but there was no shifter instinct lurking in them. No flashing talons.

"Aranya?" he said, not sure what he was asking.

Her gaze met his and something sparked between them—something warm and new. Something he wanted. What if they could move past their misunderstandings and the unfortunate beginning of their relationship?

Curse this hesitation! Curse his own caution. He only wanted to close the distance between them and—

Two *jiaun* arrows burst through Aranya's chest, her face contorting in horrid shock.

Something between a roar and a shriek ripped out of Kai's throat. He evanesced to her side, his heart raging with terror. He caught her just as her eyes shuddered shut, as a gasp slipped through her lips.

"Aranya! Aranya!" His cries turned frantic, piercing. He gripped her elbow in one hand, her waist in the other.

This wasn't happening.

This wasn't—

She's shot. She's dying. Aranya is going to—

"Get *back*, you idiot!"

That was Aranya's voice, coming from . . . not Aranya in his arms? He was too overwhelmed, too panicked, to give it a second thought. "I'm not letting you go," he growled, shifting his grip so he could lift her without jostling the arrows. "I'll get you to Delan. We'll save you, don't worry."

No time to wonder where the arrows had come from.

Then there was a boot kicking Aranya out of his arms. He gave an inarticulate cry of rage as she screamed, whipping out his knife to stab at their attacker. A blow to his wrist deflected his strike, forcing his arm upward. Then his attacker dove under his arm, snatching the hilt of his other knife before he could grab it.

He evanesced behind the attacker, unsheathing his broadsword, and grabbed the attacker's arm, wrenching it backward, and bringing his sword up to—

The blade met iron-sharpened talons.

"Phoenixes scorch you!" Aranya shrieked, straining to shove away his sword, twisting her wrist and bringing her leg up to kick him.

"Aranya?" Kai gasped, immediately letting go of her and stepping back, his gaze searching for . . . "Fathers, what—"

"Fox spirit!" she snarled, her talons glittering in the sparse moonlight.

Together, they looked down to where the first Aranya lay, arrows through her chest. She gasped, sputtered, her hands reaching up to clutch the wounds. Kai's heart twisted inside his chest so violently he nearly threw up.

No blood. Though the wounds were horrible, there was no blood.

A rock sank in his stomach.

"You didn't string the *jiaun* tight enough," Aranya growled, shifting out of her talons and pulling the weapon back out of its holster. "My shot was off, so it didn't kill the *mó guǐ* immediately."

He ought to restrain the monster so Aranya didn't get hurt, should help her finish the job, but the sight of her dying at his feet . . . Even if it was false, he wasn't sure he would ever recover. Not even when the real Aranya glared at him, loading two more arrows into the *jiaun*. When the fox spirit writhed, moaned, she placed a booted foot down on its wrist. She looked at Kai, clearly expecting him to help.

He swallowed, then caught the monster's other flailing arm and held it fast despite its struggles. He refused to look, focusing instead on the real Aranya as she aimed down.

Her breaths came fast, her throat bobbing, her hands shaking on the trigger.

She stared down at her own face.

Kai watched as she closed her eyes and fired.

The body of the *mó guǐ* slowly morphed back into its original form, its spell broken. Aranya's face melted into a snout and a pair of glazed eyes. Nine bushy tails, so silver they were almost white, protruded from the beautiful, luminescent body. In many ways, it looked like any regular fox, only silver and with more tails.

He should be dead right now.

Aranya was silent, her face grim, staring down at it. She didn't have to say it; he knew he was an idiot for not realizing the warning signs sooner. Even though fox spirits were notorious for their cunning deceptions that few could resist, he should have known the moment the arrows went through its chest, when blood didn't flow everywhere, what it was. Instead, he had been so blinded by his own fear.

"Why did you come after me?" Kai asked finally, softly.

"Delan asked me to follow you. He said that, after the siren lure, he didn't think any of us should be alone in the forest at night."

It had been a wise decision on Delan's part to send her separately, without telling Kai, to keep them both from falling into the same trap. A fox spirit's magic pertained to mind reading and illusions. It found weaknesses in the minds of its victims and personified them. Concealing the knowledge of Aranya trailing him would have kept the *mó guǐ* from learning too quickly about her presence.

They ought to burn the body.

Neither of them moved, but her eyes stole toward his. She'd heard everything, then. Every stupid word. He ran over the brief conversation in his head, how he had behaved, and closed his eyes. Only self-control kept a groan from escaping his throat.

Even if she hadn't heard, she had seen how the fox spirit had personified itself to lure him closer.

He wasn't sure he had ever felt so defeated, so humiliated, in all his life, while simultaneously being endlessly relieved that Aranya hadn't just been shot to death, and he hadn't been devoured body and soul by a fearsome and cunning *mó guǐ*.

Aranya always had things to say. Why was she so quiet now? Why wouldn't she speak? Did she think *he* would break the silence? What was there for him to say? In the span of a few minutes, too much of his soul had been bared before her. He wasn't about to offer more.

And he certainly wasn't about to start explaining or defending himself.

What she saw and heard was . . . *well*, what she saw and heard. She knew the truth now. The truth of how he thought and felt about her.

Aranya sighed, avoiding his gaze, and holstered her *jiaun*. "Delan's probably waiting. Will you burn the body while I take a load of kindling back to Delan?"

Kai only nodded.

Since Kai had evanesced and wouldn't be able to sleep, he took first watch instead of Aranya. When it was her turn for second watch, she blearily wrapped herself up in her blanket while the men slept on opposite sides of the campfire. Perhaps the warmth of the blanket would ease the quivering of her limbs.

She had always thought of the farthest shots as the most difficult. She'd never been more wrong in her life.

The closest shots were the hardest.

Even though she stared down a monster—one who had nearly just eaten her companion—pulling the trigger might have been the hardest thing she had ever done. It had stared back at her, her face, but not her eyes. Silver eyes, made of moonlight and glowing with stars and far more sentience than comfortable.

This was not like killing the qilins.

Nothing like killing the qilins.

She wrapped her blanket tighter around her shoulders, staring into the flickering flames. At least Kai had relieved her of burning the body.

It was tradition, practically law, that a fox spirit's body must be burned after killing. The reasoning had to do with how they consumed a person, body and soul, therefore in death a fox spirit ought to be destroyed both body and soul.

She didn't question it.

Death always took, it never gave. Even though it was a *mó guǐ*, this death had robbed a piece of her, a bit of her humanity, her goodness, and replaced it with a warrior's hardened edge.

Was this truly the life she wanted? Being a warden was different; they protected the innocent and vulnerable from danger within and without. Even when they encountered brigands, they were never trying to kill, only apprehend.

There simply weren't very many *mó guǐ* brash enough to enter a city.

Being a warden had allowed her to serve her people and contribute to the greater good of humanity. This? This was—well, it was still doing those things, but it came at a higher price to herself.

Whatever the cost, however . . .

Her eyes drifted to Kai's sleeping form. He had been so close to . . . Her heart faltered within her chest, but she clenched her jaw and firmed her resolve. She would do what she had to for the sake of protecting her comrades.

And she most *certainly* would not think about what she had seen and heard before she'd shot the beast. She wouldn't think about what it meant that the personification of Kai's weakness was *her*.

CHAPTER 12

"ARE YOU SERIOUS?" Delan cried.

Aranya urged her horse closer to his, lifting a branch and ducking under it. "What's the matter?" she called ahead.

"Yes, we're serious," Kai called out dryly from even further behind her, lost somewhere in the dense foliage.

She might have spat back, *"Not helpful!"* but just then, Delan said, "The bridge!"

Aranya dismounted and fought through more branches and bundles of leaves until she broke through and stood on the edge of a chasm. The drop was so steep she couldn't even see the bottom for the fog. When she lifted her attention from the great gorge, Delan stood with his legs planted wide, fists on his hips as he stared down what remained of a rope bridge. A series of hefty stakes in the ground, strung together with rope that had been cut—on the opposite side of the chasm. She took several steps closer and crouched right on the edge of the cliff, bracing her hands on tufts of grass between sharp stones. Below her, drifting slightly in the wind, was the rope bridge hanging listlessly, disappearing into the fog.

Something grabbed her collar, and she glanced up to find Delan scowling at her. "Don't go diving off the cliff now, shifter."

She chuckled at his grumpy protectiveness, then sat back on her haunches and twisted to look behind her as Kai emerged from the forest, a few leaves stuck in his hair.

"I'd bet you just about anything that those brigands cut this bridge so we couldn't follow," Delan growled.

And even if they found a path down into the chasm, it would be too much for their horses. "So . . . we go around?" Aranya asked.

Delan's grunt was laced with annoyance as he grabbed his horse's lead and marched away from the cliff. "The way around is very, *very* long and will set us back significantly, but there's no other option."

"East or west?" she asked.

"West. Going east and getting on a ship would possibly be faster, but with the seasons turning, it's too much of an unknown variable. The worst-case scenario would be to go all the way to the coast and then have to turn around because there's no ship to board. West—we'll head west. But first we need to find water for our horses. I think I smelled a waterhole back that way."

As they fought their way through the underbrush again, Aranya chewed on her lip and tried not to steal glances at Kai. She wasn't sure if she should try to repair their somewhat antagonistic friendship after all the . . . *awkwardness* as of late.

Maybe I care about you, he'd said.

She swallowed stiffly, quelling the rising heat in her cheeks, and said blithely, "Tromping through this brush makes me think of Academy Hunts."

Kai didn't respond.

"Did you ever catch a *mó guǐ* during the Hunts?" she pressed, trying not to let her brow furrow in irritation.

"No," he said.

"Did you *try* to catch one?"

A side-eye was the only response she got.

"If you weren't trying to catch a *mó guǐ*, then what did you do all night?"

"I went back to my dormitory and slept, of course."

Her mouth dropped open, but her heart lifted at the faintest pull of a smirk on Kai's lips. "You really were a rogue," she said.

The smirk disappeared, and he went back to being the solemn-faced, brooding Kai she'd come to dislike very much. She drew a deep breath in through her teeth. There was nothing to it; she'd just have to prattle.

"In the last Hunt, Cao Renshu caught two dragons," she said. "Didn't even have a scrape from the encounter. Maybe that's because he's a feral-wielder with insane strength."

"Did you fancy him?" came Kai's drawl.

"What?" She popped something in her neck with how fast she craned to him. "No, of course not. He was just one of the top students, along with Fen and Shangdi and all the rest in the top ten. I just *admired* them all. Nothing like . . . like that."

"You can't blush while you're lying. It gives you away."

She glared at him, lips parting in a snarl as fight surged in her blood. Kai was fully smirking now, one eyebrow raised.

"Which one was it?" he asked, attempting to school his features into the expression of a trusted confidante. "I heard everyone fancied Shangdi at one time or another. I mean, I imagine it would be hard not to, what with being the top student of our class, and apparently being *almost* as handsome as me."

He was grinning now. Aranya continued scowling.

"Or was it Renshu? With all that physical strength? Wasn't there also a shapeshifter too? What was his name? You know, if you married *him*, you could preserve the shapeshifting magic in your bloodline." Kai took another glance at Aranya, raised both of his eyebrows. "Wait, was it *all* of them?"

"Not at the same time!" Aranya snarled, and immediately regretted it when that slyness crossed Kai's face. "I was at the Academy since I was five! There were a lot of years—"

"And you were criticizing *me* for my—"

"That's different! You were kissing all of yours!"

"Was I?"

"Weren't you?"

He only lifted one brow. "Maybe someday, if you ask *very* nicely, I'll tell you."

"I don't want to know, Kai," Aranya said sharply, not sure what to make of her suddenly throbbing heart and the inexplicable tightness in her chest. She flashed him her most patronizing grin, and then quickened her step so she outpaced him.

"Delan!" she called. "When you were at the Academy—"

Delan stopped abruptly, raising a hand.

Aranya's pulse quickened. "What?"

He frowned, sniffing. "I think . . ."

Just then, there was a screech overhead. She instinctively ducked, eyes darting wildly above them in search of—

A shadow passed over her face, blocking the sun. Light glittered off its ruby-red scales, its serpentine tail, its silvery talons.

Aranya immediately drew her *jiaun,* but Kai appeared at her side and snatched her wrist, lowering her weapon. She was about to shoot him a furious retort when he jerked his head sideways, eyes widened.

She followed his gaze, followed Delan's gaze, to an outcropping that dipped out of the forest and into a ravine. There, perched on the rock, was a beast. Its body was coiled in sleep, sunlight dazzling along its emerald scales. Its long snout was tucked into the ends of its tail. It wasn't very big; it was about the size of a medium-sized dog.

A sunbathing, napping dragon.

Kai released her wrist as her arm flagged and her jaw hung open.

There were at least two and shooting one would alert the other. But if there were two here . . .

"Looks like we're not the only ones here for a drink. I hate getting this deep into the wilderness," Delan muttered under his breath, gaze darting from the dragon, to the edge of the ravine where the waterhole must be, to the tail-swishing horses they guided. "Kai, scout ahead."

Kai gritted his teeth, but vanished. He reappeared not far from the dragon, moving with painstaking care as he peered over the edge of the outcropping into the ravine. Aranya kept her *jiaun* loaded, snapped into firing mode at her side, as she and Delan waited.

When Kai turned around toward them, his eyes were even wider than before. He met her gaze, then beckoned her to join him. She glanced at Delan and though his jaw was tense and his eyes full of warning, he nodded once.

Not having the luxury of instantaneous distance travel, it took her several minutes to tread carefully to Kai's side, the presence of the sleeping dragon burning into her side as she moved. When she crouched next to him, his face was grim. He nodded his head to the view, then watched her as she looked.

She couldn't restrain her tiny gasp.

The ravine cut deeper than she expected, hard rock lining the descent into the waterhole. But worse than the impossibility of getting their horses down to the water at this pass, was . . . was . . .

It was *infested.*

Infested with *mó guǐ.*

Some were sprawled like the dragon near them—draped across rocky overhangs, napping, or lazily swishing their tails in the air. Others, like the qilins she saw on the opposite side of the waterhole, took their time drinking their fill. More flew overhead, dragons and . . . *phoenixes.* She hadn't ever seen a phoenix before, and the sight stole her breath away.

One streaked across the sky, a trail of fire and smoke, and landed near the edge of the water, right next to a qilin. It looked so small, seeming much less vicious next to the terror of the qilins, yet it still must have been thrice the size of a swan. It preened feathers of burning flames, rifling through them with its beak. The only parts of the phoenix's body that weren't fiery were its black eyes and black beak. Then it bent down, scooped up a beak-full of water and arched back its head to swallow, its neck bobbing.

Of all things, it hopped its way into the water and began ducking its head under and rolling back to let the water fall down its feathers. The water sizzled on its flaming feathers, whistling and evaporating into a column of steam. Six or so more watched it, as though debating if they should take an afternoon swim too.

There were dozens of *mó guǐ.* No—*more* than dozens. Perhaps even a hundred, all different shapes and sizes. She couldn't even be scared. Though the tiniest sneeze could be her death, she couldn't help staring in open-mouthed awe at the beauty of the sight. So much raw power, gleaming in the sun against the blue of the water and the green of the forest. The bright colors, the strangeness, the otherworldliness—it was like nothing she'd ever seen.

"Same," Kai whispered beside her.

She glanced sidelong at him, not caring what showed on her face. He stared back, and he started, almost as if to reach out to her, but he stopped himself. He planted his hand on the rocky ledge instead, turning his face away from her.

She swallowed, blood suddenly humming with something entirely different from awe at the monsters. She glanced back at Delan, who was angrily holding up both hands as if to say, "*Well? What is it?*"

How could she communicate without words, across this distance, what she saw?

Kai vanished and reappeared at Delan's side. Their conversing voices were so low, she couldn't catch even a thread of sound. Instead, with a wary glance at the sleeping dragon—it let out a large, unnerving sigh in response—she returned her focus to the waterhole.

They really ought to leave. Find another source of water. But then, from below, movement caught her eye.

It wasn't the movement of so many *mó guǐ* milling around. It was the swift, purposeful movements of a man.

CHAPTER 13

HER FOCUS SNAPPED to sharp clarity. She leaned forward, both hands gripping the rocky outcropping now, her braid falling over her shoulder, over the long drop.

The man wore black. He was tall, his frame broad and strong. His dark hair grayed along his temples, and it was pulled back into tight braids against his scalp. He wore a heavy cloak trimmed in fur, despite the midday heat. Behind him, bound in chains, hunched an older man in a ratty cloak. His white beard caught and blew in the breeze.

The first man approached the *mó guǐ* with no fear in his gaze, no falter in his steps. Aranya frowned as she squinted against the reflecting water. He strode toward the same phoenix she'd been watching, never slowing.

He pulled something out of his cloak. A small black bag. He reached inside, removed something so tiny she couldn't discern what it was. Then, with gritted teeth, he wheeled back his arm and threw it at the phoenix. His movements were uncannily like a lassoing motion, though she saw no rope.

But she *did* see shadow.

The phoenix stiffened, let out a cacaw of outrage, and spread its wings to fly. It shot into the air, only to be yanked down to the ground by some invisible force. Aranya barely smothered her gasp of horror. It struggled, jerking its neck like it wore a collar, flapping its wings. It opened its mouth, fire spewing forth, but almost as quickly, its mouth clamped shut.

The man in black stared at the *mó guǐ*, then muttered a few clipped words.

The phoenix stopped fighting. Instead, it hobbled on its clawed feet toward the man. The man pointed one long finger, and the phoenix followed his direction and settled itself primly to one side.

Magnificence *bound.*

Aranya's eyes burned.

He moved to the next phoenix.

The air grew hotter, hotter, as the strange man in black bound one phoenix after another. Aranya gaped, her talons lengthening and digging into the sandstone. This—this was *wrong.* Killing *mó guǐ* to protect the defenseless was one thing. But binding them as though they were slaves?

At the same time, she couldn't begin to guess how this man could harness such power to bind and use the magic of another—

She stopped.

Her mouth dropped open all the way to her toes. She stared, realization shining brighter than the sun on the surface of the water. The old man, the one in chains—he was one of the missing wielders, wasn't he? He looked different from his picture in her packet from the Secret Services, but not unrecognizably different. He'd vanished twelve years ago.

Du Liuxian. The evanescer.

The man in black, then, was none other than Fang Zedong.

And *this* was why he kidnapped magic wielders. He had a means of controlling them and harnessing their magic. Unusual magic. Illegal magic.

Black magic.

If that was indeed the missing evanescer, one that could carry other people when he evanesced, then that would explain how Fang managed to be so far from Butagin, with no sign of a travel party.

Before she could move, Du Liuxian glanced between Fang and the forest, then down again at the chains binding his wrists. Did they prevent him from evanescing? Was there some kind of magic woven into those chains to suppress his power? Could she save him?

She didn't have another minute to consider the question, because Du Liuxian turned and burst into a run—away from Fang. Disregarding the *mó guǐ*, his chains, and his own aging and frail body, he tore into the forest.

Fang whirled, and the phoenix he'd just captured ripped its neck backward as if a cord had wrenched it. The bird hit the ground, its flaming feathers flapping to right itself. The other *mó guǐ*, so peaceful a moment ago, whipped their attention to the sudden sound. Some scurried off or slinked away, while others spat hissing warnings and got to their feet.

"Stop where you are," Fang barked at Liuxian. "Or it will be worse for you."

Liuxian paid no heed, stumbling as he tried to run.

With a sweep, Fang pulled a loaded *jiaun* from a holster hidden in his cloak and—before Araya could even blink—shot the evanescer.

She gasped, covering her mouth as Liuxian hit the ground with a pained cry, two arrows stuck through his shoulder. Fang holstered the weapon with a dark expression on his face and ignored the struggling firebird as he marched toward the fallen evanescer.

"Get to your feet," he growled.

Then Fang leaned down and grabbed the arrows just beneath their heads as they protruded from his shoulder.

"No, please!" cried Liuxian.

Fang yanked.

The scream that rent the air nearly made Aranya vomit. Rage was fast on the heels of queasiness. She whipped out two arrows from her quiver and slotted them in her *jiaun.* It was a far shot, but if she could take out Fang now, it would be so much easier to save the other wielders. Feiyan, Zuan Wan, the princess, all the rest. She lined up her sights, staring down the shaft. One shot—and this could all be over.

Kai reappeared just then beside her, his hand already darting out to grab her wrist, to stop her from shooting. But he appeared so suddenly, his hand coming out of nowhere.

Aranya startled.

She jolted, the movement harsh and abrupt, and without intending to, she pulled the trigger. She flung herself downward, and the movement was enough to throw the arrows off trajectory, sending them shooting into the air.

If their sudden movement or the bits of outcropping crumbling around them and tumbling into the water didn't give them away, the whizzing of the arrows through open sky did.

Fang—along with the entire dozens upon dozens of *mó guǐ*—turned to look at them.

Kai had already ducked below the ledge. But Aranya stared back, caught like a stunned deer in the sapphire blue gaze of the strange man. Then Kai grabbed her upper arm and yanked her down.

"What were you *thinking* pulling out your *jiaun*?"

"What were *you* thinking, startling me so badly? Did you see what happened?"

"I didn't—"

A nearby hiss made them both turn.

The emerald dragon woke up. Its tail uncurled from around its snout, and it raised itself up on its haunches. Beady golden eyes, with slits like a cat's, fixed on where they crouched only a few feet away.

It spread its leathery wings, iridescent in the sunlight, and shrieked.

"I swear, I'm going to *kill* you both!" Delan growled from where he'd stayed guarding the horses, already mounting up.

The dragon's head swiveled toward him, toward the flesh of the three horses, and it threw back its head and shot a pillar of fire into the air. Wings flapped, smoke curling out of nostrils.

Aranya scrambled back, trying to reload her *jiaun*. "Over here, you big idiot!" she called to the dragon. Kai spewed out frustration, unsheathing his broadsword.

But the dragon merely shrieked again and shot into the sky, flapping its beautiful wings. She watched it go, her hand stilled where it gripped an arrow. Kai paused, too, lowering his sword and glancing warily back at her.

She scooted in the dirt back to the ledge, carefully peering out again.

Fang Zedong stared back at her. By now, he'd captured and bound four phoenixes, which sat stiffly behind him while the evanescer lay moaning in a pool of blood. Even from this distance, his eyes flashed the brightest blue she'd ever seen.

Unnatural.

He lifted one hand into the air and snapped his fingers. In one accord, the phoenixes behind him rose into the air. Aranya's throat went dry.

The firebirds came zooming toward them.

"*Run!*" she screamed.

She shot to her feet, barreling toward Delan and the horses. Kai had vanished, and Delan was already kicking his horse into a gallop, leading Kai's. He dropped the lead to Aranya's, so she could leap up and follow him.

Wind pummeled her from behind.

She stumbled to her knees, but sprang up again as her horse bucked and shrieked. "Easy, girl!" she cried, snatching the flailing lead out of the air. Her hands fumbled, but she caught hold of the saddle horn as the horse landed back on all fours. She swung herself up into the saddle and kicked her horse into a gallop.

She turned just in time to see how fast the phoenixes gained on them. *Run.* Her body screamed with fear, with the anticipation of a fiery death. She kicked her horse faster. "Faster, faster, *faster*!"

When she angled forward again, she had no time to even scream before she hit a low-hanging branch.

She flew from the saddle.

Her foot caught in the stirrup.

She hit the ground hard—and fast. Her horse didn't stop; it charged forward at the same galloping pace, dragging her with it. The uneven, rocky ground ripped into the vulnerable flesh of her back. She twisted, gasping in shock and pain.

But there was no time to think. She'd be dragged to her death if she didn't do something. Fire burst near her, scalding her face with sudden heat. With a cry, she shifted her hands and, using every last bit of her strength, curled upward and sliced through the leather.

She stopped so suddenly it was painful.

Overhead, the phoenixes careened past her.

She might have laid there, her back burning, her head throbbing, but one of the phoenixes wheeled and banked toward her.

Aranya sucked in a pained gasp of air, tasting blood on her tongue, and scrambled up to her feet. She fumbled for her *jiaun*, realized it was missing, and right as the phoenix screamed and opened its gaping, teeth-lined beak, she tore off into a sprint.

Into the depths of the forest.

She couldn't outrun it, but if she could find wood too dense for it to penetrate—

Fire shot through the air, incinerating the trees above her. She threw up her hands, futilely shielding her head from falling debris.

Her heart thundered in her chest, her breaths coming in bursting gasps.

Seeing denser foliage, she circled right and straight into the underbrush. Immediately, she regretted the decision. She stumbled, barely leaping over tangling vines instead of falling face first into them.

Aranya ran. Kept running. She ran until her lungs nearly burst out of her chest.

But she couldn't stop.

Crashing sounded overhead, and she didn't look as another blast of fire demolished a patch of wood right in front of her. She screamed, barely wheeling to the side. It was going to kill her. She couldn't outrun it. The forest couldn't save her.

Another burst of fire came alarmingly close, but she ducked under a branch and skirted around a tree, sprinting again.

Ye Ye.

She refused to die. Not while her grandfather still breathed. Wherever Kai and Delan were, she could only hope and pray they were faring better than she was.

Renewed, she ran faster, cursing her short legs and her short strides.

Her legs buckled, caught on something. She plunged headlong into a tangle of underbrush and vines. She was already moving as she landed, her whole body shaking with flight.

The phoenix flew past her again, shooting up in the air to circle around to her.

She couldn't outrun it. But perhaps . . .

She had no *jiaun,* and a sling was nothing against a phoenix. Setting her teeth grimly, refusing to give into the impulse to *run,* she yanked her knife from its sheath and faced the oncoming phoenix.

It squawked, its cries a monstrous version of a bird's call. Beady eyes fixed on her, flame and smoke trailing in its blazing path. There was so much more intelligence in those eyes than she expected.

Stay.

Her muscles jerked. It was painful to stay still, to not run when death stared her down. But she had no intention of dying, and she'd looked her own death in the eyes before. She would not cower now.

The phoenix burned through the treetops, coming straight toward her. Wind from its mighty, flaming wings battered her back a step. Her palm sweated around the hilt of the knife she held. Suddenly frantic, she patted herself down and realized it was her last weapon. No more knives—just this, and her claws.

That was it. *This* was it.

The phoenix opened its beak, fire shooting straight toward her.

Only when she saw the light and smoke burbling at the back of the creature's throat did she leap with all her strength out of the way. *Desperately*—for her life.

The fire left nothing in its wake. Only blackened ground. Heat blasted her back, then her face as she whirled. The monster careened past her like before, but it wheeled so quickly she could hardly draw back her arm.

Win or lose. It was time to kill or be killed.

Aranya flung her knife just as the creature turned around.

It struck the phoenix's throat.

The *mó guǐ* froze in midair, its eyes widening with shock, with pain. With knowing—understanding. Those eyes fixed on her, on her outstretched hand. Then it fell, impacting so hard the ground shook.

Its fire snuffed out like a candle.

Aranya let out a shuddering sob. "I'm sorry!" she gasped. "You were a prisoner, controlled against your will, and I—I . . ."

The bird's long, feathered wing spread over its face, shielding her from the view of its death wound. She had always thought firebirds were orange, but with its fire gone, the bird was charcoal black.

It smoked. Like smoldering ashes.

She collapsed to her knees.

CHAPTER 14

DON'T FORGET YE Ye," Aranya gasped, bracing her hands wide in the dirt to keep herself from completely collapsing. If the firebird had killed her, she would never have returned to Ye Ye. Neither would she have been able to continue their rescue of the missing wielders and the princess.

The firebird was doomed the moment Fang Zedong cursed it.

No amount of reasoning, however, could quell the shuddering in her limbs or absolve the guilt in her heart. Killing the fox spirit had been hard enough; killing a phoenix with intelligence and no will of its own was another kind of excruciating. It marked her soul. She wasn't just a wielder now, or even a warrior. She was a killer.

But she had no time to weep over the corpse of the monster sent to kill her. She steeled her spine, forced her limbs to obey her, and dragged herself to her feet. With each breath, she fortified herself against the pain radiating down her back.

That was when realization hit.

"Kai?" she called, dread knotting her stomach. Louder: "Delan?"

The silence of unending woods stretched before her. Its own foreboding answer.

"No, no, no," she breathed. "No, no, *please* no."

At first, she moved slowly, turning in a circle on her unsteady feet. The only familiar thing in the entire forest was the blackened corpse nearby.

"Delan?" she cried, trying to quell her rising panic. "Kai?"

Wind rustled the branches. A soft, gentle breeze; it was cooling, sweeping the summer heat into autumn. In the green surrounding her, some leaves were already turning colors. Sunlight filtered through the foliage, drifting dangerously low on the horizon.

She drew in a deep breath and shouted as loud as she could, "KAI! DELAN!"

Nothing.

She ought to think clearly, to be rational. She couldn't have run that far; they couldn't have been separated by much. If she retraced her steps, she could go back to the waterhole and follow the trails to find her missing companions.

She wouldn't panic. Nothing merited panicking yet.

It was only the woods. Sure, she didn't have any weapons, but she had her talons. She would never be entirely helpless. There was her knife, too. She could approach the phoenix corpse, pull back the feathers, and—

No, she couldn't. She knew what she would see. Eyes still open in shock, beak gaping with pain, its lifeblood—No, no, she couldn't bear to face it and extract the knife.

Her talons would have to do.

She made to walk past the corpse, but a hissing sound stopped her dead in her tracks. She froze, breath catching in her lungs. Every muscle braced; her hands tensed to shift.

Something slithered near her foot.

She shrieked and leapt back as something gray and sinuous flashed through the underbrush. It was big; thick as her arm and at least five feet in length. The size didn't frighten her so much as the stories she'd heard in class of *this* creature's venomous bite.

But it wasn't coming for her. It went straight for the corpse. Aranya watched in horror as the snake-like thing slithered up to the blackened firebird and sank its fangs into its spine. The snake-monster's body convulsed, and it took her a second to realize it was sucking.

More hisses filled the air. Terror froze her blood.

The ground began moving.

Out of nowhere, called by the stench of blood, dozens, no *hundreds,* of gray, patterned bodies slithered toward the carcass. She turned to run, but they were coming from every direction.

She was surrounded.

One bumped against her foot, and when she jerked back with another shriek, the creature reared its head and flashed its fangs at her. She barely had time to shift her hands and swipe at it before it struck, deflecting the deadly blow.

Then she was scrambling up the nearest tree, her body screaming in protest as she swung herself into its high branches. Bark dug under her fingernails, so sharp it drew blood. But she didn't care. All that mattered was getting away from the swarm of scavenging monsters.

They could slither up trees. If they did, she was dead.

She could only pray they were preoccupied by the phoenix. At that thought, she twisted on her branch and peered out toward where it had been. Her stomach convulsed. Where the phoenix had been, there was now a writhing mass of gray bodies. She pressed a hand to her stomach, trying to avoid heaving up its meager contents. Instead, she clung to the tree, pressing her face into its prickly bark, and watched as the sun dipped lower and lower into the horizon.

More skittering creatures came, ones that looked more like a bug version of a rat. It was a swarm of *mó guǐ*, their sounds alone making Aranya so woozy she nearly toppled off her perch.

Instead, she clung tighter.

Each breath was a heaving shudder. She watched the hours slip by, watched as night slowly descended. She ought to climb down while the monsters were occupied, but it seemed from every corner of the world more kept coming, skittering and slithering.

"Where are you, Kai?" she whispered, a sob catching in her throat. Between his magic and Delan's, they ought to be able to find her quickly enough.

Unless . . .

Unless they had fared even worse than she had. Unless, even now, monsters feasted upon their corpses.

Aranya choked as panic, full and all-encompassing, descended upon her. It welled in her throat, cutting off her air, tightening her chest. She couldn't stay in this tree forever, and if her comrades needed her, she ought to face the monsters below. Night was almost here, and with it, all hope of retracing her steps would be lost.

At best, she'd been a mediocre tracker in daylight.

Ignoring her body's protests and the blood staining her tunic, she lowered herself on shaky arms to another branch. The movement, though slight, elicited a hiss from the monsters. She froze, her breathing turning frantic.

They returned to their meal.

She moved again.

This time, a few stray snake-monsters came slithering her way. She scrambled further into the tree, panic driving her higher than safe. But the monsters began coiling their way up the trunk of the tree, and something within her snapped.

Tottering precariously, she broke branches and hurled them down at the beasts. They hissed, and she successfully knocked one off. It landed on the ground, but immediately began climbing again, unperturbed.

She suppressed a sob, hair in her face and snagging on leaves and branches. She ripped off bigger branches, throwing them harder and harder at the creatures. More fell, but one very persistent one reached the top.

She couldn't climb any higher. The monster hissed, baring its fangs and striking at her feet. She screamed, catching hold of an upper branch, and swung her legs out of the way barely in time.

It hissed, snapping its jaw in fury, and slithered up further.

More curled up the tree's base now, and Aranya spared a glance back toward the phoenix. A sudden bolt of queasiness hit her as the monsters peeled off the corpse.

Except there was nothing left. Not a single bone, feather, or bit of its sharpened beak.

Now they came for her.

The sun disappeared. Night fell around her.

She released one tight grip on the branch she swung from, hanging from only one hand now. Her other hand, she shifted. With a feral snarl, she swiped at the close monster. It struck at her, but she was barely faster. She pierced its scaley hide with her talon and, before it could bite her, flung it as far as she could.

They kept coming, and she was in the worst possible position.

More struck at her feet. Her grip turned sweaty on the branch, her core straining. Not knowing what else to do, she glanced toward the neighboring tree.

There was a branch that was . . . sort of close.

Swiping three monsters off the lower branch with her talons, she released her hold and dropped onto it. It cracked, and she nearly pitched forward. But she balanced just enough to leap off the branch toward the next tree.

The first branch cracked more, throwing off her jump.

She went hurtling through the air, her feet missing the branch. But, despite the slickness of her hands, she caught it and stopped her fall. She spared one glance backward and saw the tree wriggling with beasts.

She nearly vomited then and there.

Instead, she swung herself to a lower branch, then dropped herself straight to the ground. She landed in a roll, barely catching her balance, before she stumbled.

Then she was running.

She didn't care what direction. Didn't care how her body screamed in agony. She just had to get *away.* And then, despite knowing it was utterly idiotic, she screamed at the top of her lungs, "*Kai!! Kai! Delan!*"

There was no rescue. No tall evanescer to sweep her up into his saddle and carry her to safety. No stocky feral-wielder to toss her a weapon and say he had her back.

No, she was alone. In the wilderness, at night, surrounded by *mó guǐ.*

Her last bits of sanity disappeared. Panic burst across her senses, and she was suddenly frantic that she would never be free of this night, of these monsters, of her own helplessness.

How long could she run until she gave out entirely?

How long till another monster stumbled upon her? Caught a whiff of her prone flesh, the blood pounding in her veins and bleeding out her back?

Aranya sobbed as she ran, losing her sense of direction until she heard the sound of running water. Something exploded inside her, something desperate beyond explanation. She ran, half stumbling, not even sure if she was still pursued, following that sound.

That was when the world split in two.

She skittered to a stop, eyes going wide as her brain balked at what she saw.

To her right was a garden. A vivid, sunlit garden, with colors so bright they nearly blinded her night-adjusted eyes. Its beauty was exquisite, so stunning it nearly brought more tears pouring down her cheeks. It seemed to rip through the seams of the world, rending it and pasting on top of it this . . . this *vision.*

To her left was a cave.

It was dark, such a contrast to the warmth of the glittering garden that beckoned her. Brain aching from the two sights, trying to understand *what was going on*, she only panicked further.

She ran toward the cave.

The instant she bowed beneath the gaping stone mouth, the light of the garden vanished. She was pitched back into darkness, and all around was the echoing sound of water dropping. Not flowing, like she'd heard only a minute ago, but a steady *drip, drip, drip.*

She plunged deeper into the cave, not sure if she was seeking refuge from the *mó guǐ,* or if some other unreasonable instinct compelled her. All she knew was that she had to keep moving.

Her step splattered in liquid.

At once, the stench of the place clogged in her nostrils, and she didn't have to bend down to touch the liquid to know it was blood. It dripped at the back of the cave, pooled around her feet.

Kai's blood?

She froze, her breath coming hot and fast. "Kai?" she called softly, but her voice echoed throughout the chamber, bouncing off rock and blood. "Delan?"

The shadow that emerged from the depths of the cave was neither Kai nor Delan, yet Aranya recognized him almost instantly. Her heart stopped.

The brigand. The illusionist.

"This isn't real," she demanded, as she gestured to the cave surrounding them. "This is one of your illusions, isn't it?"

The shadowy form slowly stepped forward. "It is one of my memories."

She stared, trying to keep herself from bolting, trying to keep herself *reasonable.* Rational, calm. "And the garden?"

"I made it."

Made it? The dazzling beauty she'd seen was the product of his imagination? She shifted her hands into claws and growled, "Why are you here?"

"I've hunted you," he responded plainly, his voice dead.

"Why?"

"To kill you."

CHAPTER 15

ARANYA BARRED HER teeth, flicking her wrists to lengthen her talons. She stepped through the pooling blood, approaching the illusionist.

"You won't kill me," she said.

He tipped his head and said nothing. Neither acquiescence nor denial.

"Whose blood is this?" she asked, approaching him. Without fully realizing it, her movements turned more animalistic, more predatorial, despite *her* being the hunted one. She slinked closer, muscles tensed. She didn't care if her words were snarls, if her teeth flashed in the darkness. "It's your memory. Whose blood is it?"

"I was sent to kill you."

"I don't *care,*" Aranya snapped. "You're not killing me, and that's that. Now make this illusion go away."

Silence.

She charged.

He deflected the first swipe of her talons, ducking under her second. She growled like a wildcat, leaping again. This time, her talons sliced along his sleeve, but he moved so fast she only cut through fabric.

He snatched one wrist, yanking it behind her. Her cry was that of a girl in pain, but she followed it with another wolfish snarl. She twisted in his grasp, trying to pivot and duck, but he slammed her against the wall of the cave.

"You're right," he said, his voice low as he pinned her. "I'm not going to kill you. But then I must trap you so my comrades think you're dead."

"Nope," she gasped, face plastered against icy stone. "You can also let me go. You can let me kill you."

"I cannot."

Then the world shifted around them. And the illusionist, with a final wrench on her arm, shoved her to her knees. He turned and ran. She whirled, leaping to her feet, just in time to see him vanish through the cave opening.

Chasing after him, she barreled over rocks as blood spattered on her garments. She focused on the scraps of moonlight she could see through that opening.

The cave twisted.

The opening disappeared, swallowed up by stone. She choked on her own air, frantically spinning on her heel to find it again.

There it was. On the opposite side of the cave. Aranya growled, breaking into a run toward it. But the moment she got within a few feet, it shifted again, and she ran straight into a stone wall.

She pummeled the wall with the side of her fist. "You dragon-blasted illusionist!"

It wasn't real.

So why were the cavern walls solid beneath her touch? Why was the splattering blood wet on her legs as she ran? She turned for the opening and didn't immediately see it. But as she kept moving through the cave, she caught the barest trace of moonlight. She plunged deeper into the cave after it, all the hope in her soul tied up in finding her way out of this place.

She dodged around stalagmites, ducked under stalactites, chasing that fragment of light. It led to an opening in the wall. She jumped down to the floor beneath.

More blood. Deeper this time.

Aranya sucked in a shuddering breath, but did not let her pace flag. If anything, she was faster. Chasing down the light, even though it would be gone the moment she had it within her grasp. She ran through the cave until she found the opening. She sprinted as fast as she could, trying to fling herself through it before it disappeared.

Her shoulder was met with solid stone.

The opening reappeared to her left.

What else could she do? She dragged herself upright, but she couldn't bring herself to chase it again. It *didn't matter.* She would always be too late.

"It's not real, it's not real," she whispered into the darkness. She pressed her hand against the icy stone, as though to pass straight through the barrier.

It was solid.

She slid to the ground, not caring that she sat in blood. Curling up into a ball, she let her talons vanish. Sobs wracked her chest, and she pressed her face into her hands.

Aranya wept in despair.

She would never see Ye Ye again, never see Kai or Delan, or anyone else. Fathers! If she could but have one more chance, she would never be cross again. She would never be angry with Kai, and her landlord could take all her money. As long as she could be with Ye Ye, with Kai, with Delan, she didn't care if they lived out in the wilderness and ate nothing but rice cakes.

Anything to be free of this night.

Maybe this wasn't real. Maybe she was dreaming, and soon she would wake up with crusty eyelids to find Delan shaking her awake and telling her it was time to ride. More tears came, but these weren't the wracking sobs of earlier—they were soft, mournful weeping.

Not real. Not real.

None of this was real. She wouldn't believe it.

Kai. She'd tried so hard to hate him. But she couldn't keep lying to herself anymore. She longed for him to be here with her like he had been during her nightmare. She wanted his arms around her, his voice in her ear telling her that everything would be alright. Her entire life had been spent with only Ye Ye, but now . . . Ye Ye wasn't enough. She wanted Kai.

He wasn't here.

Eventually, oblivion claimed her.

When Aranya awoke, the world was bright.

Brighter, at least. Legions brighter than the cave, though it was still night. She scrambled up and realized she stood on *grass*. On a grassy ledge, overlooking a stream that cut through woods.

No ensnaring cave. No blood—none, except her own staining her clothes.

Her limbs trembled so much with relief that she collapsed back onto the ground on all fours. She stared at the grass, illuminated by the early dawn, and she thought she had never seen anything so beautiful in her life.

Finally, rallying the last reserves of her strength, she stood again. She tried to take stock of where she was, to find out what direction to head. It wouldn't do to simply wander off in a random direction. She needed to stay close to the stream so she wouldn't get lost. Delan and Kai would need water.

If they were still alive.

Her best bet was to wander up and down stream with the hopes that she'd find someone. Drawing in a deep, fortifying breath, she began trekking upstream. She shook with hunger and the remnants of last night's despair. But the sun was shining, and no matter how weak she felt, she would *not* give up.

She would see this through.

She wouldn't wonder about what she would do if Delan and Kai hadn't made it. It only made panic bubble up like more choking sobs in her throat.

Stick to the stream. One foot in front of the other.

Swiping filthy hair out of her face, she took one determined step, then another. It seemed like hours, though from the slant of the sun it couldn't have been long.

Then, to her shock, she found crushed grass, as though it had been trampled underfoot. When she looked for more, a trail that someone had walked, she didn't find anything. To anyone else, this would have been discouraging. For Aranya, who looked for an evanescer, this sent her blood pounding so hard she could barely think. There—there was a smear of blood on the grass. Not good, but . . . perhaps Kai *wasn't* dead. He would have had to be alive to evanesce.

She hurried further down the stream, discovering another spot. *Oh fathers, please.* She needed to find him. She needed *him*. And then she looked up—

There was a person.

Aranya's heart quickened, the desperation in her soul focusing on that one point. A man, propped against a tree, not that far away. His head lolled, and she had a horrible thought that he was dead.

But when she burst into a run and cried in broken sobs, *"Kai!"*, his head snapped up.

It was him. It was Shi Kai, leaning against that tree, and suddenly stumbling to get to his feet. He seemed to buckle beneath his own weight, collapsing back against the tree, but he called out, his voice laced with the same frantic relief as hers. "Aranya!"

Her limbs wouldn't carry her fast enough, and a few times she stumbled, but after what seemed a thousand years, she fell to her knees beside him—fell straight into his open arms.

"Kai," she gasped, not even caring how desperately she wept. She only wanted to be as close to him as she possibly could.

He pulled her against his chest, so tightly she could barely breathe. His own breaths were ragged, one of his hands fisting in her tangled hair. "Oh, bless the fathers, you're alive," he gasped. "I couldn't find you—I looked everywhere!"

She whimpered, her arms tightening around his neck.

"Aranya," he said again, gripping her closer.

She lifted her face from where it was buried against his collarbone, and his hazel eyes met hers, peering out of a dirt-smudged face. His hair was possibly even worse than hers, his garments torn and singed.

Impulse overcame her. Choking on another sob, she pressed a kiss to his mouth. She tasted salt, copper, and dirt, but that didn't stop her from kissing him over and over again, all across his face.

Kai caught her by the back of the head and dragged her into a long, deep kiss.

Kai had thought he'd lost her. He'd lost her when the phoenixes set upon them, chasing them to different corners of this wretched wilderness. He'd tried to track her down, but no matter how hard he searched, he couldn't find her. Neither was there any sign of the phoenix who'd pursued her.

There *was* plenty of blackened earth. Phoenix fire was known for leaving nothing behind.

But now she was here, in his arms, *kissing* him. Her haunted eyes were shut as she peppered his face with desperate kisses. Seeing her fire gone, seeing her fearlessness reduced to these tear-streaked cheeks and trembling limbs, it made him *angry*. And somehow, the incessant kisses only made him angrier.

He caught her and drew her into a furious, desperate kiss of his own. She melted against him, kissing him back fervently, and he tightened his hold on her.

He wasn't ever letting her go again.

Then she whimpered and wrestled backward, unwrapping her arms to plant her hands against his chest. He released her, and her eyes were the size of moons in the dawn as she stared at him. Her panic was clear across her face.

"What am I doing?" she cried, pressing a hand against her mouth, red blooming across her cheeks. "I didn't mean—oh!"

He caught her face in both his hands, and her eyes widened even more as they flicked from his to his mouth. That look—she wouldn't resist him if he kissed her again. But he had no intention of doing that.

Instead, he studied her face. "Aranya," he said gently, willing the frantic light to go out of her eyes. He quelled his own alarm, focusing instead on what her face betrayed.

There it was. The fear that had hounded his fearless companion through the night.

"Aranya," he said again, brushing the hair out of her face with his thumb. "You're not alone anymore. You're with me, now."

The sob that shook her small frame nearly split his heart in two. She flung her arms around his neck again, pressing as close as she could, burying her face against him. He let her cry, holding her like he'd always wanted to.

She's alive.

She's safe.

He stroked her hair but didn't touch her back. Blood stained her shredded tunic, the bits of exposed skin covered in crimson and purple. He almost didn't want to ask what happened, but they would have to worry about their wounds later.

For now, he just held her.

He felt the moment she drifted off to sleep, the moment the last bit of tension eased out of her, and her ragged breathing turned steady.

Though his own body ached, he was certain he never experienced anything so wonderful as knowing that Sun Aranya trusted him enough—felt safe enough with him—to fall asleep in his arms.

CHAPTER 16

ARANYA WOKE TO blinding sun.

She winced, burying her face away from the light. She was aware first of how hungry, weak, and *hurting* her body was. Then she was aware of her face against someone's—Kai's—neck, his head resting atop hers, and his arms holding her in the crook of his side. Her hand gripped the front of his tunic, tightening as sunlight flared in her vision.

Kai let out a soft moan, shifting when she did. He must have fallen asleep too. He lifted his head from hers, blinking against the light.

No longer beside herself with panic, she registered how close they were . . . and how much she didn't want to leave his embrace. That thought alone was enough to make her push away from him, to try to get her feet under her again.

His grip tightened, drawing her back against him, his eyes still closed. "Stay," he murmured.

A blush flared hot across her cheeks as she looked up at him. "Don't you think we ought to get up?" she asked, hands flattened against his chest, ready to push if necessary. "We need to find Delan."

He opened one eye, peering at her. He shifted toward her, leaning his head against the tree, and, as if to reiterate his order to *stay*, wrapped both arms around her. "We almost died," he mumbled. "I want snuggles."

"Snuggles?" she squawked, suddenly bristling as she blushed deeper. "We need to find Delan! We have a mission to accomplish!"

"Delan will find us," he replied, wrestling with her halfhearted attempts to pull away. "It's best if we stayed in one place and wait until he sniffs his way here. Oh, stop your flapping about! Just five more minutes?"

He offered up a sheepish grin.

"It's been hours!" she cried, standing and freeing herself from his hold. "We need to find food, and you—you've been injured. You couldn't stand up when I first found you!"

They both glanced down at his leg, at the blood staining his trousers. His sash was tied haphazardly around the wound.

Kai leaned his head back against the tree and shrugged. "I only was bitten by a dragon."

"Bitten by a dragon!" she cried, falling to her knees next to his injury. She began pulling at the fabric, untying the bloody sash, and rolling up the leg of his trousers.

He raised one eyebrow, his mouth slipping into a lopsided smirk. "Kiss me, and it'll make it all better."

She shot him a glare, which he returned with a grin. "You don't seem to be in much pain. Perhaps I shouldn't—"

"Oh, the pain!" he cried, draping his arm across his forehead dramatically. "I can hardly bear it!"

"You're not helping your case."

He dropped his arm and rolled his eyes. "Fine. Would you believe me if I looked at you seriously and told you it hurts so bad I'd rather be in *diyu* right now?"

She stared at the quirk in his lips, the sparkle in his eyes, and remained unimpressed. "I'm going to assume the pain level is somewhere between agony and nonexistent."

He gave a disapproving snort in return but said nothing as she rolled up his trousers until she found the wound on his mid-calf. He jerked when she reached it, proof that it *did* hurt. She grimaced at the blood, the torn flesh.

"Did it injure the bone?" she asked, feeling carefully for sign of breakage.

His jaw clenched, but he shook his head. "Don't think so."

"We don't have bandages. I can clean it off, but there's little else I can do."

He gave a grunt and a shrug. She eyed him, but he maintained his composure. Pulling a handkerchief from her robes, she swallowed her own grunt of pain as she got to her feet and neared the edge of the stream to wet it.

She drank first, having not realized how parched she was. Then she squeezed the excess liquid out of the handkerchief and made her way back to Kai. The first pass of the cloth over his skin dragged a hiss from him, but he gritted his teeth and offered up a wan smirk.

"You bled a lot," she said. "How did it even bite you?"

"I accidentally evanesced on top of it when I tried to get away from the phoenixes."

She couldn't help her snort. It took her two trips to the stream to rinse the handkerchief before his leg was clean. Or as clean as it was going to get for now. As soon as she was done, Kai waggled his eyebrows and said, "Want to help distract me from the pain?"

"We're professionals, *Kai*." She gave him a dour look.

"Indeed, and we've already kissed"—he stopped to count on his fingers—"quite a few times. A few more can't hurt anything."

"None of those were supposed to happen!" she protested, shoving back up to her feet, face hot. "It's best if we pretend they never—"

He caught her ankle.

"Hey!" she squawked. "Let me go! Don't make me pull out my talons!"

"Sit down! Your back has been shredded to ribbons. If you took care of my injury, I can take care of yours."

"I'm not—"

"Sit!"

With a huff, Aranya plopped down on the ground, arms crossed. Kai shifted his weight behind her, coming closer to inspect the damage. Carefully, he gathered her hair and swept it over her shoulder to keep it out of the way, sending tingles shooting down her spine.

"There," he said. "Now it'll stay out of the way."

She swallowed.

When he touched her back, however, she hissed.

The frown was audible in his voice. "This is going to be tricky. It would be best if the tunic was removed, so I can clean the wounds thoroughly, but it appears that it has stuck to some of them. The shirt is pretty torn up, but I imagine you would object to me cutting it off."

"Indeed, I would," she said. "As long as it's the only tunic I have, I'd prefer it remain somewhat intact."

"Hmm." He cast a glance toward the stream. "I think I have an idea. Come to the water. What happened, anyway?"

"I was dragged by my horse," she said sourly. "I was knocked off by a branch and my foot was stuck in the stirrup."

"Dragons," he cursed. "I suppose that's also to blame for the purple lump on your forehead."

She touched it, wincing as she did. Kai evanesced to the waterfront.

"What's your idea?" she asked skeptically once she'd caught up to him.

"You're not going to like it, but I figured you'd like it better than taking a cold bath in your clothes."

"*What* is your idea?"

He scooted to the edge of the water, rolled his trousers up to his knees, and stuck his legs into the stream. Immediately, he jumped from the cold of it, but then flashed her a grin. "You sit next to me, facing away from the stream, and we'll lower your back into the stream. Then, after a few minutes, it'll be easier to detach the garment from the wounds."

She scowled. "This sounds like a terrible idea."

He only grinned.

He wasn't . . . He *was,* wasn't he?

"You were going to dunk me!" she cried.

He gave a coughing, choked laugh. "N-no! Absolutely not!"

"I'm not doing it."

"I *promise* I won't dunk you," Kai said. Then he added, "On purpose."

"Kai!"

"Come *on*!" He grabbed her wrist and pulled her down beside him. "I will do my best to keep you from falling, alright? Do you believe me?"

"No," she muttered, even though it wasn't the truth.

He took that as consent for him to grab her upper arms and start lowering her backward into the water.

"Wait, I'm not—"

"It's alright; I've got you."

She glared at him, and despite his reassurances, her core braced, her legs scrambling for purchase on the grassy bank. "This seems like a very, *very* bad idea. My hair is getting wet!"

He shot her an exasperated look. "Your hair gets wet, or all of you gets wet. Here we go."

She gripped his arms as he lowered her so far she was sure she'd fall, and then the cold flared across her skin. She yelped and jerked, but he only lowered her further.

"There," he said, his grip on her almost painfully tight. He strained, but maintained a solid hold. "Now we wait."

"For how l-long?" she chattered, trying to suppress her urge to flinch away from the cold.

"I already told you. A few minutes. Just until it's easier to access the wounds and assess the damage."

She huffed through a shiver. He smirked at her. She glanced away. Kai's face seemed the only place for her to look except the blazing sun, but she didn't exactly want to stare at him. Best to come up with a diversion.

"I think you should tell me about your family," she said.

He flinched so hard water splashed in her face.

"Don't go all brusque and mysterious on me. I'm your friend and comrade. You can trust me."

He gave a dark, low chuckle, glancing off to one side.

"You know I won't tell anyone—"

But he said, "*Friend,* Aranya?" His echoing chuckle was mirthless. "Sometimes I'm not sure if you're just playing with me."

She stuttered, taken aback. But that clench in his jaw and the look in his eye . . . He was trying to distract her from asking about his family. Aranya had no intention of being distracted, no matter how his words made her heart trip over itself.

"I have a few theories about your family," she said instead of responding to him. "I've been thinking a lot about what you said that day, about how they had Gebei under their thumb—"

"Sometimes I think you're playing hard to get, other times that you're oblivious, or perhaps in denial?"

It was a game now. He would try to fluster her with confusing words, and she would try to trip him into admitting something.

"Having Gebei under their thumb is *illegal*, which means that your family is probably involved in something illegal. And that's aside from the whole traitor thing and clearly being in collusion with Fang, which you didn't know about. That means your family is involved in something *else* illegal that you knew about before we ever stepped foot in Gebei."

His eyes snapped to hers with such sharpness, it only confirmed her theory.

"I'm right, then," she announced, shifting her hips on the bank to a more secure position. "My best guess for why you ran from them is that you don't want to be involved. Hence your mother and brother talking about you *shirking your duties*. That's my guess for a noble motivation, that is."

"Aranya," he warned, giving her a hard look. A look telling her not to press further, not to push him, not to prod.

Icy water swept against her back, and her skin slowly went numb. In such an uncomfortable situation, she thought she was allowed a little prodding. She chose her weapon carefully.

"Well, if you ever wanted to be *more* than friends"—she watched his eyes widen slightly. Good, she'd caught him off guard—"then you can't leave me in the dark on this forever. Plus, if you do, I'll just figure it out on my own."

He tightened his grip on her arms and hefted her up onto the bank. She gasped, both from the ice dripping down her legs and the way the blood rushed to her head.

"Don't go poking around my family," he said, and he seemed more scared than angry. "Just let it drop. Let me see your back now."

CHAPTER 17

ARANYA WRAPPED HER arms around herself against the chill, her wet hair sticking to her skin. "Tell me, Kai."

He tipped his head, glaring at her. Then, while she was staring at him, he vanished.

"If you appear behind me *one more time,* I'll—"

"I'm trying to tend your wounds, alright? Stop being so irksome," he said from behind her. Much less gently than last time, he moved her sopping hair aside, and pulled carefully at the fabric.

Most of it was fine, but a couple times the tunic was still stuck, and when he peeled it away, she jolted and hissed.

"Sorry," he mumbled, continuing his work. Once he'd finished, he reappeared in front of her and scooted so he faced away from her. "Now you can take it off."

"I—"

"It's only wound treatment. You don't need to blush so."

He wasn't even looking at her.

"I'm not blushing," she growled, trying not to be self-conscious and completely vulnerable as she began working to remove the garment. Her movements were jerky, and it took everything to not let out a cry or a hiss at the sharp pain. But that would give Kai cause to turn around, and she couldn't have that.

Once she had covered herself with the tattered, torn, and *wet* tunic and drawn her knees up to her chest, she swallowed and mumbled, "It's done."

He vanished again without even turning around, and his warmth reappeared at her back.

Of the things to be most worried and awkward about, she hoped her shoulders didn't appear bulkier when bare. He'd already made fun of them, and she wasn't sure she could bear it while so prone.

He made no comment, only began dabbing at painful spots with the handkerchief. She braced herself against each pass of the cloth, squeezing her eyes shut and trying not to allow stray tears to leak out. She swallowed each hitch in her breathing.

There was only one thing she could think of to distract her from the pain and from his heat at her back.

"I think your family is connected to the brigands."

His hand froze. When he spoke, his voice was that dark, low tone he'd used with her when she'd first threatened to betray him to them. "Don't provoke me. You're *quite* disadvantaged presently."

"I'm not provoking you! I'm only trying to understand. I'm trying to understand *you*. Why you'd be willing to compromise our mission to keep your secret. Besides, no matter what you say, I know you won't hurt me."

"That's not it at all—*Aranya*!" Her name was a growl on his lips. He appeared in front of her, catching her face with both of his hands.

She flinched, clutching her tunic tighter to her chest and scooting backward. "Kai—"

"You know why I don't want to tell you?" he growled.

She stared up at him, breath caught in her lungs, her heart racing. She gave her head a small shake.

"Because my brother knows your name, knows you, and it will take him very little time to gather your personal information. He knows you're associated with me, and he has reason to believe I care about you, which means I'm more likely to entrust this sort of information to you. Which means *you* will be very useful to *him*."

Everything in the world narrowed to his face, his hands on her jaws, his furious, beautiful eyes. Oh, fathers. She was a lost cause. Shi Kai would be the downfall of her in more ways than one.

Kai didn't stop. "And do you know what he will do with you? He will use you against me, and he will know exactly how to make you bend to his will."

"How?" she asked stupidly, her mind spinning, but not quite able to fully understand. "I didn't bend before."

"He'll use your grandfather."

He could have punched her in the gut. Her jaw fell open, the air gone from her lungs. She stared at him, grappling with what this implied and with what he wasn't telling her. The theories about his family that had been stewing in her mind now swarmed to the forefront of her thoughts.

Kai must have believed her placated because he evanesced behind her again. She straightened her back instinctively, trying not to flinch too much when his long fingers gripped her shoulder, and he continued wiping away the blood and painfully working out bits of debris that had gotten lodged under her skin.

"What happened back there with your mother and brother?" she asked softly. "When you went into that room with them?"

His fingers pressed into her collarbone as he gripped her shoulder harder. Then he sighed and allowed hesitantly, "They were threatening me, that's all."

"Nothing new?"

"Nothing new."

When the sopping, red-stained kerchief finally made its last pass, her shoulders sagged in relief. Behind her, there was shuffling, and when she carefully turned, she was just in time to see Kai shrug out of his own tunic, only his thin undershirt retaining his propriety. Her cheeks went hot. She quickly averted her gaze.

He held out the garment to her. "I know, I know, it stinks. But I thought it might be better than your wet tunic. We can hang yours up to dry."

Why wouldn't her tongue form words? Her mind fogged up, but she nodded mutely and accepted the tunic. Like before, he evanesced in front of her, back facing her, so she could see him and the scant privacy he offered her.

She worked quickly, her wounds and skin prickling in the cool breeze of the wind. The garment was much too big, hanging down past her knees, but she wasn't about to complain. It smelled like him, albeit a slightly stinky version of him. She didn't really care.

She got to her feet without saying anything to him, carrying her wet garments to the tree and hanging them up, angling the undergarments away so he wouldn't see them. Then, crossing her arms across her chest, she eased herself down to a sitting position by the tree they'd napped under earlier.

Kai's head was cocked.

"You can turn around now," she said, drawing the neckline of his tunic closer self-consciously.

He evanesced right to her side, flung an arm around her shoulders—surprisingly carefully—and tucked her in close. "*Now* we can snuggle. Hey, you look good in my shirt."

Aranya squawked wordlessly, flailing her arms in surprise. She stumbled to her feet, out of his reach, and sat down again. Away from him.

"No, *now* we have to figure out a plan for food. And for finding Delan."

Kai glared at her.

"Besides, we need to discuss Fang Zedong."

"Why?"

"Because that was him, back at the waterhole. I'm sure of it."

"I thought so too," said Kai.

"I think the old man he had with him was Du Liuxian, the evanescer. That would explain why he was here, so far from Butagin. Liuxian is an evanescer who could cross leagues at once, so it appears Fang is using him as a sort of . . . traveling aid?"

He propped his elbow on his good leg. "Du Liuxian could evanesce with other people, so that must be how Fang is using him."

"You remember that from the packet they gave us at Suguan? I thought you didn't read it." Aranya couldn't help the way the words came out a touch wryly.

The look he gave her was withering. "I can be studious when I want to be, love."

That one word sent her heart tripping over herself. She set to ripping up blades of grass and splitting them into smaller and smaller strips. Anything to avoid Kai's gaze.

"But actually, I knew that because he's a powerful evanescer. Back before his disappearance, my parents had hoped he would have a daughter that Yong or I could marry."

It made sense. Aranya still felt like an idiot when the only thing she could think of to say was, "Oh."

"He never married, however. At some point, many years ago, his name just stopped coming up in conversation. My parents focused their matchmaking efforts elsewhere."

Aranya forced her hands to stop touching the grass. "So he's a powerful evanescer that Fang captured and continues to use to further Fang's own purpose. It stands to reason that the rest of the missing wielders are likewise imprisoned against their will and being used."

Kai nodded grimly. For a moment, their eyes met, and then he said softly, "I'm glad you're safe, and that we found each other again."

Her throat tightened until she could only manage a nod in return.

They passed the afternoon making camp and avoiding starvation while they waited for Delan. Kai watched Aranya closely as she tried to piece together her fragmented sense of control. His flirting wasn't helping with that, but it *was* distracting her. And he couldn't let her spiral back down to where she'd been this morning.

So, he kept throwing out comments that turned her cheeks red, and probably too many requests for kisses. Anything to keep her snappy rather than scared.

Since Aranya was the more mobile of the two, he'd handed over his *jiaun* and sling and she'd gone hunting. When she came back with two rabbits, that creeping fear lurked in her eyes again, returning as sure as night fell.

"What if Delan doesn't find us?" she said by way of greeting. "What if something happened to him? What if a *mó guǐ* finds—"

"Then we wouldn't have to worry about someone badgering us to keep things professional between us." He waved his hand. "Oh, wait—you do that, anyway. Never mind. I suppose that would be a conundrum if he doesn't find us, wouldn't it?" Kai took the rabbits from her and began skinning and skewering them to roast over the fire he'd built while she was gone.

Her face twisted into both horror and outrage, and he could only be relieved that it wasn't terror anymore. She glanced between the extra knife in his belt and the second rabbit next to him. She blinked quickly, glancing away from the carcasses, the blood on Kai's hands as he worked.

"I'll do this," he said. "Can you fill the skin with more water? I drank it all while you were gone."

She rolled her eyes, snatched up the skin, and headed toward the stream. His too-large tunic hung from her shoulders as she rubbed her arms. She glanced every which way, almost as flighty as the creatures she'd just hunted. His hands slowed at his work.

Then he bent back down over the rabbits, renewing his efforts. They both were half-starved and if he wasn't careful, he'd cut himself with his jittery hands.

"Will you be able to walk again soon?" Aranya asked when she came back, sitting on the opposite side of the fire and rubbing her palms near the blaze. Through the mess of her hair, her dark eyes lifted to his.

There was that fear again.

He suspected it wouldn't totally be gone until they got out of this dragon-blasted situation and were back on the hunt again. Or would it continue to haunt her even then?

He glanced down at his leg, rebandaged with his sash. The pain was still substantial, but he wasn't about to admit that to her. He waved a hand. "Pfft, I can walk. But I will walk much *better* tomorrow, I think."

She smiled a little at that, dropping her gaze to the fire as he began roasting the meat. They sat in silence, the sizzle and smell of rabbit filling the air. Her smile slipped into a pensive, faraway expression.

"Come eat," Kai said.

She blinked, eyes coming into focus again. "Food! Finally."

With jerky, pained movements, she got to her feet and came to his side of the fire. He handed her a stick ladened with meat. She took it with a mumbled thanks, not looking at him, and as she turned to retreat to her side of the fire, he reached out to her impulsively. Just as quickly, he retracted his hand.

It was covered in blood. Blood and fur.

Disgusting.

"There's more coming," he said lamely, nodding toward the other meat cooking over the fire. It was the only way he could express what he *wanted* to say.

Please stay. Please, please stay.

She bit her lip, and as if reaching the end of a long inner debate, sat down next to him. He closed his eyes in relief, then focused back on roasting the rest of the meat while she ate. Once it was all skewered and over the fire, he evanesced to the stream to clean his hands and fingernails.

He evanesced back to her side, crossed his good leg—leaving the other stretched out—and chanced a look at her face.

"Tell me about your grandfather," he said, removing another skewer from the fire and blowing on it. He purposefully occupied himself with these mundane movements, refusing to meet the sudden flashing of her attention toward him. "All I know is that he's a shapeshifter, prefers to be a white cat, and likes to rack up fines at your tenement."

She gave a mirthless chuckle, her hand pausing on its way to her mouth with a bite. When she spoke, her gaze wouldn't leave the fire's dancing flames.

"He's cared for me as long as I can remember. Always good-natured, quick to laugh, slow to scold. I still managed to earn a lot of those," she said with a sheepish smile. It faded into a thin line, her bruised forehead furrowing. "Somewhere along the way, however, it slowly switched from him caring for me to me caring for him. It happened so gradually I almost didn't notice, but it became harder and harder with the Academy. The later years, I was always getting special permission to leave so I could go check on him. I'll never forget . . ."

She stopped. Swallowed hard. The skewer of meat remained untouched in her hand.

Kai waited.

Her eyes closed. "I'll never forget when I came back after being gone for two days, and he . . ." Her voice caught, her throat bobbing furiously. When she finally spoke again, her voice was barely above a whisper, as if she feared it would break entirely if she spoke too loudly. "He hadn't eaten. Because he couldn't cook anymore. He hadn't eaten in two days. I found him collapsed on the ground. I thought he was dead, and it was my fault."

Kai's lips parted. She sniffed, wiping the back of her—*his*—sleeve across her eye. Then she drew in a deep breath, wrenched meat off the skewer, and set to eating vigorously.

He ate much slower, his stomach knotting with each swallow. He had to ask; had to know why she had been alone. "Where were your parents?"

She had just taken a particularly large bite, and Kai waited while she chewed. But then she just shrugged, her mouth trying to twist into a smile—another attempt to keep from crying.

"They're gone," she growled, stuffing more rabbit into her face. "Died when I was little."

"Both?"

"They got sick. Apparently we lived out of the city then, and I guess it was one of those things that came and went so quickly, they just . . ."

"How old were you?"

She snorted. "Ye Ye said I was two. He believed I was too young to have any memories of them, but I *do* remember. One or two things. They're fuzzy, but I remember trying to climb out of my bed and getting frustrated. Ma was *there*. She put me back to sleep. But by now . . . I sometimes wonder if I only remember my memory of them, like the memory itself has become too faded over the years . . ."

"Where's the rest of your family?"

"That was it. Just me and Ye Ye."

"But . . . your parents had no siblings? No family of their own?"

She shrugged, biting her lip. "I guess not. Ye Ye . . . He didn't want to talk about my parents. When I was younger, I used to ask a lot about them. He was never cross with me, but whenever I asked, he would get . . . His hands would tremble a little. He always redirected the conversation."

"Was he your mother's or father's father?"

"Mother's. It wasn't until I was older that I began to piece together what happened. What troubled Ye Ye about them. About *him*."

She wouldn't look at him. Hadn't looked at him in some while now. Unconsciously, after finishing her meal, she reached up with one hand and gripped her shoulder, rubbing the skin almost nervously.

Oh. Her magic. The pieces of the puzzle finally fit together.

"Your mother," he said slowly, "was a full shifter. But she didn't marry another shifter. Your father didn't have magic at all, did he?"

Aranya looked up, her eyes bright and liquid as night fell around them.

"Your grandfather didn't approve of the match."

She shrugged. "I can't know for certain, but I suspect as much."

This was why she was only a partial-shifter. Her father's blood diluted the magic in their lineage.

"Sometimes I wondered if he feels guilty for their deaths, perhaps? Maybe not because he caused it or anything like that, or that he'd been unkind to my father, but perhaps he felt responsible in a way? It's only my speculation; I only have what I know of him and a few snippets I've gathered over the years."

The fire popped and crackled, its light seeming smaller as the darkness grew deeper. She startled slightly at a particularly large pop, her gaze darting to his to see if he'd caught the movement.

He had, but he didn't let her see that. "Was it hard, taking care of your grandfather by yourself?"

"No, no, I'd do it again in a heartbeat—"

"Good things can be hard."

She looked down, chewing on her lip. Tears welled on her lower lashes. Wordlessly, she shut her eyes and nodded. After a long minute: "Yes, it was hard. It was hard and lonely."

His hand itched to reach out and take hers. He longed to offer that bit of comfort, to show her that she wasn't alone anymore. But he didn't move.

"And you can't tell me anything about your family?" she asked abruptly.

He *wanted* to tell her. Desperately longed to tell her everything. Partially because he'd never truly talked about it with anyone—he couldn't. But also, because he wanted her to *see* him, to understand.

Perhaps there were things he could share without giving her information that wouldn't be good for her to possess.

He leaned back against the tree, feeling suddenly as far away from her as when she was on the other side of the fire, even though she sat next to him. It was stupid, but he longed to hold her in his arms again while he told her about his family. He just wanted that . . . comfort. That assurance.

He took a great swig of water, the sudden weight of her attention heavy on him. She wasn't thinking about her Ye Ye anymore, or the fragmented memories of her parents. For the first time that day since he'd cleaned the wounds on her back, he was the one fighting a flush.

Why was this so hard? It wasn't like it was some dramatic story. Why did he feel this cavernous need for her affection as he fought to articulate it?

"It never felt like a family," he said at long last. He drank more water—lots more. Aranya waited, patient and quiet. "It felt like . . . like another version of the Academy. But worse. Competition, no-nonsense, so much pressure . . ."

He wasn't making any sense. Drawing a deep breath in, he took another swig of water.

"It was me or Yong. It always should have been Yong. He was older, he actually *wanted* it. I never wanted any part in it. Mother wanted it to be Yong. But Father . . . he wanted it to be me. When he died, he left it to me. I didn't *want* it." The last words came out in a growl. "And now I can't get them to leave me alone."

When he dared a look her way, firelight danced across her face. Sharp and erratic, as the gears seemed to turn in her mind. She was putting the pieces together.

He shut his mouth.

How had he ever thought her dull? She was quicker than a whip. Her brain operated in puzzles and riddles, always trying to figure things out. His family was another riddle for her to solve, like the mystery of Fang Zedong and the vanishing wielders.

He shouldn't have spoken at all.

Aranya's lips parted, her head tilting. "Your father . . ."

Oh stupid, phoenix-scorched dragons. She *knew.* And if she knew, how could he protect her? He shut his eyes as she said the words, her voice low and breathless.

"He was a crime lord, wasn't he? A lord of the brigands."

His silence was answer enough.

"He wanted *you* to take his place," she whispered. "He made you his heir, and that is why you hid. And why your mother and brother are trying so hard to find you."

Aranya, Aranya, Aranya. His heart throbbed a painful rhythm as memories kept returning. Of his father, his cold mother, his calculating brother. All the *fights*. The family dinners turned into strategy and training meetings.

His father hadn't been just any crime lord, either. He was lord of the Hidden Ones. The most fearsome network of brigands; the network of people born without the bureaucracy's knowledge. The people who never existed, who couldn't be traced or tracked in the government's records.

"When we arrested those kidnappers back in Zushui, that siren Lehua and the earth-wielder . . ." Aranya leaned closer to him. "They were broken out of the incarceration unit that night. You did that, didn't you?"

He gave a short, bitter chuckle. "It was my responsibility while at the Academy to deal with any Hidden Ones who were caught by the Suguan wardens. I had to break them out. That was why I did so many pranks; I'd have to evanesce in and out of the incarceration unit at night, and then I couldn't fall asleep for hours. Besides, Lehua knew who I was. If I didn't silence her, she would've revealed my location to my brother. So we made a bargain."

There were so many things he knew, so many things he wished he'd never known. He *hated* these bonds, these ties, and possibly what he hated the most was that he couldn't bring Aranya into that dynamic.

Aranya.

"Kai!"

He blinked, realizing belatedly that she had come closer to him, was leaning over him. His breath hitched as he registered how close she was, how wide and concerned her eyes were.

"Kai?" she said again. "Are you alright?"

Clenching his jaw, he turned his face away from hers. He had so little self-control as it was, and the last thing he needed to see was her parted lips hovering so near.

Her hand landed gently to cover his, making his heart lurch, and before he knew what he was doing, he entwined his fingers with hers. Like they'd done at his family's house, and this little bit of contact became his lifeline. Her hand was small, but square, strong, and calloused. He squeezed it tightly—probably too tightly.

Even by the sparse light of the fire that illuminated only half of her face, he could see her cheeks flushed crimson. See her searching his face as her thumb brushed across the back of his hand.

"Kai, it's alri—"

He ignored the pain in his leg and pushed up. He reached out, impulse overcoming reason, and brushed his fingers against her cheek. She froze, eyes widening, as he slid his hand further, along her jaw.

"Is *this* alright?" he asked, his voice breaking, his heart aching and pounding in his chest.

Please let me kiss you, Aranya. Please want *me to kiss you.*

He didn't want her to comfort him because she pitied him. He wanted her to want *him.*

She swallowed, her chest and shoulders raising and lowering with every breath. He tangled his fingers into her hair, pulling her face nearer to his. "*Aranya*, tell me if you want this."

If you want me.

Her lips parted, her pulse racing beneath his touch, but he searched her dark irises for a sign of what ran through her mind, for an answer.

He saw it a fraction of a second before she closed her eyes, twisting her face away from his. His heart plummeted down through the earth straight to *diyu*. Watching her lips draw into that thin line gutted him so thoroughly he could only stare with his jaw unhinged and gaping.

He'd thought . . .

Bitterness swelled in his soul. Why did she torment him like this?

"How long till Delan finds us?" she asked, her voice wavering traitorously. She withdrew her hand from his and twisted her face free of his hold.

Kai growled, letting her go without a fight. He wasn't about to answer her question; he didn't know, and at the moment, he didn't care where in the seven valleys Delan was.

She had *wanted* to give in, but something else had won out. The same thing that had driven her into his arms this morning yanked her away from him tonight.

Her fear of being alone.

Funny how his own deep fear so mirrored her own, yet it made him reach out even as it made her flinch away. As if hearing his thoughts, she whispered, "You're not going back to Zushui."

Not a question—a statement. He didn't answer. What was the point?

She gave a dry, empty laugh. "I suppose I'll get the appointment after all." She didn't ask where he would go after this was over; she knew he didn't know. And if he did, he couldn't tell her. Not if she was to avoid becoming Yong's next target.

"I'll take second watch," Kai said instead. Moving carefully to not disturb his bad leg, he lowered himself to the ground. He stopped, finding his balled-up cloak next to him. With gritted teeth, he picked it up and tossed it a little too hard at Aranya. "Stay warm."

Then he turned so his back was toward the fire and tried to fall asleep.

CHAPTER 18

ARANYA HUDDLED UNDER Kai's cloak, the night growing colder and darker by the hour. Autumn was taking hold, readying to plunge Zheninghai into icy winter.

Her heart wouldn't stop racing. First, from how her lips burned from the kiss that never happened, then with dread as she pieced together more understanding of Kai's family and the things she'd heard at his house, and finally from the slightest movement or noise in the forest surrounding them.

She stared at his turned back, hating herself, hating how his face had changed from pleading and desperate to hard and cold. That shift kept replaying in her mind, and though it had been her rejecting him, in many ways it was like he'd rejected her too. But then he'd given her his cloak, even when he was so angry, and that had to count for something.

Why was this so complicated?

He wasn't returning with her to Zushui. What was the point of *this*—of *feeling*—if it was going to be over the moment they finished their mission? What good was a kiss when the affection and devotion it promised were gone the minute it was over?

She wasn't interested in being a passing fancy.

There *was* something she was interested in, and she doubted it was the same thing he wanted. But even if he did want the same thing, as long as Ye Ye lived, they couldn't be together. She had to devote herself to his care, and she couldn't allow him to become a pawn in Shi Yong's games.

Wind howled in the treetops, and Aranya wrapped Kai's cloak tighter around her shoulders. She glanced around, straining for any sight or sound of predators. Her hackles raised as leaves rustled, the noise so loud it could disguise any *mó guǐ* approach.

They would be fine. Kai was here, with her, and if anything attacked them, she could call for him and they'd fight together. Unless, of course, something killed her silently. Or one of those snake-monsters bit her, and she was too late to call for help.

Where were these paranoid thoughts coming from?

She tried to calm her breathing, like they had taught at the Academy. Controlling one's fears was an important part of one's job. She had to learn. It just hadn't felt so difficult until now.

Would Delan ever come? Was he hurt? Was he . . . dead?

The hours passed in slow torture until it was finally time for Kai's watch. But even then, could she let her guard down long enough to fall asleep?

Wrapped up in his cloak, she trudged to Kai's sleeping form and hesitated. He was peaceful, sleeping there, and he'd been so upset earlier. If she woke him, it would only bring back memory of . . . of . . .

She drew in a fortifying breath. But just as she was about to nudge him with her toe, she stopped and shook her head in frustration. Instead, she bent down to her knees, placed a hand on his arm, and said with a gentle shake, "Kai. Wake up."

He groaned.

"It's your watch."

Another groan. Then he reached up like he was going to fling his arm over his eyes, but instead he rested his hand on top of hers. She flinched unintentionally.

"Kai, wake up," she said, shaking him a little more forcefully now.

"Shut up, Partial. I'm awake," he growled.

"Oh. Good."

He dragged himself into a sitting position, groaning all the while, and leaned back against the tree. His eyes fixed on the dying fire, blinking slowly, and never once drifted her way.

It didn't matter.

She didn't care. All that was important was getting some rest. She shuffled back to her spot, shivering a little, and plopped down on the ground. The wind howled overhead, and her head snapped up instinctively.

"Don't worry; I won't let the monsters eat you while you sleep," Kai muttered.

She glanced at him, at his sleep-mussed hair and scowl, and impulse overtook her. "Are you angry with me?"

"Angry?" he asked, his face contracting in confusion before it cleared. "No."

"Are you sure?"

He finally looked up at her then, and if a face could be impatient, amused, and only half-awake at once, that was his expression. Then he held up one arm, opening the space at his side. "Just come here," he said, and his words were so slurred she almost didn't discern them. But his hazel eyes, glowing in the firelight, fixed on her so intently, his arm remaining poised in the air.

"Uh," she said stupidly, her blush seeping down her neck.

When she didn't move, he sniffed, lowered his arm, and turned back to the fire. He seemed more alert now. Which was a good thing if he was going to be of any use against said monsters.

But she was tired, scared, and half out of her mind. That was the only explanation for why she scooted to Kai's side, staring up at him and silently pleading for him not to turn her away, even though she turned him away.

"Ever the contrary one," Kai muttered, side-eying her. "If you think puppy eyes is all it's going to take—"

She wasn't going to wait for whatever nonsense he was about to say. She slid up to him, leaning her head against his shoulder. Her face went hotter than fire, but *here* she was safe. Not on the other side of the fire—*here*.

Kai let out a low chuckle, sighing and then opening his arms to her. She curled into his side, a relieved exhale escaping her lips.

"Oh, Aranya," he mumbled. "What am I going to do with you?"

"Nothing; just let me sleep here."

"You drive a hard bargain, little *friend*."

She didn't answer, too tired and flustered to say anything. As if sensing her mood, he drew her closer and pulled his cloak tighter around her.

"My arms are always open for you," he whispered. "No matter if I'm mad or not."

"Me and every other girl," she mumbled.

"No. Just you."

She didn't hear his voice. She *felt* it, rumbling through his chest and into her face. It was the only soothing thing in her current perception. She winced against morning light, against the crick in her neck, the ache in her back and hips.

Kai still held her, his warmth surrounding her. Somehow, she hadn't expected him to stay instead of extricating himself once she was asleep. It was a relief he was here. Her muscles relaxed, and she burrowed deeper into his chest.

"Shh, she's still asleep," Kai said in a hushed tone to . . . not her.

"Glad you two got cozy while I was gone," came the wry reply.

Aranya's eyes flew open, and her head shot up, hitting Kai's chin.

"I *said* to be quiet," he growled. "Now we've woken her up!"

"Delan!" she cried, scrambling to unsteady feet. Before Kai could catch her, or before Delan could even brace himself, she tumbled forward and flung her arms around him. "I thought you were dead!"

Now the tears were coming again—dragons eat them! She couldn't cry in front of Kai *and* Delan!

"Have a little faith in a man, dearie," Delan chuckled, patting her back lightly. "A few scrapes and bruises, but otherwise hardly worse for the wear. You don't look so . . . well, perhaps I shouldn't finish that sentence, if I've learned anything from my wife. Leave it to you two to get yourselves into all manner of scrapes. Seven valleys, Kai, what did you do to your leg?"

Aranya pulled away from Delan, swiping furiously at her cheeks as she glanced back in time for Kai to level an irritated glare at Delan.

But then they were both looking at her, and a muscle jerked in Delan's jaw at the sight of the tears she was trying to swallow.

The last thing she needed right now was their attention. She had to control herself and her emotions. The past two nights might have been hard, but that didn't give her liberty to break down now.

She sniffed, wiped her eyes with her sleeve, and walked to the other side of the tree where she'd hung the rest of her clothes. "What do we do now?" she asked, forcing her voice to steady.

"We keep going," Delan replied, matter-of-factly. "We see this mission through. And you both will thank me—I saved our horses."

Aranya poked around from the other side of the tree. "The horses?"

"Over there, by the stream. That's why it took me so long to find you; I went to find your horse first. Stupid beast was about to be food for dragons, but I saved it in time."

Her shoulders dropped with relief. She ducked back behind the tree and said, "I'll change, then we can go."

Changing with men nearby always made her nerves extra jumpy, but she worked quickly. On the other side of the tree, Delan began whispering in a hushed tone. Evidently he thought he was being quieter than he was.

"What happened to her?"

"I don't know."

"You didn't ask?"

"She didn't seem to want to talk about it. Her back was pretty bad."

Her cheeks heated, and she fought another swell of rising tears. Almost as if on cue, pain shot up her spine and she bit back a cry as she fussed her tunic on. It wasn't as roomy as Kai's, restricting her movements.

But if she made a sound, Kai would volunteer to help. And she didn't need that.

When she finished and poked around the tree again, trying to pretend she hadn't just overheard their conversation, she held out the limp garment to Kai. He was still seated on the ground, and she was suddenly afraid he wasn't as mobile as he'd told her yesterday.

"Here," she said as professionally as she could. "Thank you for letting me borrow it."

Kai shrugged, not accepting it. "Keep it. You looked better in it than I ever did."

She paused. Frowned. "I don't know what that's supposed to mean."

"Take your phoenix-scorched shirt, boy," snapped Delan.

Kai shot Delan a glare, snatched the garment out of Aranya's hand, and vanished. He reappeared in the saddle of his horse by the stream. Delan rolled his eyes, then followed. She hesitated for a brief second, glancing at the embers of the fire, then the spot where Kai had held her all night.

She shook her head, steeling herself against the blush crawling up her neck.

They had a mission to accomplish. To *finish*. They were so close. They had solved much of the mystery. Fang Zedong had kidnapped the wielders to use their magic and was keeping them imprisoned in his fortress near the border of Zheninghai. He also had magic that could capture and compel *mó guǐ* to do his bidding, and the captured wielders to obey him.

They had all but confirmed it, and when they discussed their theories with Delan, he agreed.

Now it was time to rescue the missing wielders and the princess.

CHAPTER 19

THE NEXT SEVERAL weeks passed in a blur of traveling. There was so much ground to cover, and the days slipped away with the dull clatter of horse hooves, the changing of bandages for wounds, long nighttime watches, and a handful of trips to towns to buy supplies and send updates to Suguan.

Aranya tried not to worry as they traveled. Were they too late? By the time they reached Fang Zedong's fortress, would there still be a chance to rescue the imprisoned wielders? Would their messages arrive fast enough to the capital that troops would be on their way to the same location? Or would they arrive and find themselves alone in enemy territory?

"I think we'll arrive tomorrow," Delan said, stretching his legs out by the fire and taking a big bite out of a rice cake.

Kai broke a stick and tossed it into the fire, arm dangling off his knee. Aranya watched that stick burn, turning black as the fire licked around the edges.

“What if we arrive and no one’s there?” she asked. “Do we try to rescue them on our own?”

Delan snorted. “Definitely not. We will arrive, assess the situation, and if there’s already an encampment set up—which I think is very likely, considering the amount of border patrol near Butagin—then we will meet with whoever is in charge, exchange information, and after that make plans for infiltrating the fortress.”

Aranya nodded, pinching the bridge of her nose absently. She happened to glance up and found Kai watching her. Her cheeks colored.

They settled down for the night. Aranya took first watch since Kai hadn’t evanesced that day. She fidgeted with her knife, then the strings of her cloak. Her thoughts swirled around her mind, punctuated by flashes of terror whenever the dark world around her rustled.

“What’s the matter?”

She jumped, swiveling her head to where Kai had appeared next to her. Pressing a hand to her heart as though the pressure would reduce its frantic rhythm, she gasped, “You startled me!”

“A good warrior never startles,” he replied, smirking as he drew one knee up so he could rest his elbow on it. “Say, how long do you think we have to talk before Delan smells our conversation?”

She couldn’t help her smile. “Get some sleep, Kai.”

“Not until you tell me what was making you frown so severely and startle like a newborn deer.”

“Make yourself comfortable, then.”

“Hey,” he said, much gentler. “Look at me, Partial.”

She delayed long enough to be petty, then rolled her eyes his way in a glare. “You know I hate it when you call me that.”

“Very well, *love*.”

She scowled. But his face wasn’t the mocking, satirical smile she anticipated. Instead, his hazel eyes glowed gold in the firelight, his eyebrows pinched, and his head tilted.

"You haven't been yourself since that night. It's been weeks. What . . .?" His question trailed off as his eyes searched hers.

What happened? he was trying to say.

She looked away, drawing her knees up to her chest and wrapping her arms around them. She gave a little shrug, smiling halfheartedly.

"You don't have to tell me," came Kai's gentle reply to her silence. "I just want you to know that I'm here if you *do* want to talk about it. Sometimes letting it out helps it not fester."

Her eyes followed his absent movements as he ran his fingers down the scabs formed along his leg. Then he picked up a stick and, to her surprise, instead of breaking it, he began drawing it through the dirt.

Unbidden, her heartbeat accelerated. Could she bring herself to speak of that night? It was over; it would never happen again. If she left it alone, eventually she'd recover. Her fear would not control her forever.

The words bubbled up in her throat, but they lodged there—sticky as unshed tears. Back and forth, the memories came to the surface, only to be shoved back down under the pressure and struggle of articulation.

Instead, different words came out: "Why you?"

"Pardon?"

She rocked back and forth on her heels, keeping her voice low to not disturb Delan. "Why did your father leave it to you?"

Kai's stick stilled. His shoulders crept up with the mounting tension, his jaw locking shut tightly. Then he tossed the stick into the fire.

"Letting it out will help it not fester," she teased.

"Don't throw my words back at me. I'll make a deal with you. We will confess or fester together—if you tell me about that night, I'll answer your question. What do you say?" His head cocked toward hers.

"You said I didn't have to tell you if I didn't want to."

"And you don't." His lips twisted, but just at the same time, a loud snore erupted from the other side of the fire. Both of them tensed, Kai looking ready to vanish in an instant. But Delan only rolled over, his breathing turning quiet and even again.

Aranya swallowed, squeezed her eyes shut, and whispered, "After we were separated and I was knocked from my horse, the phoenix pursued me until I killed it."

"Killed it? With what?" His eyebrows rose even as they furrowed.

"I threw my knife at it."

Kai let out a low, rumbling chuckle as he shook his head. "Seven valleys—only you, Aranya. Only you."

She wasn't sure what that was supposed to mean, but he seemed impressed. That wasn't the hardest part to recount, though. Her nails dug into the leather of her boots as she continued, trying to keep her story as sterile, as pragmatic as possible. Despite her best efforts, however, half-choked words spilled out of her lips.

"There were so many of them. All around me. Slithering and . . . and . . . the *sounds*, and then they were coming for me . . . And I didn't know if you were still alive . . ."

She was trembling all over as she kept talking, fighting the emotion that kept latching its claws into her voice, fighting the *helplessness* that settled on her shoulders. It was over, over, over. But it stayed—why wouldn't it go? Why couldn't she forget it all? She had to finish this mission, had to return to Ye Ye. She couldn't let her own qualms get in the way.

Kai's shoulder bumped hers. "It's alright."

She bowed her head, letting a few tears trail free. His solid hand rested on her back.

"You don't have to cry alone anymore," he whispered.

Those gentle words were enough to make the floodgates spill open. She buried her face in her hands, sobbing as quietly as she could to not wake Delan. Kai wrapped his arm around her, drew her slowly to his chest, and it only made her cry harder. This taste of affection, of care . . . But he wasn't coming back to Zushui. It would be just her and Ye Ye again until eventually it was just her.

Finally, her tears spent, she sniffled, sitting up straighter and swiping the back of her sleeve against her wet cheeks. "Your turn," she croaked, wrapping her arms tighter around her legs.

He slid his hand back to his lap, staring down as he played with the fringes of his robes, the seams of his trousers. "My brother was like my mother, but my father . . . He was different. Still corrupt as a set of market scales, but not the way they were." He bunched his face, like he was struggling to express exactly what he meant. "I think there was part of him that didn't want to do the . . . *business*. He at least went through the trouble of justifying it. Twisted, warped logic, but it was something. He knew I hated every part of it, and he thought that made me more suited to the task. I did everything I could at the Academy, at home, to convince my family of my aversion to responsibility, from neglecting my studies to purposefully failing exams to having those dalliances, I wanted them to believe me an idiot. I had my father fooled with the rest of them . . . until he sent an order that instead of breaking out one of the brigands from the incarceration unit, I was to kill him. How could I kill someone who was asleep and weaponless in a cell? I couldn't. So I freed him. That was when my father knew."

Aranya waited, her tears dried to her cheeks so that every facial movement felt crusty.

He gave a soft huff, lifting his gaze from his twiddling fingers to the smoldering embers of the fire. Then his eyes darted to hers, but almost as quickly fled to find refuge again in the fire.

"I'm not doing it," he said at last. "They can do whatever they want to manipulate me and coerce me into it. I won't bend. But I fear most for what they might attempt to do to you. I will need to come up with something to keep them away from you."

"Can they be stopped? Why can't you turn them into law enforcement? For being traitors and running an illegal band of brigands?"

It felt like a stupid question because surely if it were as simple as turning them in to the authorities, Kai would have already done it by now. Unless he was more loyal to his family than to Zheninghai.

"If I turn them in, I'll be killed," Kai replied, his voice empty. "Besides, the way it's structured, if I hand over my mother and brother, the rest will escape. A new leader will rise, cutthroats will be sent to dispatch me. And any connected to me."

Her lips parted, the implications of his statement warring in her sluggish mind. "So . . . as long as you're running from your family, I'm at risk."

His throat bobbed, muscles jerking in his jaw and neck. He ran a hand down his face. "I tried to keep you out of it."

"And Delan?"

"I don't know. He's certainly in a better position than you, but I can't know for certain." A rueful, thin-lipped smile. "You see why I wanted that appointment in Zushui?"

"There has to be a way to free you from your family."

He shrugged. "If the government discovered the operation on its own, then perhaps something could be done. But brigand networks are like cockroaches—they survive. There is always someone to fill any vacated space, and they are vengeful. But I won't let them hurt you."

The promise was spoken forcefully enough, yet she couldn't help but wonder how much power he truly had to keep that promise.

A log breaking and falling into the fire split the silence, sending up a shooting display of glowing sparks. Kai said nothing more, his attention fully fixated on that log as it blackened and crumbled around the edges.

"You should sleep," Aranya whispered.

"I should do many things," he replied absently. "Doesn't mean I do them."

"Heaven forbid you do what you ought."

He grinned. "Aye, indeed."

Then he sighed and got to his feet. With a cocky salute and a smirk, he laid down on his back and stared up at the stars.

"Goodnight," she said with a smile.

"Goodnight, Partial."

"Just as I suspected," Delan announced the next evening. "Signs of encampment. On this side of the river border, no less. It must be reinforcements."

Indeed, as he spoke, smoke curled out of the forest tops below the rise they stood on. Aranya stared, her heart pounding impatiently in her chest, at that sign of comrades, of rest from travel, of imminent battle. But it was what stood beyond the thread of blue river winding through the emerald forested countryside that arrested her full attention.

A bulwark guarded that hill, threatening and fierce. It was enormous, built of gray stone, with not a sign of color softening the severe edges of its menacing turrets. While Kai and Delan kept staring, Aranya kicked her horse forward. "The sooner we proceed, the sooner we arrive," she said.

Kai's eyes glittered with amusement. "The longer we linger, the more we postpone our arrival."

Delan rolled his eyes, giving his mount a sound kick. "Just think! For the span of our time here, I won't be alone on babysitting duty." At both of their glares, he only shrugged and held up both hands in a placating gesture. "I mean, forgive me, you both are competent and intellectually stimulating comrades."

Aranya should have given him a sourer glare to match Kai's, but she couldn't help her grin.

Almost there. Almost there.

It was dark before Delan sent Kai ahead to scout out the camp and ensure it was Zheninghai, not enemy troops, that camped on their side of the border. Kai was back shortly with this affirmation, and they proceeded onward to the encampment.

She was perhaps expecting a warm welcome, a bid to sit down by the fire and eat of a prepared hearty stew, or even an offer to brush down her horse and hobble it for the evening.

Instead, when they entered, the place was a frenzy of commotion.

CHAPTER 20

UM, HELLO?" ARANYA said with a tentative smile as a man with a short-trimmed beard and arms the size of tree trunks came hurrying through the camp.

"Yes?" he said, stopping briefly.

"What is going on?"

"There was a breach in the fortress. They recovered the princess."

"Oh!" What a relief! This was far better than what they'd expected. "And the other wielders? They're recovered too?"

He shook his head briskly. "Oh, no. We've only just confirmed that they're imprisoned in the fortress."

"But if there's a breach . . .?" asked Delan.

"A *small* breach. A very small breach. Not enough for us to launch another full-scale attack. I need to go—we're preparing in case of retaliation." With that, he strode off, vanishing back into the commotion of wielders.

Campfires dotted the forest, stretching farther than she could see clearly at this hour. They cast the busy wielders in relief, rendering them shadows and silhouettes as they moved like wind through the night. Tents were set up near the fires. One in particular caught her attention. Not because of the tent itself, but who stood outside it.

A young, slight woman lifted its front flap to enter. Her hair fell unbound to her hips, and blood smeared her garments. But something made her pause and look over her shoulder. Straight at Aranya.

Princess Meiling.

A pair of lovely eyes met Aranya's, set in a sweet, soft-featured, and very dirty face. She was covered in filth from head to toe. Despite that, there was *something* about her bearing, something . . . different.

Why had Fang wanted the cursed princess?

The girl ducked inside her tent and shut the flap behind her.

"This is a much more substantial force than I expected," said Delan, surveying the campsite. "The emperor must have ordered every fighting wielder on this side of the mountains here. They must be planning a full-scale attack."

A hand landed on her shoulder. She turned to find Kai nodding toward a figure in conversation with another wielder. Immediately, she recognized him from her Academy days as one of the prestigious men leading the emperor's armies.

"Lieutenant Jadaala!" she breathed. "He must be leading this! I wasn't expecting someone so . . . *high profile* to have been sent here on our recommendation."

"We may not be the only reason they're here," Delan said. "Our reports likely agreed with intelligence from other search groups. No doubt the princess's capture played a significant role. His Imperial Majesty probably wanted to burn the entire empire down to get his daughter back." In the half-light of the encampment, Delan's face was hardened, its edges chiseled. He looked like the seasoned warrior he was, his stocky form all power and muscle. He almost seemed like a different person than the one who had only hours before complained of being a babysitter. "Tether your horses."

When the lieutenant finished his conversation and they had watered their mounts, Delan strode toward him. Aranya followed close at his heels, Kai behind her.

"Lieutenant Jadaala," said Delan with a respectful bow. "Lian Delan, from Suguan Secret Services. My comrades, Sun Aranya and Shi Kai."

"Very well, very well." The lieutenant was a man of hard lines, with an extended brow and a sharp nose, a cut jawline. His eyes were slightly wide set, angled, and stern. "I fear I am busy at the moment ensuring all lines of pursuit are cut."

"Of course. We are merely reporting for your service. When the threat has been neutralized—"

"Wonderful. I shall meet with you in the morning, circumstances permitting. Now, if you would not mind excusing me."

The lieutenant strode off, leaving Delan grinding his jaw behind him.

"Never liked him," he grumbled. "Let's finish with our horses. Then I might see if the lieutenant is in a better mood. I need to tell him about how we saw Fang."

Kai sat outside the tent he'd been offered. People milled about, despite the late hour, but everything had calmed down since their arrival.

Extra scouts patrolled the area, ready to warn them should anything change. Aranya and Delan had long been asleep, and he found it strange that he didn't long for his comfortable bed in Zushui, but rather the nights under the open sky. He'd grown rather used to being able to glance to the side and see Aranya sleeping soundly, her mouth hanging open and hands clenching her blanket in a death grip.

He swallowed, running his hand down his face. He ought to go inside the tent, to wrap himself up in his own blanket, and sleep. After all, he was quite sleep deprived. But his eyes would not close.

For weeks now, the only thing that could chase away his anxiety about his family was Aranya, and she was another source of anxiety herself.

Not that she knew that.

"Your surname is Shi?"

Kai started, his gaze shooting up to the figure staring down at him. How had he been so lost in his thoughts that someone had approached him without his notice? How often had he teased Aranya about how good warriors never startle?

The man before him was—oh! *Spitfire.*

"Lieutenant." Kai barely managed to control the surprised timbres of his voice. He stood, bowed, and arranged his features into respect. He was taller, but when he tilted his face downward, it forced his eyes to look up. It made the person he spoke to feel taller.

A trick he'd learned to get out of trouble at the Academy.

"Your surname is Shi?" the lieutenant repeated, face impassive.

"Yes, sir. Shi Kai, at your service."

"From Gebei?" His frown deepened, eyes roaming over Kai's travel-soiled robes and the belt of weapons he had yet to discard for the night. "Son of Shi Mu?"

"The same."

The lieutenant's pupils sparked, his mouth curving upward. His thumb looped around his belt, resting dangerously close to the knife sheathed there. "How interesting to find you here."

Kai's heart quickened, his mind racing to understand the implications behind his words. "Did you know my father?"

"You might say I did. You have a brother, do you not?"

"Shi Yong."

"The purest line of evanescers in Zheninghai, hmm?"

"Purest line known."

At this, the lieutenant gave a dry chuckle. "And yet every single one has declined an appointment in the Secret Services. Until now."

CHAPTER 21

"YOUR MOTHER IS the only person I ever knew to not accept any appointments," said Lieutenant Jadaala.

Kai kept his movements reserved, nonchalant, but inside his heart raced. Alarm bells blared. Questions bubbled at his lips. But he wouldn't lose control of himself, no matter how dread slid down his spine.

"I did not know my family had such an honorable connection in yourself," he said.

The lieutenant gave a rueful snort. "It has always been a bit . . . one-sided."

Pause. Then, tentatively, Kai asked, "I beg your pardon?"

That hand, looped so casually on his belt, moved subtly, easily, to trail absently along the hilt. Kai tried not to look down and watch its leisurely motions. Instead, he kept his eyes firmly fixed on the lieutenant—the lieutenant who was clearly threatening him.

And there was only one reason he could think of as to why.

"What made you decide to join the Secret Services now, boy, after your family shunned them?"

"I was summoned. I could not decline."

"But you wished to decline?"

Kai hesitated, but opted for honesty. "I did."

"No explanation as to why?"

It would be so easy to extricate himself from this conversation by vanishing. But that would only complicate matters in the future and potentially get him into deep water.

These were the sort of questions that gave Kai headaches to think of an evasion for. One misstep, and he revealed his family dynamic, which would solidify his death sentence. If he refused to answer, he would look guilty of whatever the lieutenant suspected him.

"I was content with my appointment," he answered finally.

"What was your appointment?"

"I was a warden at Zushui Wardpost."

"A warden! Fathers have mercy. You cannot be serious."

Kai hoped his silence was answer enough.

"And, pray, what was so delightful about your wardenship that made you desire it over the Secret Services?"

"I don't like long hours, fighting monsters, and getting little sleep," Kai answered with more bite than probably wise. "And the injuries can be quite bothersome."

The lieutenant laughed outright at that. "Perhaps you take more after your mother than I expected."

"I do not," Kai snapped. Instantly, he regretted the words and the tone. "Forgive me," he muttered, lowering his head. His chest burned and rage simmered in his lungs, but he swallowed the emotion threatening to overtake him.

The lieutenant was silent. He tilted his head. When Kai glanced up, the lieutenant's eyes pierced his, and Kai let all the fire in his soul blaze out of his own in return.

Smart? Probably not.

But he'd already blown his cover of being ignorant and dismissive. Might as well answer the man's unspoken question, the one he was fishing so tediously for.

"I'm not sure how you're connected to my family, or what you want from me," Kai growled, "but I'm innocent of whatever you're insinuating."

"You are?" came the mock reply.

"I became a warden to cut ties with them."

His eyebrow rose, and the tilt of it gave the impression that he was somewhat convinced. "So you know why I'm interrogating you?"

"I do not, though I have my suspicions."

He chuckled. "Has anyone ever told you that you'd make a good politician?"

What did he mean by *that*? Kai bit back his sharp retorts and instead said, "I'm afraid not." It was also beside the point, and he was growing wearier with every minute that this conversation continued.

"Let me understand this, then. By having you here, I am not risking the lives of these good warriors, nor am I compromising the integrity of this mission?"

Kai's blood hummed in his veins, his throat turning dry, but he said, "You are not."

"And *you* understand that if I suspect any foul play on your part, I can ship you straight back to Suguan for trial?"

Kai's jaw clenched, but he only nodded.

"In that case," said the lieutenant, lifting his chin and squaring his shoulders, "I have a mission for you, evanescer. You are to infiltrate Fang Zedong's fortress, catalog its weaknesses, and report to me the state of the place after our first attack and this subsequent rescue. I especially want to know if he has replenished his supply of phoenixes."

Kai blinked, forcing back terrifying memories. "His supply of phoenixes?"

"He had some eight to twelve of them guarding his fortress. Our casualties from those beasts alone cost us too dearly on our first attack. You must tell me if there are more."

"When shall I go?"

"Now."

"*Now*?"

"Now."

Why hadn't he sat up inside his tent instead of being so available outside it? So much for getting *any* sleep tonight.

"I want to strike back as quickly as possible, now that they are weakened. I expect a report back by first light," the lieutenant said.

Trying to not look as sour as he felt, he swept a professional bow and said, "As you command."

The lieutenant gave a sniff, then turned to leave.

That was it? He wasn't going to tell him anything else about his connection to his family? Annoyance doubled in Kai's breast, enough that he asked, "How do you know my family?"

The man turned, and for a second, all Kai could see in his eye sockets were the dancing reflections of firelight. Then he twisted his head more, and pools of black replaced the fire. He smiled mirthlessly. "One might call it my hobby, though my wife calls it my obsession. Every spare moment I'm not serving in the military, I'm working to bring down the Hidden Ones."

Kai's jaw sagged, his lips parting.

Lieutenant Jadaala gave a clipped, "Hmmph," and left, disappearing into the night from whence he'd come.

Kai stood motionless outside his tent for a long moment. Then he clamped his mouth shut, glanced upward at the moon inching across the sky, and swept aside the tent flap to duck inside.

There were little preparations to be made, only changing his clothes so his stench didn't betray him and fully arming himself. His heart wouldn't slow its unsteady, jolting rhythm, despite how he told himself it wouldn't be terrible. He could leave whenever his life was threatened. He was trained and skilled. The errand wouldn't even take the whole night.

There was no reason to wander over to Aranya's tent and say goodbye.

Clenching his jaw, he pulled out his last knife, inspected the blade, and then returned it to its sheath. There. He was ready.

He evanesced.

When Aranya hesitantly stepped outside of her tent the next morning, she breathed a sigh of relief that nothing terrible had happened during the night. The camp remained as it had been, with people eating around fires and—wait, were they drinking tea?

"Aranya!"

She turned, spotting Delan approaching, hands full of a steaming bowl and cup. Grinning, she scurried over to him and eyed the breakfast.

"Where did you find that?" she asked, her mouth watering so much she was nearly drooling.

He shoved them toward her. "It's for you. I've already eaten."

"You brought me breakfast?" she cried, definitely far too elated this early in the morning as she sat down. "I can eat this?"

"Yes, yes, goodness gracious. Eat."

She could hardly be spared to think of anything else as she stuffed her face, savoring the heat of the tea. It was the blandest drink she'd ever had, yet the best tasting of her life.

A sudden thought made her pause mid-chew.

"Where's Kai?"

Delan frowned. "He's not here. I met with Lieutenant Jadaala earlier this morning to debrief about our intelligence and understand what we've missed. He said he's already sent Kai off on a mission."

Gruel stuck in her throat. She swallowed hard. "What? A mission?"

He shrugged, but his brow was unusually pensive. "He sent him to Fang's fortress and told him to scout it out. Typical of him to do so without as much as a warning to me."

"Kai is in the fortress right now?" she cried, forgetting the food she held in her lap. "As in . . . this very instant? How long has he been gone? How do we know he's not in trouble? Couldn't he be hurt?"

"Shh, don't fret. He's only been gone a few hours, or so the lieutenant tells me. And you know Kai. Even if he should encounter harm, he'll evanesce back here in a heartbeat. It's just the sort of task that he ought to be doing." The last words were spoken more begrudgingly than Delan probably intended.

"If Kai is busy then, what are we to do? How did your meeting with the lieutenant go?"

"We're to prepare for another attack. Our intelligence confirms everything they've been suspecting, and with last night's rescue, it's been further confirmed that the remaining imprisoned wielders are in Fang's fortress. At this point, our task is to level the fortress and rescue the prisoners."

"Easier said than done, I'm sure," she muttered as she returned to her breakfast.

"Indeed. Once Kai returns, a plan will be formulated with the information he collected. Then we attack."

"What else did the lieutenant say? What have we missed? How long have they been here? Where is the princess?"

"The princess has already left with enough forces to guarantee the safe journey back to Suguan. As for what else we missed, there was a rather large and rather devastating battle against the fortress not long ago. Apparently Fang had a force of phoenixes to do his bidding, along with an army of barbarians and brigands."

"Battle? Phoenixes? Brigands? What do you mean he has an army of brigands? That doesn't seem possible. Brigands are just brigands; there's no such thing as an army of them."

She well-remembered the illusionist, and the other brigands he was with. But they had seemed like a small, specialized group. The entire kidnapping brigade they'd discovered couldn't have been more than a dozen brigands.

So why did Delan say Fang had an *army* of brigands?

"Apparently he has a significant army of them," Delan replied, shrugging. "Which means the entire fortress is armed to the teeth with magic, monsters, and enough manpower to decimate anyone who tries to breach it."

This statement made Aranya bite her lower lip, glancing away from Delan. She picked at a groove in the edge of the wooden bowl, then scratched her ear, and huffed.

"What?" Delan asked.

She stood, taking her dishes with her. "Seems like a dangerous place for Kai to be."

CHAPTER 22

NOON CAME AND went. Aranya busied herself with sharpening her knives, procuring another *jiaun*—how many had she gone through on this mission?—and testing its sights, brushing down her horse and giving it the extra care it had missed over the last few weeks.

Kai didn't come back.

Lieutenant Jadaala instructed everyone to be prepared for battle at a moment's notice, but as the day dragged on further, she took advantage of the time to risk a visit to the river and wash out her spare clothes.

The afternoon waned. Aranya deemed her cloak filthy and, despite having already made a trip to the river, went again. She scoured the offending garment so hard she rubbed her palms and the tips of her fingers raw.

The other side of the river was enemy territory, and Delan grew fussy with how long she worked on the shore, so he came and paced behind her while she worked.

"There could be archers, you know," he growled. "I'm sure that garment is clean enough."

"They haven't shot me yet," was Aranya's returning growl. She cast a glare up at the fortress. The foliage surrounding their camp was too dense to see it, but from here she had an almost unobscured view of the hilltop and the stronghold atop it.

Eventually, Delan succeeded in dragging her away from the river and back to the camp. She pulled her *jiaun* out again, and after thumping the string a few times, decided it needed to be restrung. Despite having done this hundreds of times, she snapped the string the first two times.

"Easy," said Delan from the other side of the fire. "What did it ever do to you?"

She leveled a glare at him and shifted one hand into talons to slice through another length of rope.

The sun set, taking with it the warmth of the day. Aranya's cloak was still drying, so she ignored how cold her fingers grew as the evening stretched long. Delan eyed her much of the time, constantly following her nonstop movements, but she ignored him too.

"I'm sure he's fine," he said gently. "It's a big fortress; he probably had too much to cover in a day."

She huffed out a huge sigh. "I know he's fine."

"Good," Delan replied skeptically.

She didn't have time for his . . . his . . . *rubbish.* She shot to her feet, scooped up her *jiaun* and a quiver of arrows. "I'll be back. Just going to make sure the sights are aligned properly."

Stopping for no one and not even bothering to smile when other wielders made eye contact, she marched through the camp until she was a ways beyond it. Not too far that she couldn't call for help, should the unlikely happen, but far enough that she wouldn't be bothered.

Skewering her cloth target to a tree with an arrow, she loaded her weapon with two arrows and took aim. She stared down the sights, leveling the weapon at the center of the target. Her finger brushed the trigger.

Growling, she yanked the weapon down, pulled out one of the arrows, and then lifted it again. The balance unsteadied; its weight pitched. But instead of being a hindrance, it was a challenge. She took aim, compensating with her hand for the lack of a second arrow. Exhaled. Then she pulled the trigger.

The arrow went wide, lodging in the bark next to the target. Faster than breath, she reloaded and shot again, this time without her hand bracing the frame. It missed the tree altogether.

Over and over again, she reloaded and shot. By the time she'd run out of arrows, she was hitting the target every few shots. Never the center, but it was an improvement.

Perhaps she should have taken care to not stomp so loudly in the underbrush, but she didn't care. She stormed to the tree, collected the arrows, and then went fishing in the vicinity for the wayward ones. After a few minutes, she grew impatient and abandoned the three she couldn't locate, and trekked back to her spot.

Load. Shoot. Load. Shoot.

The movements cleared her mind, focused her soul. She let the thrill of the whooshing arrows flood her veins, let it overcome all other thought.

Load. Shoot. Load. Shoot.

It wasn't *that* hard to shoot one arrow from a *jiaun*. The masters who always cautioned against it likely had never tried to learn. She varied which slot she inserted the arrow into, purposefully throwing herself anytime she grew too comfortable or believed she was starting to get it.

Instinct. Shooting one arrow from a *jiaun* was pure instinct. The more she actively tried to compensate for the missing arrow, the worse she shot. But if she kept herself from thinking too carefully, if she let her training overtake her limbs and hone the minutia shifts of her muscles, it wasn't too hard.

Load. Shoot. Load.

"I've heard shooting one arrow from a *jiaun* too much will permanently damage the calibration of the weapon."

Aranya whirled on her heel, flinging up her *jiaun* before her. "You!" she cried. The strain of the day poured out of her, and her finger quivered on the trigger. Quivered with rage.

"It leads to irregular wear and tear, and after too long, it will shoot as unreliably with two arrows as with one. It's almost dark, anyway."

Shi Yong stood not five paces away, his long hair falling over his shoulder as he leaned against a tree, ankles crossed and hands on his hips. Instead of the gaudy, colorful, gold-edged silks she'd last seen him in, he was dressed in practical, but luxurious black. The cut was tailored, the hems shining with silver thread. He grinned, twilight glinting off his incisors.

"What are you doing here?" Aranya bit out, setting the sights directly on his chest. Then she grinned wickedly, matching his. "Should I add another arrow? Make sure it shoots straight?"

He vanished and apparently guessed her expectation that he would appear behind her. Instead, as she spun to attack him, he reappeared next to her and grabbed her jaw, yanking her backward against his chest and forcing her head up so he could smile and say to her face, "That won't be necessary."

She fired the *jiaun* over her head, the wind from the shot blasting her forehead. Yong moved too quickly, anticipating her move. While she was off balance, he vanished and reappeared, knocking her *jiaun* out of her hands.

Snarling, she shifted her hands into talons and ducked, avoiding his next blow. She leveled a blow of her own, but he deflected and caught her wrist, avoiding the lethal bite of her talons. He yanked her toward him, his free hand coming at her face. She hurled her weight to the side, dislodging his grip on her wrist and landing a hefty kick to the side of his knee. He grunted in pain, staggering before vanishing.

He did not immediately reappear.

"Have you followed us?" she growled, bracing herself and brandishing her talons. She stayed low to the ground, half-crouched as she circled in place. Waiting for him to appear and strike.

"Actually, no," came the reply from behind a nearby tree.

The moment her knife hit the side of the tree, the shadow she'd seen behind it vanished.

"Let's just say this was a happy coincidence."

"The happiest of coincidences, actually," she replied, barring her teeth in a grin. "How I've missed sparring with you."

"The sentiment is mutual." His voice came from the opposite side of the clearing.

Another of her knives whizzed through the air.

From her left: "Your aim is impeccable, even if you're too slow."

"Your brother likes my aim, too."

"Does he, now? Is that the only thing he likes?"

"He likes it when I don't talk all day."

This earned a bright, surprised laugh. "I think he likes it when I don't talk all day, as well. Look at us, Sun Aranya, so alike. Are you out of knives yet?"

Thunk.

"Apparently not!"

"Why are you here, Shi Yong? What *coincidence* brought you to the edge of enemy territory?"

Silence. Now that she was out of knives, save one, she watched for that telltale shadow, barely visible in the oncoming night. If not for the rising moon, she wouldn't have seen him at all. But there, behind that thick trunk, was the edge of a black robe. As carefully and quietly as she could, she eased her way closer.

"I'm surprised you haven't already guessed it," came the reply from behind the tree she approached. "Fascinating to me that you say we are so close to enemy territory. I don't think you know what a true enemy is."

Aranya barely contained her snort. Just a little bit closer . . .

Yong appeared right in front of her. "Looking for me?"

She punched at him, her talons plunging for his face. With a swift arc of his arm, he deflected her blow and flipped her onto her back. She let out a furious cry, rolling to get to her feet. But before she could get her feet under her, he pounced onto her.

No, no, no! She writhed, bending her knees to avoid the position he was trying to maneuver her into. But his feet wrapped around the insides of hers, keeping her legs apart so she couldn't stand. She went to roll, but as she pushed up with her arms, his hand slid underneath and yanked her elbow back toward his belt, his other hand pressing painfully into the space between her shoulder blades as he forced her torso to bend and kept her legs pinned.

"There, now we can talk," said Yong between pants. "Why is Kai in the fortress?"

"How do you know he's there?" she gasped through her clenched teeth, trying to shift herself into a more favorable position.

He wrenched her arm back so hard she cried out. "I asked you a question, love."

Something about Yong always brought out the part of her that loved to play with fire and provoke a fight. She couldn't help her ridiculous giggle as she returned, "And I asked you a question, *darling*."

With that, she stabbed at his thigh with her talons. He was fast, but not fast enough to prevent one of the sharp tips from ripping his robes and drawing blood. Furiously, he shoved her face into the dirt.

"I don't like repeating myself, but for you, sweetness, I'll oblige. Why is Kai in the fortress?"

Each panting breath was so full of dust she choked, panic seizing her with iron bands around her lungs. He laxed his grip, letting her tilt her head and gasp for clean air.

"Why would I tell you anything if I don't know what you will do with that information?" she growled. "Why do you care? He's not coming back with you, if that's what you want to know. You can't make him come back."

"Even if I closed your pretty eyes forever?"

"Seems to me like that would work against you."

"Why? Tell me, Sun Aranya, does my brother harbor any tender feelings toward you?"

"Nope. Not unless flirting counts, and I don't think it does considering he flirts with every female that walks on two legs."

He chuckled, another surprised reaction. "It seems his taste has changed from pretty idiots to pretty tigers."

"I don't think his taste discriminates much."

"Such a high opinion of the one you're suffering to protect!"

Aranya rolled her eyes, huffing out a breath. "I'm having a hard time understanding you, Shi Yong. You follow me hundreds of li and assault me, but you have yet to truly hurt me. It's as if you need something from me, but you're too scared to say exactly what it is."

"Too scared? I've been—"

"Asking veiled questions. Now ask me what you want to know and then get *off* me," she snarled.

"Very well," came his growling reply above her ear. "I want to know what Kai was looking for in the fortress."

"What he was . . .?"

Suddenly, it all made sense.

CHAPTER 23

EVERY LAST PIECE that had been puzzling her for months fit into its proper place.

With clarity came rage.

Yong relaxed his hold on her legs, so she bent her knees, broke the hold, and got one foot under her. Yong fought to regain control, but she used her free hand to push up and roll herself opposite the direction he expected. The result was strain on her pinned shoulder that was so acute she gasped.

But then, with lightning-quick maneuvers, she had him pinned. His height and weight advantage forced her to leverage her bare gain with every trick she'd learned at the Academy. His sleeve on the arm she pinned had ridden up during their fight. Enough for her to see the tattoo on his inner wrist. A nine-tailed fox, the tips of its tails curling into smoke with a crown resting atop its head.

A tattoo Kai did not have.

"You were in Fang Zedong's fortress," she seethed. He wasn't vanishing away from her grip, making premonitions trail like chips of melting ice down her spine. "You were there because you're working with him. *You* supplied the army of brigands he now has at his disposal. Traitor!"

"I guess Kai *did* tell you then about our little family business."

His grin, his huffs of laughter sent shivers down to her toes and anger burning through her blood. "And you saw Kai. Where is he? Why hasn't he come back?"

"Because Fang got a hold of him, that's why! And I can't rescue him."

Despite the sudden terror that clenched around her heart, she wrenched his wrist tighter. Aside from his sharp intake of breath, he gave no sign of pain and did not fight her. "What is Fang going to do to him? And why aren't you glad for it? Shouldn't you be thrilled to have your birthright back?"

"Fathers, he told you more than I expected."

"*Answer me.*"

"The inheritance will never be mine. My *beloved* father made sure of that in the terms of the inheritance. As for Kai, I don't know what Fang intends to do to him. I found him, and we had a nice conversation, and then Fang arrived and restrained him."

"A conversation that looked like ours?" she spat. Of course Kai would have been discovered if he was fighting Yong!

"You can be sure."

"How could Kai have been restrained? An evanescer cannot be bound."

The moment she said the words, he vanished from under her, making her hit the dirt hard. He reappeared a few steps away, but made no move to attack her. "That is the general belief, isn't it?" Yong replied, and his voice . . . his *eyes* . . . There was a flash of true fear there. As if he only now realized how easy it would be for his co-conspirator to turn on him in a blink.

That sent a bolt of terror straight into Aranya's gut. It took everything in her to keep her composure, to not race back to camp, yelling the entire way about Kai's capture.

But she had to deal with the man standing before her.

Kai will be fine. Kai will be fine. He's not gone. He's still alive.

"You want Kai free of Fang," she said as coolly as she could manage. "But you don't know how to do it. So . . . you want my help?"

Yong lifted one eyebrow, belying the tension in his shoulders. "No. I want to know why he went in the first place."

"Use your brain and figure it out yourself. It's obvious as the mud on your face."

Meeting her gaze levelly, he reached up with his sleeve and wiped his cheek. "They're planning another assault on the fortress, and they wanted Kai to scout it out for them."

Her smile was sweet and sticky. "Look at you."

He evanesced to her in a flash, grabbing her jaw and yanking her head up so fast her neck popped. At this angle, she couldn't swallow, but she met his hatred with hers, fury with fury. She wouldn't break under the force of his wrath.

"I don't need your patronization. Be glad I've deemed you more valuable alive than dead for now." He caught her wrist before she could plunge her talons into his gut. Never breaking her stare, he growled, "I think I'm finished here."

Then he vanished.

"Calm down, Aranya. He's going to be fine. Just sit—"

"I'm not sitting down! And stop trying to put that blanket around my shoulders! I'm not panicking. I'm just trying to figure out what we should do! Where's the lieutenant?"

Delan gripped both of her shoulders and firmly set her down on the ground. "Shut up, girl. You're shaking. Sit down and eat a rice cake. Here's some tea. Someone's gone to fetch the lieutenant and he'll be here shortly. Give me your hand. It's bleeding."

"He's trapped, Delan. You said evanescers can't be bound. Why is he bound? Why can't he escape?"

She *was* shaking, enough that her tea kept spilling. Delan managed to get the blanket around her shoulders despite her multiple attempts to displace it. But she wasn't panicking. She was being rational, trying to understand how they would rescue Kai.

"We will find a way to get him out," Delan said sternly.

"I *know*. But we're wasting time here! They could be hurting him, and we're just sitting here all cozy by the fire! We need—"

She was shoving aside the blanket again, trying to stand, when Delan crouched in front of her, his face hard, and slapped her.

Aranya blinked, stunned, her cheek burning. She turned wide eyes up to him, one hand reaching up toward her cheek, but he grabbed both of her wrists and held them firmly.

"Get a hold of yourself, girl! You're letting your own fear and emotion get in the way. You're a warrior. Keep your head on straight. This is what serving our country looks like. This is the call of duty. This is what you were trained for. If you lose your head, you're no good. Not to Zheninghai, and certainly not to Kai, who needs our help. You cannot be overtaken by your anxiety or your impulses. It may feel like we're wasting time, but if we're to have the best chance at rescuing the evanescer, we need to plan carefully. And that means there will be time spent sitting around and feeling useless. Chin up, little shifter."

She stared at him, her breathing coming in short bursts. His face softened with each heartbeat, enough for her to see his own worry glimmering in his irises. But it did not overcome him; he was still the cool, collected, reliable Delan.

She lowered her head into her hands and cried.

"I'm sorry. You're right. I just . . . I just don't want him to be hurt."

"I know," Delan said, gripping her shoulder tightly. "Maybe it shocks you to hear, but I don't want him hurt either. Don't give up on him yet. Kai's a bright one, with enough raw talent and skill to be a match for almost anyone. Have a little faith in him. *Seven valleys.* I hate it when my wife worries about me. It's like she thinks I'll let myself get killed or something stupid like that."

Aranya's response to that was something like a snort of laughter and a choke of sobs. She dabbed at her eyes, trying to regain control of her breathing.

"I don't care about the tears. I've seen plenty of them," said Delan. "Between a wife and three daughters, there are a lot of tears in my house. And every single one is a crier. You'd have thought with the odds, one of them would be a shouter or a silent pouter. No, indeed not. The worst times are when all four are crying at once."

She laughed again, shuddering and sniffling. "What's your wife's name?"

"Genji."

Just then, heavy strides made them look up to see a furious lieutenant marching their way.

"What is this I hear? The Shi boy has been imprisoned? That's impossible!"

Aranya straightened. Beside her, Delan exhaled through his teeth, looked to the heavens, and then turned to greet the lieutenant with a serious countenance. She opened her mouth, about to confirm the lieutenant's statement, but—

Her blood ran cold.

Behind the lieutenant, from the dark forest, a tall figure stepped into the glow of the firelight. She knew that form, the shape of those shoulders, the face illuminated by flickers.

But she hesitated.

It was Kai. It had to be Kai. Wasn't it him? Why wasn't she sure?

"Aranya?" came Delan's voice, even as his head turned to follow her gaze. "Your face is as white as . . ."

"Kai?" she breathed, certain he was too far away to hear her. But his head jerked at the sound of her voice. "Kai?" she choked.

Lieutenant Jadaala was the last to turn around and see Kai. He heaved a hefty sigh and waved a hand. "Finally. Come immediately to my tent to report."

Aranya was already scrambling to her feet, her heart pounding wildly in her chest. He was here, he was alive, he was alright! Before she could run to him, Delan grabbed her arm. She twisted, about to growl something, but the heavy warning in his eyes made her stop.

Kai said nothing.

"Will you answer me, boy?" snapped the lieutenant. "I require a report."

One moment, Kai was standing, and the next he collapsed into a crumpled heap of long limbs and dark cloak.

"Kai!" Aranya twisted, brought her knee up to Delan's gut, and broke free of his hold.

He grunted, then snapped, "Get back here, girl! You don't know if—"

"He's hurt!" she cried, racing past the lieutenant until she reached Kai's fallen body. "Someone get a medic! Kai, can you hear me?"

She rolled him over so he lay on his back, and jerked involuntarily to find his eyes wide open, fixed on her. For the worst moment of her life, she thought he was dead. But then his eyes drooped closed—and then people were surrounding them and pulling her away.

"No, no, I need to take care of him! Let me go!"

Her protests were to no avail. Aranya was dragged away, and Kai was borne off to be examined by the resident medics.

"Have him inspected," the lieutenant was ordering. "The moment he's able to report, tell me."

CHAPTER 24

DELAN WAS BY Aranya's side again, saying things, but it was white noise to her. She stared after the group that carried Kai away, her heart shriveling into a rotten mess of confusion, dread, and anxiety.

"Aranya—"

"I'm fine, Delan," she snapped, pulling away from him. But then she stopped and looked back. His brow was lowered, the lines of his face taut. She sagged and ran a hand down her face. "Forgive me, I'm doing it again. I'm *not* going to lose my head. I'm going to stay rational, and I'm not going to panic."

She offered up a little smile, hoping it would mend some of the damage of her short words. He accepted it, giving her a hearty shoulder squeeze and saying, "Get yourself to bed. You can check on him first thing in the morning to see how he's doing."

That was a good idea. It would keep her from waiting around the fire all night for news. She should just go to sleep, and morning would be here before she knew it. Surely he would be in a much better state by tomorrow. She hadn't seen any blood on him, so that had to be a good sign, right?

What if it's something more serious? What if there's internal damage I couldn't see, and while I sleep he—

No. She wouldn't think like that.

Kai would be fine.

She should simply be grateful that he was back safe and sound, no longer imprisoned in that wretched place.

Focusing on the crunch of twigs beneath her boots, the cold wind rustling the treetops, and the murmur of the milling people around the camp, she marched to her tent, shivering as she went. What had made her think late afternoon was the perfect time to wash her cloak?

It was now too cold for her to strip down to her underthings without the added warmth of her cloak, so the moment she was inside the security of her little tent, she kicked off her boots and wrapped her blanket around her fully clothed self. She unwound her hair, raking her fingers through the long dark strands to undo the braid.

Then, with all the resolve in her heart, the will in her mind, and the determination of her soul, she plopped onto her bedroll, laid down, and closed her eyes.

She didn't sleep. So she knew the moment he appeared inside her tent.

Aranya startled, nearly yelping in fright, and scrambled into a sitting position. Her fright was quickly overcome with relief. "Kai! Are you well? What did the medics say? I have been so worried about you!"

He said nothing, only stood before her. His robes and tunic were gone—likely due to the medics' inspections—leaving his torso and arms bare. He wore only a pair of trousers to ward off the cold.

A chill raced down her spine.

Slowly, careful not to startle him, she reached out. Her fingers brushed the hair of his wrist, and a jolt like lightning shot up his arm. Then his fingers entwined with hers, squeezing so hard the muscles in his arm flexed. It was like he feared if he let go, he would be lost forever. He closed his eyes, his face almost shuddering—a contrast to the powerful lines of his body.

"It's alright," Aranya whispered, reaching up with her other hand so she held his in both of hers. She squeezed his hand back, holding tightly enough that he would know that she wouldn't let go. "You're safe, and you're not alone. You're safe."

She ran her thumb down the back of his hand, stroking soothing lines as she repeated those words softly. *You're safe. You're safe. You're safe.*

What had he endured under Fang's hand?

He made no other move as his hand began clenching tighter and tighter around hers. She winced until she was afraid he might actually crush her bones.

"Kai—"

Then his eyes changed.

His pupils dilated, like a cat's before it pounces. His free hand was moving. It came shooting toward her. Light from nowhere caught a glint. A sharp, lethal glint—a blade.

She didn't have time to scream, to make any sound at all. Instinct kicked in, far more reliable than rational thought, and she dove to the side. Fast, but not fast enough. A strange *thwump* sound. Pain burst behind her eyes, across her scalp. She let out a cry, trying to keep moving, but her neck snapped backward. She was caught. He'd lodged his knife in the bedroll, stabbing straight through her long hair and pinning her.

"Kai!" she cried. "What are you doing?"

He still held her hand, clutched it so tightly she couldn't begin to free herself. She shifted her free hand into talons, trying to angle backward to cut her hair free of his knife.

But then he yanked his knife out. It came plunging for her again.

She rolled in the opposite direction, but his grip on her hand restrained her. His knife grazed her shoulder blade, slicing through robes and skin as it sank into the bedroll.

This time, she wasn't pinned except by his grip on her hand. Before he could get his knife up again, she leapt to her feet, slid her free arm under his, and pivoted her weight so her back was to him. Using all the momentum and leverage available to someone her size, she grunted and bent, flipping him over her back hard onto the bedroll.

It was enough to break his hold on her hand, giving her more freedom.

But then he caught her left shoulder and threw her off balance, so he could yank her down to him, that knife darting out to slice her neck.

Blood roared in her ears, her pulse so frantic she could hardly think. She could only move, only wrestle against his hold. But that knife—that knife was coming. Too fast. Leverage! She needed leverage! She had no leverage in this position. He was too big, and without his shirt, there was no disguising the strength rippling through his body.

She choked, a pitiful version of a scream.

Shift, shift, shift!

But if she shifted, she would hurt him.

At the last second, Kai rolled, throwing his weight, and instead of piercing her jugular, his knife sliced under her jaw. Another graze, but blood flowed, trickling down her neck as his knife plunged yet again into the bedroll.

He was trying to kill her. But he also . . . wasn't?

Would that knife ever stop coming for her? He yanked it out of the bedroll and raised it above her head. She snatched her chance, throwing her weight against his arm and wrapping her arms around it.

She could attempt to restrain him, but he was stronger, and the last thing she needed was to fight him strength against strength. Instead, she shoved on his arm, maneuvering to his side. With a quick twist, she yanked his arm behind him.

"Kai—stop!" she gasped.

He vanished.

Before she could tell where he reappeared, he clipped her legs out from under her, slamming down hard on her shoulder. She landed against the canvas of her tent, and the flimsy structure buckled around them.

No, no, no! She couldn't get tangled up in canvas!

Then Kai was over her, his knees braced against her waist, one hand slamming her arm to the ground. He pinned it over her head, his sweaty face only two hands' breadths away from hers, a sheen over his muscular chest, and he lifted the knife.

Ready to plunge it into her heart.

But his eyes locked on hers, and there was . . . *struggle.* A battle. Not with her. He gasped, his hand trembling, and then his eyes dilated again—black eclipsing beautiful hazel.

Fang got a hold of him.

The phoenixes. The siren snare. Zuan Wan's uncuttable bonds. A curse. *A compulsion.*

That knife came plunging toward her.

Aranya twisted her wrist free and shoved up, her heart raging in her chest, and wrapped her free arm around Kai's neck. She felt the kiss of steel before the ice of his lips, but didn't pull back. Not even when pain sliced into her. She dragged his face to hers, kissing him with all the desperation and fevered hope of midnight and the first blushes of dawn.

The tent collapsed around them, and the scratchy, coarse canvas enveloped her as the knife was ripped back. A brief second—Kai kissed her back. Then, in the same breath, a broken sob shattered through the obscuring darkness of the tangle of material. When she expected his kiss to continue, to deepen, he pulled back. For a half second, he remained where he was, and she could only see the glimmer of his eyes in the black.

"Aranya," he choked. "I—I almost—"

Then he vanished.

There was no place to stop. The moment he evanesced to another dark, empty spot in the woods—nearly ramming into trees or falling into ravines as he did so—his skin itched to be gone. He couldn't stay. Couldn't . . .

He vanished. Reappeared. Vanished. Reappeared. He broke into a run, evanescing around his obstacles instead of altering his course to avoid them. Sweat poured down his face, corrosive rivulets—the only tears he could cry.

Away. Away. Away.

Never had he known shackles. Never had his own hand belonged to another. Never had he dreamed he would plunge a knife into her chest. If not for her quick thinking, he would have murdered her and as many of the other warriors as he could in cold blood.

He never wanted to hurt her.

Now, he knew the depth of his brother's corruption, the heights from which he had fallen. If he would be so treacherous, what would keep him from killing Aranya?

A Shi would kill that girl. Whether it was him or Yong, one of them would do it.

But if he ran, if he vanished into thin air, if he disappeared again, perhaps she could be spared. Perhaps her grandfather would fill the length of his days. Perhaps . . .

A branch hung out in front of him. He evanesced to the other side, then to the far side of the tree it hung from. Nothing would stop him. Nothing would bind him again. He would keep himself and the disaster that followed in his wake away from her.

Evanescing can't solve all your problems, boy.

Qigang's words flashed through his mind, quick as lightning and just as distracting. Kai tripped over a tree root, and was too stunned by those words he didn't even evanesce away to prevent his fall. Instead, he landed smack on his face in the dirt.

Inhale. Exhale.

The world was quiet around him, the pregnant stillness of a forest at midnight—the softness of a predator lying in wait for its prey. He breathed, hands planted flat on the ground.

Evanescing can't solve all your problems.

In, out.

Fire. No, not fire—smoke. He smelled smoke.

Slowly, he lifted his head.

Not three paces away, an obsidian dragon stared at him. Its large, cat-like eyes gleamed like marbles, too glassy to be real. Smoke trailed from its nostrils, curling into the dense foliage and obscuring Kai's view of the moon.

The dragon did not move.

Its haunches tensed, however. Its wings weren't tucked into its side, but lifted and half-folded. Ready for flight or attack. Kai watched the pupils of those golden eyes widen, constrict into slivers, then widen again, oscillating.

Kai lowered his brow. Angrily, he pushed off his arms, standing up.

The dragon skittered back a few paces, its eyes dilating and wings spreading further. It opened its mouth, spitting a few hisses.

"What?" Kai asked, raising an eyebrow. "You think I'm going to eat you? Don't flatter yourself."

With a sweep of his cloak, he evanesced away.

"What happened?" a wielder Aranya hadn't met yet asked as he pulled the canvas off her. "Some crazy nightmare?"

She pursed her lips, quickly wrapping herself up in her blanket and pressing a hand over the throbbing wound in her chest. It wasn't deep, but it was enough to bleed. And hurt.

"A nightmare indeed," she mumbled in response.

He didn't ask further questions, just helped her reassemble the tent and offered a few stupid jokes about not tearing down the rest of the camp when she went back to sleep.

"I'll try," she said. "Thank you."

Once alone, with her hands shaking, she retrieved her set of bandages and set to work, binding up the shallow wound on her chest. The others were such hairline cuts they'd already stopped bleeding.

Kai had fought the compulsion with everything in him. The little cuts attested to that. If he hadn't fought it, he would have killed her thrice over.

Where had he gone?

At least she had broken his curse with her kiss. He should be free now, and he was free from Fang. That would be enough, right? She finished the bandage, readjusted her clothes, and then sat on the edge of the bedroll. She stared into the dark corners of her tent, not even sure what to think.

And then there was Kai.

CHAPTER 25

ARANYA'S HEART NEARLY exploded in her chest with sudden fright. She jerked backward, shifting both of her hands into talons and holding them out before her. She rearranged her feet, so she was in a better position to defend herself.

But Kai didn't come close. He knelt on the ground, and her quick once-over revealed he carried no weapons that she could see. The eyes that fixed on hers weren't manic. They weren't haunted—not in the same way they had been earlier. They were huge in the darkness, but gold glittered in their depths.

Her mouth was hanging open, her tongue shaping words she didn't say. He held up both hands, his eyes searching hers with painful focus.

"Aranya . . . I'm sorry."

She stared, keeping her talons in front of her. The only sounds between them were the huffs of her heavy exhales, the space stretching full of starless darkness and stale air. She closed her mouth, swallowing. Her rational mind told her he was safe. But another part said that he was dangerous. That he could easily kill her if he tried.

"I'm sorry."

She believed him. But did that mean she should trust him? This was probably exactly the sort of thing Delan had the forethought to be concerned about and why he had prevented her from going to him when he first returned.

"I know," she whispered.

His gaze dropped to where her hand instinctively guarded against her chest, then her chin. "Are you . . .?"

"I am fine, yes."

"Are you certain?"

"I am certain. And you?"

"I am . . . better."

"Fang Zedong captured you?"

"Yes."

"Did he . . . harm you?"

"Nothing lasting. He wanted me fit for . . . his errand."

"To kill me?"

"To kill everyone in the camp."

"Oh."

The silence extended, longer and longer, until Kai said quietly, "You keep your talons up? I don't blame you."

She lowered her talons, but didn't shift them away. "I will trust you again very soon. Forgive me for not letting my guard down."

"Don't apologize."

More silence. If her senses weren't so jumpy they threatened to explode, she might have broken eye contact with him. But she dared not give him even a shred of advantage, should she be wrong about his curse being gone.

"I will go back to the infirmary so they don't notice I'm gone," Kai said, the words barely discernable in his low voice. "I'm so sorry." Then he vanished.

Aranya waited a long time before lying down on her skewered bedroll.

The next morning, when she left her tent, she went quietly to stand in line for food. On her way, however, there was a cluster of people she recognized sitting around a fire, speaking in hushed tones. Lieutenant Jadaala spoke to Delan and Kai and a few others. It was a small group, but the lieutenant seemed to be asking Kai questions.

Was she supposed to be there too?

Kai looked up. A shadow passed over his face when he saw her. He turned back to the lieutenant, and Aranya could barely make out him saying, "I'm sorry, could you repeat the question?"

She'd ask Delan later if there was anything she needed to know. Right now, she couldn't sit next to Kai as if last night hadn't happened. If he was reporting to them about the curse and how she'd broken it, she had even less inclination to be there.

As it turns out, her questions were shortly answered when the lieutenant called a meeting of the entire camp a few hours later.

"The earth wielders have been tunneling for the last few days under the east wall," the lieutenant said, pointing at the unfurled scroll on the table. "By their predictions, if unhindered, the wall should fall at dusk tonight. Last time we sent a company around the other side of the main attack site to catch them by surprise and that did not go as well as planned. This time, we will send three companies over the collapsed wall. Because of the evanescer, we know Fang has managed to get himself more phoenixes, but not as many as before. There were four when he was there yesterday, but if he can get them that fast, we must anticipate that he will get more. That is why I have other earth wielders tunneling under the south entrance a much smaller tunnel, one that won't cause the wall to collapse. The rest of our army will enter there."

Aranya stood on her tiptoes, trying to see over the shoulders of the men in front of her.

"Want to get on my shoulders?" whispered Kai beside her.

She glanced up at him, flinching almost imperceptibly. His tone was light, but there was a questioning lilt to it; he didn't know if she would accept his teasing so soon. Despite her best attempts to remain unruffled, her face hardened.

The lieutenant continued. "Again, because of Shi Kai's intelligence, we were able to directly pinpoint the location of the prison where the remaining eight missing wielders are imprisoned, along with others who were taken prisoner after our last attempt to take the fortress."

"Eight?" Aranya whispered to Kai. "I thought there were eleven."

"Some are dead," said Delan from behind her.

"Which ones?"

"Ye Min is dead. And . . ." Kai trailed off.

"And who?"

"Guardian Zuan Wan."

Her mouth opened, and her hand strayed to her chest where the bandage was hidden beneath her clothes. *Dead?*

"The second tunnel will run straight to the prison," said the lieutenant. "It is evidently a maze of tunnels and doors, so you must take care. Our first priority is to rescue our own who still live. Capturing Fang Zedong is of secondary importance. So, while the three companies are keeping Fang's forces occupied here at the eastern gate—archers will be placed here and here to bring down the *mó guǐ*—the others will enter through the smaller tunnel, break into the prison, and escort the prisoners back to camp. The prison should be long evacuated before Fang realizes what is happening."

The plan for invasion thus explained, Lieutenant Jadaala straightened and faced the gathered crowd. Though his face was always hard, this was different, as if the edges of his face were etched into granite.

"Our own beloved and revered Guardian Zuan Wan was one of those who perished in this fortress. *No more.* Not another wielder of Zheninghai shall die in that cursed rot. It is up to you to save these prisoners. *You* are to be the guardians of Zheninghai—every one of you."

He paused, and no one moved a muscle or even let out a breath. They waited—Aranya most of all—for whatever he would say next.

"Now move," he growled.

Aranya hadn't worn armor often. At the Academy, they were taught how to put it on correctly, how to do so *quickly,* how to fight when they weighed an extra hundred pounds, and of course they studied the different types of armor used in warfare for the last several hundred years.

But that didn't mean she was comfortable in it.

Clonking heavily outside, she was suddenly glad for the nippy air. If it had been the heat of summer, she surely would have melted in all this metal.

She stopped.

Kai and Delan stood with their backs to her, talking to each other and watching the camp prepare for tonight's battle. They wore their own armor, swords strapped to their belts.

Had Kai gotten taller?

She shouldn't think . . . but *oh* he looked handsome suited up like this. His long hair was partially pulled back to stay out of his face, cutting his strong jaw sharper. The sun glinted off the metal plates on his broad shoulders, his long legs planted in a wide stance. Despite having fought many battles at his side and seen his fighting prowess, something about his armor made him seem that much more of a deadly warrior. After last night, however, she didn't think she would ever forget how easily he could kill.

Even Delan looked better, his bulky frame looking extra strong. She highly doubted the armor was quite as flattering on her, as it probably made her shoulders look several li wide.

Bracing herself with a deep breath, she marched up to them and stepped next to Delan. She couldn't bring herself to fully let her guard down with Kai. "Any news about which company we will be in?"

"You and I will be with the prison rescuers," said Delan. "Since we have more information on who they are."

Aranya blinked, tilting her head. She caught herself before she glanced over at Kai. "And him?"

"Scout," came Kai's low reply. "To alert your company if the rescue is discovered."

That made sense. Thinning her lips, she drew a deep breath through her nostrils and offered tentatively, "I suppose Lieutenant Jadaala is very happy to have an evanescer at his disposal."

"I believe he has mixed feelings," Kai said dryly.

"One of these days," growled Delan, "you'll learn how to answer a question straight. Not everything needs to be mysterious, boy."

Kai crossed his arms over his armored chest, a smirk playing at the corners of his mouth. "Ladies love mystery."

"Play up the mystery too much and then the lady will be disappointed when she learns the truth," said Aranya, refusing to look his way.

Out of the corner of her eye, she saw his head swivel toward hers. She didn't give him the satisfaction of meeting his questioning gaze.

Delan, between them, planted his hands on his hips and glared at the sky. "Fathers have mercy on a poor soul caught in the crossfires of a lovers' quarrel."

"I think you meant a rivals' quarrel," Aranya interjected with a scowl.

"I meant what I said, shifter. Keep fighting me and you'll prove my point."

She huffed, crossing her arms over her chest. It was risky, but she chanced a glance over at Kai, expecting to see one of his roguish smirks. Instead, his face was utterly blank except for one pensive line that ran between his eyes.

Aranya was a bundle of jittery nerves as they filed into the tunnel. The ceiling was low, the space between the walls hardly wide enough to fit a person. And inside: complete darkness. They were eerily close to the fortress, but still had a good distance to walk until they reached their destination. Her nostrils filled with the heavy and grounding smell of clay.

Two of the earth-wielders who had carved this tunnel led their crew. They would be responsible for breaking into the dungeon. One had the ability to easily manipulate dirt, while the other could move stone. How they were planning to break through iron bars, she wasn't sure.

"It's impossible to be quiet with this armor," Aranya whispered to Delan behind her.

He gave a short shush in response.

Kai was *somewhere.* She wouldn't let her imagination run through everything that could go wrong. She wouldn't picture a repeat of his capture. Instead, she focused on this dark, claustrophobic tunnel, and the sounds of chinking metal and dozens of pairs of boots.

After ducking beneath the low ceiling and twisting sideways through thin places for what had to be an hour, their progress halted. Muffled whispers sounded ahead, but the words were too difficult to distinguish.

Then a strange rumbling noise punctured the stillness. She turned, trying to see Delan behind her. It was too dark.

"What's that?" she whispered.

"The earth wielders breaking us into the dungeon."

"It's so loud. How can they not hear us?"

"Just wait a minute."

She fidgeted her weight between her feet and adjusted her helmet, then checked her sword. Fathers, she wished the broadsword wasn't the preferred weapon for attacks like this. She hadn't been as diligent in swordplay as in archery, and though she had her *jiaun,* it would do her little good in a dark dungeon.

A dull roar filled the cavern. The ground around them rumbled, shook, and dirt rained down from the ceiling. Terror flashed through her at the thought of being buried alive in this tunnel.

I won't think about that. These earth-wielders know their work.

The rumbling didn't stop, only growing louder and louder. It wasn't coming from ahead, where the earth benders were breaking into the dungeon. It came from everywhere, from all around her.

"The eastern wall is caving," said Delan, bracing his limbs against the walls of the tunnel. "Perfect timing."

Her helmet rattled on her head from the force of the destruction.

"Are they sure it's safe to be underground while a wall is crashing down?" asked Aranya.

Delan chuckled but didn't respond. Almost as if he was afraid of the same thing as she was.

Finally, they started moving forward again. Her heart leapt in her chest, her restrained breathing turning ragged. She caught herself and forced her breathing to steady despite the sudden flood of adrenaline in her veins.

They were almost there.

Her first real battle. The conclusion to her first secret mission.

She crossed her fingers as she placed one foot in front of the other, the speed of the warriors in front of her quickening as the seconds slipped away.

She *really* hoped this wouldn't be her last battle.

CHAPTER 26

ARANYA EXPECTED TO crawl out of the floor into the dungeon. By now, she ought to have learned to not trust her expectations, considering how often they were wrong. When she reached the end of the tunnel, instead of a floor, she found a long drop waiting for her. Squatting, she braced one hand on the edge of the dusty stone, the other on her dangling sword, and hopped down.

The wafting smell she'd encountered in the last leg of the tunnel now hit her like an avalanche—the smell of rot, decay, of aching muscles and torn flesh, of slick stone and dank darkness. She wrinkled her nose, wincing and covering her nose with her sleeve to stifle her urge to cough.

Delan dropped down behind her, already wearing his lavender kerchief tied over his nose, and she forced herself to follow the other wielders up the hewn steps—each movement sounded so loud in the echoey chamber!—and not stare at the iron-wrought bars stretching floor to ceiling. On impulse, she reached out and barely let her finger brush the metal.

Ice flared through her skin. She pulled back.

The wielders filed out of a door at the top of the stairs. Once she passed through it, she craned her neck to see the room they entered. From the shuddering light of a torch a wielder carried at the front of the line, she could make out that the chamber was nigh identical from the one they exited. Three cells lined the wall with a small walking path to the stairs that led up to another door. But when she twisted further, she found the door she'd just come through to be one of three.

"Where do those doors lead?" she whispered to Delan behind her.

"Probably to more cells," he whispered back.

"Why are these empty?"

"Probably because they don't have enough prisoners. Now hush."

She hushed for a minute. Then she leaned back again, pressing the back of her hand to her nose. "Do you have an extra kerchief?"

He glared at her as he shook his head.

An unintelligible order was whispered ahead, and a couple wielders broke out of line to approach those unopened doors. They heaved their weight against the hefty doors until they gave, and a shrill squeak pierced the air, followed by a low groan. She winced.

Delan's own grimace was ghoulish in the torch's stuttering flicker.

She hurried on, heart pounding and palms sweaty, almost forgetting the stench of the place as she mounted the stairs and exited through another door. It remained the same. Three cells, three doors that led deeper into the bowels of the dungeon, and one door that led upward at the top of a staircase.

Except these cells weren't empty.

Two inmates occupied the foul space. One sat unmoving against the bars, his arms crossed over his knees. Long, blanched hair flowed down over narrow shoulders and pooled on the ice-cold stone floor.

The other clutched the iron bars with weathered, knobby fingers, pressing his face into the space between, and his white beard hung to his elbows. He sat like a frog, propping up on his feet with his knees splayed.

Du Liuxian.

One wielder reached out and gripped the bars with both of his hands. The metal flared, turning orange with heat. Another wielder set to work on the other cell—one of the earth movers—planting her palm on the stone wall. With a great heave, she shoved the stone, so it recessed deeper into the wall, leaving a gap. She continued on the stones above and below it, giving the prisoner a chance to slip out.

"You," a sharp-nosed woman said, edging her way with a torch past the cells toward Aranya. At first, Aranya thought she was talking to her, but then realized she addressed the man behind Delan. "Tell them back there that we've found Pen Tao, high seer, and Du Liuxian, evanescer. You escort them through the tunnel." Then she turned to Aranya and held out the torch. "Check those chambers."

Aranya accepted the torch, glancing back at Delan. "You want to come with me?" she asked, giving an uneasy grin.

"He'll check the other chamber," said the woman, producing an unlit torch and handing it to Delan.

She didn't mean for her hands to shake as she held the torch out to Delan's to light it. But adrenaline coursed through her veins, and every sense peaked in alertness. Delan gave her a reassuring smile—visible from the crinkle of his eyes—then busted open his chamber door and disappeared.

Taking a deep breath, she did the same.

She left the door swinging open on its hinges, gritting her teeth at the flurry of sounds above her and the whining of the rusted metal.

"You're not taking me anywhere!" came a snarl from above, the voice gravelly with disuse.

"We're rescuing you, sir."

"You'll murder me!"

"Shh, no one is going to hurt you. Come this way."

Aranya bit her lip, squeezing her eyes shut for the barest second, and then hurried down the steps. They were uneven, and a little too close together—the perfect combination to cause stumbling. She gripped her torch in one hand and the wall with the other, forcing her pace to steady as she plunged into the pitch blackness.

This chamber was empty, matted and damp straw the only thing in the cells. She continued forward, her heart rate climbing, and faced another set of three doors.

A labyrinth of a dungeon indeed.

She licked her lips, bracing herself, then threw her weight against the first door. It gave much easier than the one before it, and she nearly went pitching down the staircase. Swallowing to keep her stomach in place, she gripped the sharp edges of stone sticking out between the crumbly grout and held still for several deep breaths.

Then she was in motion, the sounds she left behind growing fainter with each awkward step. When she reached the ground floor, she held up her torch and peered into the cells.

Nothing.

She refused to let her spine crawl as she turned her back on the empty chamber and hurried back up the stairs. The adjoining room proved just as empty, though somehow even darker.

When she entered the third chamber, however, she almost couldn't even force her feet to step over the threshold.

The stench was so overpowering it brought tears to her eyes. She nearly choked on her own gag, and through blurry eyes, she held her torch down over the drop to the floor below.

There was something in one of the cells. She could hardly breathe, but she pressed her sleeve over her nose and mouth and descended the stairs carefully. When she reached the cell, she paused, squeezing her eyes shut.

Then she forced them open and held the torch up to the bars.

They weren't like the other bars from the other cells. These were wreathed in . . . in *vines.* Brown, cracked vines with thorns the length and breadth of her thumb. They wound up the iron, drooping down from the top bar at the ceiling. The tips of the thorns were so sharp they almost glittered in the light and shadow playing from the torch.

Inside, encased in a coffin of briars and dead weeds, was a corpse.

There was no doubt in her mind.

Lord Zuan Wan. One of the elite guardians of Zheninghai.

Aranya stared, pressing her hand harder against her face. The sudden urge to cry welled up in her chest, burning the back of her throat and hollowing out her gut.

But there was no time for that.

She hastened back up the steps, swallowing furiously as she went, and then hurried up the other set of stairs into the chamber where Pen Tao and Du Liuxian had been freed.

Unfamiliar faces hurried in both directions, squeezing around the mutilated cells of the prisoners. Aranya stopped in the doorway, her tongue stuck to the roof of her mouth, and stared at the passing figures.

"Guardian Zuan Wan," she managed, but it was too quiet for someone to hear.

Nevertheless, a young girl—probably not much older than Aranya—happened to look up and see her standing with her mouth open at the door.

"The guardian," Aranya repeated, nearly gasping. "His . . . his . . ." She shook her head. She was a warrior! Not some weak-kneed damsel. She straightened her spine and growled, "Lord Zuan Wan's corpse is in the final chamber on the left."

The girl's lips thinned in a grim expression, but she merely nodded and said, "I'll tell one of the leaders. You go on ahead."

Aranya scurried past the girl and up the chamber's stairs to the next level of the labyrinth. Delan was nowhere to be seen, and she tried not to let that turn her breathing fast. There remained no sign of Kai, but that was to be expected. She made a few inquiries, found that wielders had been sent down the doors on this level, and proceeded higher.

Before she knew it, she'd reached the end. Stepping carefully through the door, she found herself in a hallway of doors. With only one other person. It was the same sharp-nosed woman as before. She looked severely at Aranya, though not necessarily with displeasure. Or perhaps it was merely how the light of the torch played on her harsh features.

"That door," she said, pointing to the last one on this side of the hallway. Presumably wielders had already descended into the others.

"How is the battle going?" Aranya whispered, her feet refusing to move.

"I do not know."

"But they haven't discovered us yet?"

"It appears not yet, though we best not try our luck. Hurry, girl! We must comb through this entire dungeon to be sure we've rescued everyone."

With that exhortation, Aranya obeyed and went to the last door. She wanted to hesitate, to protest heading down into this entire section of the maze by herself, but she couldn't. She wouldn't falter now.

Furrowing her brow in determination, she shoved open the door and descended into pitch blackness.

When the door swung shut behind her, she jumped. But then she gritted her teeth and pushed onward. She wouldn't think about how the darkness seemed to swallow up the light of her meager torch. She wouldn't worry about if it had enough fuel to last a trek through these chambers. She wouldn't imagine what monsters could be hiding in the shadows.

And she would move *quickly*.

The faster they finished, the higher the likelihood of their plan succeeding, and the more lives would be saved. She all but ran down the stairs, flashed her torch into the empty cells, and plunged into the right-most door.

Empty, empty, empty.

Until she reached the very bottom floor.

She pushed open the door and was immediately met with a low voice.

"Who's there? You're not one of the guards."

Aranya nearly leapt out of her skin in her fright, but she mastered herself and scurried down the steps two at a time. "I'm Sun Aranya. We're here to rescue you."

"Bless the fathers," came the relieved reply. "I didn't want to get my hopes up."

This voice sounded very different from the haunted, half-crazed tones she'd heard from Du Liuxian as they freed him. It was distinctly male, and surprisingly . . . not insane? Perhaps he hadn't been imprisoned long.

She held up her torch as she approached, and the prisoner, who was standing, winced and covered his eyes. He was a large man, certainly as tall as Kai if not taller, and definitely broader. His clothes were ragged and filthy, but similar to the ones she wore beneath her armor. It wasn't until he squinted and looked up into her face that she recognized him.

"Cao Renshu?" she breathed.

CHAPTER 27

RENSHU BLINKED AGAINST the light, gripping the iron bars, and peered at her, as though trying to get a better look at her. "Forgive me, but have we met?"

"Oh!" Aranya gave a sheepish grin. "Uh, no. That is, not officially. We just were in the same graduating class, and you were one of the top students."

"Ah, I see. It's a pleasure to finally make your acquaintance, Aranya."

"Likewise." Her smile quickly faded into a frown, and she tilted her head. "Aren't you in the Emperor's Guard? How'd you end up here? And don't you have feral strength? Why haven't you broken yourself out?"

His voice was accommodating, and not at all snappy, despite her questions. "Yes, I'm in the Emperor's Guard. I'm here because the emperor sent much of his personal guard to this fortress to rescue

Princess Meiling, but I was captured. Yes, I have feral strength, but it appears I am under some sort of curse. I cannot access my strength or my other senses."

Was this how Fang had imprisoned Kai? By somehow dampening or restraining his magic with a curse?

She bit her lip, considering the situation. "Then I'll have to run back up and let the other wielders know you're here so they can rescue you. I cannot break you out, unfortunately. Unless . . ."

An idea struck her, one that made her heart lurch and her cheeks heat. As much as she wanted to discount it, it was a good idea. Besides, she was a professional. This was her job. It would only be awkward if she made it so.

"Unless what?" Renshu asked, his wide hands still gripping the bars—heedless of their cold.

She swallowed, flushed, but kept her voice steady when she said, "I could perform the Yanzhao Technique to free you, if it is a curse. Then you could break yourself out of the cell."

Renshu was quiet for just a smidge of a second longer than Aranya had hoped for, and self-doubt crept up the back of her neck. She forced a neutral expression on her face.

"Clever thinking," he said, though his tone betrayed the slightest reluctance. But he didn't hesitate when he pressed his face into the space between the bars. It didn't fail her notice that he bent his knees, making himself shorter for her.

Professional. Professional. Professional.

This was just part of the job—kissing strangers to break curses when necessary. She held the torch out to one side, her neck going unusually hot, and stepped forward. Her heart pounded, but she refused to falter.

You're betraying Kai.

The voice in her head stabbed her so sharply she sucked in a breath. It should have been too quiet for Renshu to hear, but he immediately pulled back. "If you're not comfortable with this, I will wait for other help."

She blinked up into his concerned, dirt-smeared face, and couldn't help the simultaneous burst of gratefulness in her heart and the sudden flush of shame that followed it. Neither could she prevent the next thought that shot through her mind.

Kai's kissed dozens of girls. And none of them were cursed.

Resolve tightened her jaw. If Kai was allowed his Academy dalliances, she was allowed one professional, curse-breaking kiss. It would be a waste of time and lives to hesitate now.

Besides, it wasn't as if she and Kai were . . . anything.

"No, it's fine," she growled.

With that, she reached up and grabbed the front of his shirt through the bars, pulling his wide-eyed face low enough that she could stand on her tiptoes and press her lips to his.

"Aranya? Aranya? Aran—!"

Aranya gasped, nearly choking as she wrenched away from Renshu to whirl and find Kai standing in the doorway, mouth agape. He was almost entirely shadow, but she could see with pristine clarity the shock on his face.

It morphed into a tight, glittering snarl of a smile. "Forgive me for *interrupting*. There's trouble. I was sent to warn you. Keep searching this sector for prisoners, but be prepared for confrontation."

She meant to explain the kiss, but the word that spewed out of her mouth was, "Trouble?"

Behind her, Renshu grunted, and iron groaned. She turned just as he planted his legs wide and wrenched open the iron bars with his bare hands. She stared, eyes round, until she heard a huff from the door.

"Looks like you're in good hands," came Kai's sour growl as he turned and swept out of the chamber in a flurry of cloak.

"Oh, don't be an idiot!" Aranya cried after him as he vanished.

Renshu squeezed through the opening he'd created and pursed his lips. "Sorry if I complicated . . . something."

She waved a hand, glaring into the space where Kai had vanished as she ran up the stairs. "Don't worry about him. Are you in any shape to . . .?"

"Go with you and break more prisoners out of cells? Absolutely."

She grinned. "We've got some two dozen cells to check left, I believe." Together, they made their way to the upper chamber. Renshu busted open a door with probably more force than necessary, gave a sniff, and shut it.

"What?" she asked, watching him do the same to the second door. "You're . . . smelling for occupants?"

"It's a little faster," he said with a quirked grin, then bounded up the stairs to the next level.

"You seem rather spritely for a newly released prisoner," Aranya gasped, trying to keep up with him.

"I haven't been here *too* long, thankfully. And I feel so much freer with that curse broken."

"Has it been bad? Here, that is?"

"You have no idea. Hey, there's someone in this one."

They hurried down the stairs, Aranya nearly wiping out on the last one, and Renshu was already bracing to bend the bars with his hands. Giving him a wide berth, she approached the cell and shined her torch into it.

A woman lay on the ground, her hair covering her face and splaying out on the stone. Her body was twisted, the sharpness of her gaunt form visible through the folds of her tattered robes. Hip bones, elbows, ribs, and shoulders protruded from the fabric.

And yet, it was as though the placement of each limb was precise, perfectly calculated to induce pity, to think, *"What a poor, beautiful woman to rescue!"*

Aranya knew her without even seeing her face. Even in repose—the only stench in the air was that of dungeon, not that of death—she was so distinct, Aranya would have known her anywhere, despite having never met her before.

Kang Lei. The missing siren.

Renshu stepped aside from the hole he'd created, enough for Aranya to twist sideways and slip through. He took the torch from her, holding it high to illuminate the chamber. She knelt next to the woman, quickly brushing aside the hair from her face and shaking her shoulders.

"Lei," Aranya said. "Wake up."

"Oh," was the responding groan. The woman pulled her hand free when Aranya tried to grip it and instead flung it across her eyes. "Oh!" she said again, but did not otherwise stir.

"Get up!" Aranya growled, shaking her harder. "We're running out of time!"

Nothing.

"Here," Renshu said, handing the torch back to Aranya. She stepped back out of the cell and waited as he reached inside, grabbed hold of the woman's upper arm, and dragged her to the edge. She tried not to wince at the rough treatment as he pulled her through the opening—Aranya had to run to his side and help with her floppy limbs—and then he scooped her up and slung her over his shoulder.

"Oh!" the woman moaned.

"We've got to keep moving!" said Renshu, his face tense.

"What?" Aranya asked, following him back up the stairs.

"I can hear them coming," he said, gritting his teeth.

"Who?"

"Soldiers. Fang's soldiers."

"How can you tell it's them and not ours?"

"Because I can hear fighting."

"Oh," she said lamely, panting to keep up with his lengthy strides.

Renshu stuck his nose into the other doors on this level, announced them empty, and they charged up another flight of rocky, inconsistent stairs. Down, they plunged again into another leg of the fortress through another series of doors. "Twenty more cells," he muttered.

"I'll check this one!" Aranya said, splitting off from him. He nodded, not glancing her way as the siren's arms swung and dangled behind him. Her adrenaline urged her faster and faster, almost to the point of carelessness on the flights of stairs. "I found one!" she called after a few minutes.

She hurried to the cell, shining the torchlight into the wincing face of a skeletal prisoner.

"It's alright, we'll get you out of here," she assured the prisoner before calling, "Renshu!"

Heavy footsteps echoed from the floor above, and soon enough, they reached a crescendo outside the open door. Aranya turned.

"Renshu! Can you—oh dragons!"

She threw herself to the ground, rolling on impact, narrowly missing an arrow to the chest. Her torch slipped out of her grasp, sputtering and snuffing out on the stone. Blackness enveloped her and her attacker.

It had been so fast, but she was pretty sure she'd seen a barbarian guard in that door—definitely not Renshu—but whoever he was, he was clearly armed and aiming for the kill. Aranya kept moving, hating the clank and clamor of her armor with every step. The guard had the upper hand, being on higher ground. Another arrow whizzed dangerously near her, and she leapt to the side, toward the stairs and away from the prisoner. Its iron tip clunked against the stone and skittered across the floor.

Ignoring the sword strapped at her waist, she unholstered her *jiaun* and, as quietly as possible, loaded two arrows into the slots. Then she dove, correctly guessing that her attacker had found her again in the dark. An arrow hit stone and bounced against her boot.

She maintained her bearings in the pitch black, and, taking wild aim in the general direction of her attacker, fired her *jiaun*.

A garbled cry of surprised and unfamiliar syllables erupted from her attacker. Not a cry of pain. Aranya slotted one arrow—no time for a second!—and fired toward that cry. But he'd already moved, and she bolted, running alongside the staircase to get away from his next shot.

Then the door smashed open, banging into the stone.

Renshu.

Probably. Hopefully!

This time, as she moved, she loaded two arrows. Her aim had to be solid! Her attacker hadn't shot another arrow toward her yet, so she guessed he was distracted. Relying far more on instinct and the sounds of what she hoped were Renshu's steps, she fired.

This time, a howl of pain cut through the air.

"Nice shot!" came Renshu's voice. "I'll finish him."

There was a sickening thud, and Aranya grimaced, lowering her weapon. "Are there more?"

"Yes. Not far behind. Where'd your torch go?"

"It's out. Can you free this prisoner?"

"It would be my pleasure."

Renshu navigated the dark quickly, and Aranya spared a thought that it would have been wonderful to have Delan's night vision right about now. The groaning of metal filled the quiet, followed by a puff of exertion from Renshu. He grunted once more, and then said between huffs, "Good sir, are you able to walk?"

No response.

"Aranya, can you help me get him out?"

She holstered her *jiaun* and followed his voice, hands outstretched and fingers splayed. He caught her elbow and said, "Here." Then, moving as though blind, she felt her way through the bent bars and tentatively reached out further for the prisoner.

Her hand touched matted hair first.

"Here, let's stand up," she said gently, hooking her arm under the prisoner's armpit. "Can you stand?"

Nothing.

"They're coming," Renshu said through gritted teeth. "Just pull him if you have to."

"Sorry!" she squeaked, and then she hoisted the limp man over her back. He was surprisingly heavy for being nothing but sagging skin and a rack of ribs. She stumbled to the opening, grateful when Renshu reached out his hand to guide her.

He leaned into the narrow space, grabbed the prisoner, and hefted him out and onto his other shoulder. "Follow me," he said, grunting as he readjusted the two humans slung over his shoulders.

They maneuvered their way up the stairs. Aranya opened the last door on this level for Renshu to sniff, and he proclaimed it empty. Seventeen left to check before they could get out of here.

Then, even in the dark, she heard his head whip to one side. He bent and hoisted his burdens to the ground.

"Are they here?" she whispered.

"They're here."

The door above them burst open.

CHAPTER 28

TORCHLIGHT FLOODED THE darkness. Aranya was still loading her *jiaun* when Renshu leapt forward on all fours, racing up the stairs, and pounced upon the five guards that poured through the opening.

She braced herself beside the prisoners, feet wide and shoulders back. Her blood raced with the urge to shift, to let herself run wild like Renshu, but she maintained her self-control. If she'd learned anything, it was that a clear mind was her biggest asset.

With a sweep of his arm, Renshu sent one guard hurtling over the edge of the stairs. He shouted as he fell, and Aranya gritted her teeth, aimed, and fired as he hit the ground.

Her shot was true. His cries ended abruptly.

Her first true kill.

Hands fumbling with the next reloading, she clenched and unclenched her jaw. Renshu killed a second, then a third, and she almost hesitated to shoot again for fear of hitting him. But then the fifth guard raised his sword to hack into Renshu's neck while he was in the process of dispatching the fourth guard.

Aranya shot straight over his shoulder at the fifth guard.

Renshu's reactive swipe knocked the already-dead man down the stairs. As he fell, Renshu caught the torch out of his hands. His eyes met Aranya's across the chamber, and he raised an eyebrow.

"Who taught your shooting class?" he asked as he cleared the bodies and hurried down the stairs to scoop up the prisoners again.

"Master Quan for my first five years, then Master Xu."

"You got Master Xu?" Renshu exclaimed, bounding up the stairs with limp prisoners bouncing on his back. "I'm so jealous! I tried to register for his classes every year, but they were always full!"

"Did you register on the first day?" Aranya asked, grinning despite herself as she scampered up behind him.

He sighed. "No, I didn't. I always waited until the second or third day. I was the sort of person who procrastinated *just a little*, but I always paid for it."

She laughed. "Novice mistake." Not that it cost him much in the end.

"Indeed. Phoenixes scorch this place—there's more coming!"

"How many?"

"Three this time. Hey, do you think you can take them out with your *jiaun*? Because we can move faster if I don't have to set the prisoners down."

A thrill raced through her veins, whether from his faith in her or the excitement of battle, but she immediately said, "I think so."

"Good. One more door and then they'll be here."

By now, her thighs ached from all the stairs, but she refused to slow down. They were nearly running, little caring how much sound they made, as they continued scouring this leg of the dungeon for more prisoners to rescue. *Twelve cells left.*

"Get ready!" Renshu whispered.

She had her *jiaun* loaded and aimed for the door the moment it opened. Her arrows flew straight, hitting the first guard in the gut. He toppled back, and the second leaned forward to yank the door shut. Heart racing, she slammed one arrow into a slot and fired. The door barely shut in time, her arrow bouncing off the door handle.

"Well, that's a new trick," said Renshu.

Her pulse was racing so fast, the high of the thrill so intoxicating, that she grinned. No matter that she had just killed a man. This was *war,* and she was proving herself a valuable foe.

Then the door opened fast. Just a breath, and an arrow came whizzing straight toward them. It hit right between Aranya and Renshu, and she squeaked as she toppled to one side.

But then she was running, dodging around the iron-barred cells. The moment the door opened again, she fired her double arrows straight through the narrow gap. The door slammed shut, but Renshu had already divested himself of his burdens and pounded up the stairs like a lion. He wrenched the door open, nearly breaking it off its hinges, and grabbed the second guard by his collar and flung him into the air. Aranya shot him before he landed and reloaded in preparation for the third.

But Renshu had already sliced his jugular with the guard's own sword.

As Aranya lifted the hollow-eyed man to make it easier for Renshu to sling him over his shoulder, a new form appeared in the doorway. She dropped the prisoner and wrenched up her weapon.

It was Kai.

Just then, the earth around them shook. Stones fell from the ceiling, clattering to the ground.

"Get out!" Kai cried, his voice hoarse. "The mission has been compromised. Orders are to *get out.*"

"Through the tunnel?" Aranya said, already bounding up the stairs.

Renshu glanced between them, the two prisoners back on his shoulders.

Kai's fists clenched, his throat bobbing, his eyes sparking with fury. "They discovered the tunnel. It's . . . it's a bloodbath down there."

Her jaw sagged, her mind scrabbling with possibilities. "So . . . what's the escape route?"

Kai's chest heaved. He blinked rapidly, the muscles in his neck twitching. Then his eyes met hers, wide and terrified.

"There is no other escape route," Renshu growled. Then, firmly, fiercely, "We'll just have to face the bloodbath. The three of us can do some damage."

"What about the other prisoners?" Aranya gasped. "We haven't finished searching this wing! There's twelve cells left to check."

The three of them exchanged looks. Around them, the world shuddered and groaned, the pebbles on the ground rattling against stone.

Then Kai said, "Give me that torch. I can search faster."

"You stay and defend the prisoners, Aranya," said Renshu, sliding them back down to the ground. "I'll search as well."

"If we're not back within ten minutes, you get yourself out of here. And you leave the prisoners, understand?" Kai's eyes were hard.

Throat suddenly dry, she could only nod.

Then Kai vanished and Renshu raced out the door.

Aranya braced herself in front of the prisoners, *jiaun* slotted and ready. She stared at the door above her, those jagged and uneven stairs. Beside her, the ice of the cell's iron bars grappled for her. She suppressed a shiver.

The siren moaned from where she splayed on the floor, dramatically romantic in her rags and flung limbs. The light from the torch she'd propped up against the wall illuminated the other prisoner next to her. He stared blankly, mutely, as though his mind had fled his body ages ago. Probably one of the other missing wielders, but she wasn't sure which.

She swiveled her gaze away from them, from the haunting shadows playing across their gaunt faces, cast by the sputtering torch. Best to focus on calming her breathing and counting the passing seconds so she didn't lose track of time. Her limbs quaked, though not exactly from fear. The urge to fight or flee raged in her blood, and when she tried to hold still, her hands began trembling. She settled on a swift pace back and forth in front of the prisoners.

Long minutes passed with no sign of friend or foe. Only ghastly light in a dark place and two mute companions.

It only made her more anxious.

She walked faster, the sound of her boots filling the space. She ought to listen more carefully to signs of pursuit, but . . . but . . . She paced faster, harder, heavier. When would they be back? How many minutes had it been? Probably only two, but it felt like seventy.

"They're going to get him."

The sudden, hollowed voice echoing behind her made Aranya nearly shriek and whirl. Instinctively, she flung up her *jiaun*, fingers dancing along the trigger. Through her sights on the weapon, she watched as the male prisoner twisted his neck. Unseeing eyes pivoted in sunken sockets toward her. They fixed directly on her. He whispered something, shaking his head slowly.

"What?" Aranya said, lowering her weapon.

The whispers continued, a bit louder, but still unintelligible.

Aranya softened her tone, tilting her head as she leaned closer to him. "I cannot understand what you're saying. Is something wrong? Are you in pain?"

The poor man covered his face with his hands. He wouldn't stop shaking his head. His hands moved to cover his ears as the shaking grew more vigorous. The murmurs grew louder until Aranya could finally make out what he was saying over and over again: "They'll get him. They'll get him. They'll get him!"

Aranya's lungs tightened.

He was mad.

After hesitating, she touched the man's shoulder with two fingers. "We'll get you out of here soon. Don't worry."

The man's hand clamped down on Aranya's, pinning it to his shoulder when she tried to draw back. His eyes were wide, pleading, distress painted in every line of his face. "They'll get him! They'll *get him*!"

She gave another tug on her hand, but when he clutched it tighter, she relinquished. If her touch comforted him, then it was the least she could do. "I know, I know," she cooed softly. "Just try to be patient. They'll be back soon, I promise."

She cast a helpless look at the door above the stairs. Where were Kai and Renshu? Why hadn't they come back yet? It must've been ten minutes by now, and Kai had told her to leave. But she couldn't just abandon the prisoners.

She'd stay a little longer. *Hurry back, Kai. Please.*

"They'll get him. They'll get him!" the prisoner kept crying, his voice growing louder and louder, pleading with her.

Aranya gritted her teeth, flinching when his bony fingers squeezed her hand so hard she feared it might break. "Hush!" she whispered. "You need to be quiet or else they'll find us!"

He shook his head so vigorously that spittle dripped between his sagging lips. "They'll get him."

Aranya ran through the remaining wielders in her head. Then she started, whipping her attention to the prisoner. "Are you Cai Fu? The high seer?"

His only response was crushing her hand in his. Aranya's eyes bulged as pain flared, and then she pried his hand off her, scooting away and rubbing the sore palm with her thumb.

If this was Cai Fu, clearly he'd gone mad. But what if he wasn't *only* mad? What if he'd seen a vision?

A vision about Kai.

"They'll get him," whimpered the prisoner.

"Who?" Aranya demanded, dread settling like a rock in her stomach. "Who? Who will they get?"

He shook his shaggy head. "They will. They will!"

"*Who*?"

The prisoner stopped, holding still and remaining quiet for several long heartbeats that rang like death knells in the darkness. Slowly, he lifted his head, staring straight ahead as though he watched something she couldn't see.

"Ye Ye."

CHAPTER 29

THE NEXT MOMENT, Aranya had the prisoner's shoulders pinned against the wall, her face a finger's breadth from his.

"*What*," she seethed, "do you know about Ye Ye?"

He wheezed, eyes rolling. She didn't care her back was exposed to the door, that an enemy could enter and shoot her down in a blink. Her hands shifted into talons, and animalistic instinct flooded her senses.

"Tell me!" she demanded, fighting the frantic pounding of her blood that demanded violence. "*Who* is going to get Ye Ye?"

"Fang."

Aranya released the prisoner, already leaping up the stairs, talons gleaming. Kai and Renshu didn't matter; they could rescue the prisoners without her.

She needed to rescue Ye Ye.

How in the seven valleys and eight phoenix-scorched wildernesses did Ye Ye get brought into this? She was so frantic, she was almost in tears. She flung open the door, raced through that chamber, and up the next set of stairs.

Ye Ye was back in Zushui, safe and sound and being watched by Na. How could anyone have—

Yong.

She skittered to a stop, every drop of blood draining out of her skin and into the rock beneath her. Kai had said Yong would do anything. He would use Aranya to get to Kai. And to get to Aranya—

Talons ripped into her hair. She gasped, lungs constricting. Stumbling to the nearest cell, she vomited between the iron bars. Even after her stomach was empty, it convulsed like she was about to heave her guts up, too. She had to find Yong. Limbs trembling, she broke into a run. Wherever he was, she would find him.

And then she would murder him.

"You'll not find him there."

Aranya froze, one foot on the stair in front of her. Her breaths came in gasps, sharp as knives in her lungs. She turned to look over her shoulder, back to where that strange, rasping voice had come from. Torchlight danced on the edges of stone and iron, illuminating the barren chamber.

No one.

Icy, phantom fingers crawled up her spine, tickling and making her shudder.

"Who's there?"

"Only me," came the voice, this time from her left. She spun, shining her light into nothing. "Just a nightmare, that's all." The voice came from her right, disembodied but solid. Firm.

And oddly familiar, though she couldn't place it.

The room grew darker, blacker. Her torch struggled, the popping flames of the fire spitting with protest. She swallowed, blinking furiously, chest heaving.

Whatever was happening, she didn't have time for it.

She turned to run toward the door. And immediately froze again.

The door had multiplied.

In front of her, instead of stairs leading to one door, she faced seven staircases. Some were straight, some twisted around on themselves, spiraling upward. Others looked like they might crumble into nothing if she applied her weight. At the top of each staircase was a door.

"Shuren, you dragon-blasted illusionist!" Aranya shouted, her voice breaking. "Quit with your games!"

There was a chuckle behind her. She clenched her jaw, refusing to turn, knowing no one was there. But that voice kept chuckling, louder and louder as she growled at the staircases before her.

"Give me back reality," she said. "Give it *back*!"

"This isn't an illusion," said the voice behind her, full of mirth. "Can an illusionist enter your mind? See your fears? Manifest them before you? Oh no, powerful as they are, their illusions can only come from their mind."

The familiarity of that voice struck her then. She couldn't help herself as she whirled, flinging up the torch toward that voice.

To her shock, a person sat cross-legged on a little red embroidered mat, holding a covered box in his hands.

"Lim?" Aranya said, not able to disguise her bewilderment. "My . . . landlord?"

Lim smiled, still wearing his apron, his long, skinny features stretching wide. His fingers danced on the cloth covering the box sitting in his lap.

"What are you . . . Why are you here?" she said. She shook her head, wincing. There was no time for—for whatever this was! She had to find Yong. She had to . . .

But those seven sets of stairs winked at her when she looked over her shoulder. Her lungs tightened with the creeping return of the despair, hopelessness, and *helplessness* that had imprisoned her that horrible night.

"Yes, this magic is quite nasty, isn't it?" said Lim. "Dark stuff. You don't see it much these days, since it's illegal."

"Black magic?"

"You *have* heard of it, then!"

"All illegal magic is called black magic," Aranya said, bite lacing her tone. "What are you doing here? How do I get out of this? I *need*"—her voice broke—"*need* to get out of here."

"Hey, Sun girl!" a new voice called from the opposite side of the chamber. That same familiarity, then fumbling confusion, followed in its wake.

"Na?" Aranya turned again, holding up the torch. Now she was shaking, and not at all from adrenaline.

There Na was, exactly how Aranya remembered her that first day at Zushui Wardpost. She had a slight limp when she walked toward them, her weapons strapped on over her practical robes. Her face was grim, a face unaccustomed to smiling, though not necessarily an unkind face.

"I'm sorry, girl," said Na, shifting her weight to her good leg and crossing her arms. "I did my best, but I couldn't stop it."

"Couldn't stop what?" Aranya nearly shrieked, her talons catching in her hair. "What. Are. You. Doing. Here?"

Na pointed at Lim. No—*not at him.* At the covered box he held. Lim shrugged, his face utterly nonchalant despite the fact that he sat in the middle of a black magic-filled dungeon.

"It's your own fault," came a new voice. Those smacking, fat lips shaped the syllables with hard punctuation. *Qigang.* The supervisor of Zushui Wardpost. "You're impulsive. You don't think through the consequences of your actions. You're negligent. How could Na have stopped it? Capable as she is, you left her with your problem for weeks! *Months.* And you think something wouldn't happen?"

"Problem?" Aranya breathed, her heart suddenly freezing in her chest. Denial burst across her senses, panic flaring fast behind it.

Then, all pairs of eyes in the room fell to the box in Lim's hands.

Every molecule of air sucked out of the room.

She couldn't breathe. Couldn't move.

No, no, no, no, no.

Lim swept the covering off the box.

It wasn't a box. It was a cage.

And inside, lying motionless—not breathing, not twitching his whiskers, not flicking his tail—was . . . was . . .

A fluffy white cat.

Aranya flew across the room, tossing away the torch. Her talons caught the meager light as the torch rolled on the floor, the flame fighting harder than ever to keep its spark of life. She was shrieking—roaring—like a wild animal. She didn't hesitate, didn't blink as she plunged her talons into the smug face of her landlord.

He vanished. Him, his now bloody visage, and his mat.

The others vanished around her too, but her entire world was focused on the cage she held. "Ye Ye?" she choked, fingers trembling as she fumbled with the latch. "Ye Ye?"

It was locked.

She couldn't open it.

With an animalistic roar, she sliced her talons along the iron frame. The impact sent pain screaming up her arm, and the cage remained intact.

"Ye Ye? Ye Ye! Please, please, I don't understand, Ye Ye! Tell me what happened. Tell me you're alright—Ye Ye!"

She shifted out of her talons, sliding one finger through the narrow openings in the cage. That first brush of fur on the pad of her fingertip released the dam holding back her tears.

"Ye Ye!"

She cradled the cage in her lap, far more tenderly than Lim had done, and willed herself not to panic, to think rationally about things. He might just be asleep. This couldn't be real—there was dark magic here, filling this room.

But while the others had vanished, Ye Ye remained here.

Gently, though not as gently as she intended, she shook the cage. Her heart nearly stopped in her chest.

The fluffy white cat was stiff.

The back of her throat burned. It burned with the heat of a forest fire, an insatiable and unstoppable blaze. It wasn't real. This wasn't real. This wasn't her life.

The torch sputtered and snuffed out.

The world went dark.

Aranya clutched the cage to her chest, sobbing. It wasn't real. It wasn't real. But the fluffiness between her fingers was real. The cold of the wretched, despicable cage was real.

"A cage," she choked, spitting out the words into the darkness swallowing her. "He's a human! Not a *problem*. Not an *inconvenience*. He's *mine*. Ye Ye, *wake up*! Oh please, let this not be real. This can't be real."

Her sobs filled the emptiness until it wasn't empty anymore. Another miserable voice sounded: "I'll get him. Don't worry. Getting the grandfather is key to getting the girl, and once we've got the girl, we can get Kai."

That was Yong's voice.

Coming closer.

Frantically, Aranya leapt to her feet, hugging the cage with Ye Ye close to her chest, and she broke into a run. Away from that voice.

No one—*no one*—would take Ye Ye from her.

Never again.

Snarling like a wildcat, her hands shifted back into talons as she ran. Her boots echoed on stone, loud enough to announce her presence to anyone in the vicinity. But she just had to *get away*. Or she would fight. Let them fight her! She would kill them all.

She braced one arm out in front of her to catch herself before she smashed into a wall. But a bracing arm couldn't warn her when the floor fell away into stairs.

Aranya fell too fast to scream. Too hard to catch herself on the stairs and minimize the

impact. Too wildly to keep her grip on the cage in her hands.

She hit the ground. Her body screamed in pain. Panic sent her rolling, shoving up to her knees that felt like they had knives stabbed into them.

"Ye Ye?" she cried, voice breaking. "Ye Ye!"

She fell back to her knees, crawling on the ground and searching for the cage. It couldn't have fallen much farther than she did! Where was it? Where *was* it?

She was sobbing again. Losing control of herself in the pitch blackness. But she couldn't find him. Her hands kept closing around empty air, kept bumping into frigid and sharp-edged stone.

Then, she stopped.

She sat back on her heels, rocking. "You're no use to anyone if you can't control yourself," she whispered to herself. "Not even to Ye Ye. Get ahold of yourself, girl! No panicking. Stop panicking!" She smacked the sides of her head hard, trying to bang rationale back into her brain. Trying not to lose herself to the utter terror enveloping her.

"I'm going to find Ye Ye," she said, half choking and half gasping. "And then I will get out of the dark. I will find my way out of the labyrinth. I will not be careless. I will not worry about Ye Ye being . . ."

She couldn't say the word. It threw her into a mess of shredding anxiety. No, she couldn't think like that. She wouldn't worry about how long it might take to find the cage in the dark or if she would ever make it out of here alive.

With a huff that was more like a sob, she got to her feet. This room she was in was probably like the others, which meant it was small and bound by walls. She should find a wall and follow it around the perimeter of the room to maintain some semblance of direction while blind.

A strange sound pricked her ears. Her senses shot to high alert.

She wasn't alone.

She froze, telling her fear-crazed mind not to tear off like a maniac again. If she did, she would lose Ye Ye forever. No, this time, she would be still and quiet. Silent as a ghost.

The sound grew louder, and at first it sounded like the panting of a warrior who'd just won a difficult battle. She braced herself, reaching for her weapons. A weird smacking sound punctuated the panting.

It sounded eerily like a kiss.

Aranya tensed, quieting her own frantic breathing so nothing would betray her presence. As though whoever was down here wouldn't have heard when she and her entire suit of armor fell down the stairs.

More panting, then another smacking sound. Then, a sigh, and finally—a voice. A voice so familiar it sent a punch straight to her gut.

"You're beautiful," said Kai's unmistakable deep voice. "So, so beautiful."

He wasn't talking to Aranya.

CHAPTER 30

ARANYA'S MIND STUTTERED to a complete halt.

"Beautiful?" said a woman's voice.

Jie. One of Kai's girls from the Academy.

"So beautiful," Kai repeated. More kissing sounds followed the words, then a giggle.

"You came back for me," said Jie. "Shi Kai, who never goes back to the same girl. What did you tell me once? *'I never play the same game twice,'* weren't those your very words?"

Darkness chuckled in response. "Prove interesting enough, and perhaps I'll make an exception to my rule."

"You arrogant, preening phoenix." The way Jie said it, it sounded more like a compliment. "I'll assume then, that this is your apology for kissing that Sun girl?"

Kai's devilish smirk was audible. "I apologize for nothing, love."

Standing alone in the dark, bereft of her beloved grandfather, those careless words should have cut like a knife through Aranya's heart, carved it out, and served it up on a platter.

But they didn't.

Her heart still beat in her chest, albeit a ragged rhythm. Her mind twisted and turned over the things Lim had said, the things that the seer, Cai Fu, had said.

It was the magic. It fed on her insecurities, her fears.

This wasn't an illusion. It was a manifestation of her worst fears. That she would lose her grandfather—that it would be her fault, that it would be because she left him. That Kai would grow tired of her, that his kisses and flirtations had no depth or meaning, that he would betray her the moment she admitted herself in love with him.

That she would be alone. Alone, in the dark, with no escape, and no hope.

Lim, Na, Jie, Ye Ye, even Kai—they weren't real. They were only illusions.

But if her fears manifested around her, then she could face them head on. She could look them in the eyes, hold them by the scruff, and tell them to eat dragon scat.

Aranya got to her feet, her armor clanking loudly. "Come on, Kai, you should know that no girl wants to be kissed in a dungeon. You should also know that no girl wants to hear about other girls while you're kissing her."

Around her, the air shifted. Her limbs suddenly lightened, like she'd been dragging a ball and chain behind her this whole time, and she'd just used the key to unlock it.

But spouting off at an imaginary Kai was one thing. Walking out of here without her caged grandfather was another.

Was she *sure* this was not real? That Na, Lim, Qigang hadn't done something to him? That Yong hadn't? That he was still safe at home, curled up with his tail wrapped around his pink nose by the hearth?

Was the entire nightmare false? Or was that one piece of it true? Could she risk believing it to be false? Could she risk leaving here without her grandfather? Would she go home to Zushui only to find the nightmare at Fang's fortress was reality?

This magic surrounding her, permeating the stone and the iron and earth, was pure evil. Of that, she was absolutely certain. Her heart pounded, her hands slick as a mossy river stone. Eyes open or closed, it made no difference. She was utterly blind.

"Ye Ye," she whispered. Her voice broke, but she summoned it again, this time stronger than before. "Forgive me if I'm wrong. Oh!" A sob caught in her throat. The pain in her heart was so sharp she could have believed she plunged her own talons into her chest.

But then Aranya marched, resolve firming in her heart. She faced the pitch blackness, the swirling evil in the air. She had a mission to accomplish. No matter the lies that surrounded her, she wouldn't believe them. She would rescue the wielders who had found themselves imprisoned in this hellish place. It didn't matter how her limbs trembled, or how weak she felt, or how hard it was to fight the groping fear.

She would see this through to the end.

When Kai met back up with Renshu, he was half carrying an emaciated prisoner with two more behind him. Renshu had found two prisoners, one of whom was in better shape like himself, but the other looked like a walking corpse.

"That should be everyone," Renshu said.

Kai nodded, swiftly turning on his heel and herding his group of prisoners up the stairs. He didn't *want* to talk to the man who'd just been kissing Aranya—it didn't matter that it was only to break a curse. He was determined to be wounded and petty, which he thought was reasonable considering the phoenix-scorched mess of a situation they were in.

As much as he didn't want to talk to Renshu and would prefer leaving the man in the dark, he muttered begrudgingly, "You and Aranya can watch the prisoners while I evanesce down to the tunnel to get a read on the situation."

He was actually telling someone his plans. Delan would be so proud. Kai scowled. Informing someone of his plans meant he was bound to stick to them.

Kai ended up following Renshu's nose back to where Aranya guarded the prisoners. He swallowed his fear, telling himself Renshu's keen senses would likely have picked up any significant disturbances like a battle. There was nothing to worry about. Aranya could hold her own.

Renshu, apparently trying to lighten the mood, said, "I assume you are well acquainted with Aranya?"

Annoyance prickled down Kai's spine. The prisoner clinging to his shoulder chose that time to pitch forward, and Kai had to react swiftly to catch him before he smashed his brains out on the unforgiving ground.

"Yes, we are well acquainted," said Kai.

"She's sniper level with that *jiaun*." The appreciation was obvious in his voice.

And despite his determination to be jealous, Kai smirked. "She's just as good with a sling."

"Really? Nobody's good with a sling these days. They practice shooting with their *jiauns* instead."

"I saw her hit this brigand once with a shot from her sling at some seventy or so paces. Straight to the belly."

Renshu let out a laugh. "Wish I could have seen it."

"Sure you do," Kai muttered under his breath, back to being sour again.

"Here we are!" said Renshu, reaching a door and moving to open it. Almost as quickly, he froze.

"What?" Kai demanded, shoving his clingy prisoner to one of the stronger ones.

"I can't smell her. She's not here."

He was already opening the door, but Kai evanesced into the room.

The woman prisoner was sprawled on the ground, unconscious, but the man was awake. He swayed on his backside, hands over his ears as he muttered something unintelligible under his breath. He seemed utterly oblivious to the fact that his rag-like pants had split.

"Where is she?" demanded Kai, evanescing to the man's side and pulling one of his hands away from his ear. "Where did the shifter go?"

"It's the magic. It's the magic!" he cried, bowing his head toward his knees as if to hide.

"Don't hurt him, Kai," said Renshu.

"I'm not hurting him," snarled Kai, but he let go of the man's wrist. "What magic? Where is she?"

"He must mean Fang's magic."

Kai whirled, his stomach plunging to the floor. "Fang's magic?" His voice came out in a croak, memories of shadowy black manacles chaining his hands above his head flooding his mind.

Renshu's face had gone pale, grim.

"Is she prisoner, then?" Kai demanded. "Did Fang find her? How do we—"

"I don't know," Renshu said, cutting him off with a growl as he readjusted the prisoners on his shoulders. "But with your magic, you could find her faster than anyone. I'll take the prisoners to the tunnel."

"By yourself?" Kai might dislike Renshu, but not *that* much. "With *all* of them?"

"I can fight too," said the strongest prisoner, one eyebrow lowered in a glower.

"See?" said Renshu with a crooked grin. "We've got this. Go find Aranya and then come join us."

After grinding his teeth and warring with his sense of responsibility, Kai nodded and told them where the tunnel was. He didn't wait to watch Renshu toss the incapacitated prisoners over his shoulders as his mottled crew begin their escape. He was already evanescing away with his torch, calling Aranya's name into each chamber he entered, and trying not to let his imagination spiral out of his control.

Don't lose your head. Don't lose your head.

For all he knew, Fang hadn't caught her. She could have just been making her escape like he'd told her to. She was probably fine. But the longer he searched, the more frantic he grew, and the more clearly he saw her—the haunted turn of her eyes, the misery filling her soul when she'd come out of that night-darkened forest alone and ran into his arms.

She was alone. Probably terrified out of her wits. And all these festering dragon-blasted chambers were empty!

"Spitfire," said Kai, cursing vehemently. "*Spitfire.* Aranya!"

Movement caught his eye; made him turn.

The form that emerged from the darkness into the flickering ring of his torchlight wasn't the short, strong frame he desperately hoped it was. Instead, it was one even more familiar—a tall, masculine form. One that mirrored his own.

"Yong," Kai spat. Question after question hurled through his mind, but he refused to give voice to them. Showing ignorance was showing weakness. And he never let his brother see his weakness.

"Kai," said his older brother, the faintest curve of a sardonic smile playing at the corner of his lips. "What a game this has become. You always loved games."

Game.

It was only then that Kai noticed the changes in Yong's stance, the way he kept his hands by his side, the way the darkness seemed thicker there, so thick it almost obscured the edges of his flesh to Kai's view.

Forget hiding his weaknesses. Kai evanesced to his brother, grabbed the front of his robes with one fist, and yanked him closer. He channeled every ounce of the dripping venom that ran in their Shi blood. "You did something to her, didn't you?"

"Zushui, was it? A warden, *really*, Kai? But you *were* the one always gifted in disappearing under peoples' noses, weren't you?" Yong grinned, an absolutely garish grin, his eyes glittering. Smoothly, he lifted his hand and flicked Kai's nose. "My evasive little brother. But I have you now, don't I?"

The knife was flashing between them, pressing into the soft flesh of Yong's throat. "What did you do to her, *brother*?"

Another evanescer would have vanished away from the blade. But not Yong. No, he only grinned wider and cocked his head to one side.

"She's trapped right now. In a magical nightmare of Fang's concocting. If you come back with me to Gebei, if you take your rightful place as Lord of the Hidden Ones, I'll let her go. I won't harm her. I'll even be certain to get her out of this fortress. Alive."

"Of course you would. You can't kill the only leverage you have on me."

Yong's mouth twisted, the realest part of his mock smile. "I know you too well, brother. You cannot pretend she means nothing to you. She's different. Different from all the rest. And you would do *anything* for her."

Kai sheathed the knife, despite how empty his hands felt when he did. He had to play this carefully if he was to get Aranya out of this. Counting on his twitching fingers, he began dryly, "Things I would not do for Aranya. One, commit treason. Two, murder. Though there might be one or two exceptions to that. Three, kiss your backside—"

Yong snarled. His hand flung out in a wide arc, a fast one, and Kai barely evanesced out of the way. "Quit with the games!"

"Everything's a game," Kai snarled in response. "And I know exactly the one you're playing. You'll spare her life, but you'll keep her under your thumb. You'd have me accept my inheritance and then Aranya would be the string by which you, the puppeteer, would work me, the puppet. I might be named Lord of the Hidden Ones, but you would be the true master. So yes, I *would* like her free and away from here, but it will be on my terms, not yours. Never yours."

With that, both brothers vanished, reappeared—and the battle was begun.

CHAPTER 31

KAI UNSHEATHED HIS broadsword the same moment Yong did. They circled the dark room, eyes never blinking away from the other.

"I've told you before," Kai growled, "I will be no one's puppet. You cannot make me, and neither could our wretched father."

"How dare you speak of him so?"

"Oh, and neither can our heartless mother."

"She had a heart, if you would have stopped running long enough to see it. But now—"

"Had?" Kai's voice faltered.

The expression that passed over Yong's face was a terrifying thing. It was made of raging forest fires, the blood of broken hearts, and the flint of an iron-wrought soul. "You haven't heard?"

"Heard *what*?"

Two words: "She's dead."

Dead? No, no, that couldn't be. She'd been strong when he'd last seen her. She'd been everything his horrible mother had always been. "I don't know what you mean," Kai said stupidly.

"She's been dead for weeks, you qilin-spawn. If you hadn't run, you would've known. You should have been there with her. She's gone because of you. You made her sick."

Kai's steps faltered. He was so sick he might vomit. It took everything to focus on Yong a mere few paces away, their swords between them. He wanted to throw down his weapon and walk away, to find a darkened corner to swallow him up.

Aranya.

This was about her, about finding her. This wasn't about his past or his mother or his broken family. This was about fighting with every ounce of strength in him for the one good and beautiful thing in his life.

Yong's teeth flashed. "I am *done* losing everything I care about to you."

That was when Yong finally vanished. Kai slammed himself back against the wall, his instincts flaring as he searched for that telltale glimmer. Yong's most hated magical tick. They both had them. But, in typical Yong fashion, he waited to strike. Waited, not reappearing, wanting Kai to let down his guard and turn his face away. As if Kai would abandon the wall and leave his back exposed.

There!

Kai evanesced, swinging his sword at the same moment that faint muddling of the air gave away Yong's reappearance. But Yong ducked, vanishing again. This time, he didn't wait to reappear, and Kai didn't have time to get his back against a wall.

Sword clashed against sword, parry, and block.

"I suppose this was bound to happen," Yong growled.

They both disappeared at the same time, reappearing on opposite sides of the room. In one swift movement, Yong withdrew a knife and flung it. Kai only barely evanesced behind him, slicing with his sword. But Yong didn't waste time spinning on his heel—he evanesced to Kai's side and thrust his sword straight toward Kai's chest.

"This is not my fault," replied Kai, dodging the blow. "You hate me for reasons outside of my control, and I hate you for reasons entirely inside your control."

"Are you this arrogant with *her*?" Yong snarled.

He vanished, this time not reappearing. He loved that trick, the suspense it accommodated. He wanted Kai shivering in his boots, wondering where he would reappear next. But Kai didn't have time for stupidity.

"Ladies love confidence," Kai said, forcing a wicked grin onto his face as sweat slid down his temples.

Still, Yong did not reappear. Kai could almost feel the palpable displeasure in the air.

"You should try it sometime," Kai drawled. "Maybe a girl will finally notice you."

Yong smashed into Kai's chest, slamming him into the wall. Kai evanesced away, but not before he let out a loud, "oof!" His sword darted out, taking advantage of Yong's fury. But Yong wasn't as distracted as he appeared, and with a quick clip of his sword, Kai's blow was deflected.

"I hate you," said Yong, evanescing to stand with his back against the opposite wall.

"The sentiment is mutual," drawled Kai.

"If Father had just—!"

"Indeed. Then you'd be able to fully express the monster you are."

In startling succession, Yong reappeared to Kai's left, then right, then left again, letting loose wild, lightning-sharp blows. Kai could only barely deflect the first and second blows. On the third, he couldn't change momentum that quickly. He evanesced, but Yong evanesced with him, hammering him relentlessly. Evanesce. Strike. Evanesce. Strike. Strike. Dodge. Evanesce.

As much as Kai hated to admit it, he couldn't get the advantage. Neither of them could, and all he could do was provoke Yong into a further rage. But instead of making Yong clumsier, it made him sharper, more bloodthirsty.

The hatred shining in Yong's eyes ran even deeper than Kai's, and it had burned for longer. Since the moment Kai had been born, they'd been sworn enemies.

"I'll leave her in the nightmare," snarled Yong. "It'll kill her. The magic will consume her mind and soul, and if there's anything left of her body, it'll disintegrate like burned parchment."

"You'll free her," Kai growled back. "You need her."

But Yong's eyes glowed, glittering blacker and blacker, and suddenly Kai wasn't so sure. He remembered those cursed bonds, the wretched compulsion that nearly forced him to kill Aranya.

"I'm sure Fang could whip something up for me," Yong said coldly between blows. "Something that might make you more *receptive* to my bidding."

Those spellbound phoenixes burned in his mind. The feeling of the dagger in his fist as the tip pierced Aranya's flesh. No, if Yong had any leverage with Fang—which he probably had, considering the forces he provided him with—then . . .

"I'm not letting her out," said Yong. "Hope you kissed her goodbye."

They were nearly chest to chest, the blades of their swords the only things between them. Kai refused to look away from his brother's eyes, refused to back down from the whorls of intensity, emotion, and hatred. He faced it, pushing back with all his might.

Then a sharp twang.

Yong's eyes went wide with sudden shock. Shock and pain.

Kai evanesced away, expecting a trick, but when he reappeared a few feet away, he was stunned by the sight he saw.

An arrow pierced Yong's gut, blood darkening his robes and slipping through his armor. One arrow, not two.

And there was Aranya, standing in the doorway of the third opening at the far side of the chamber, staring furiously down the sights of her *jiaun*.

Had he died? Was he imagining things? Yong said she was trapped! Yet here she was, her hair a wild shock of black, her face smudged and ever bruised. And her eyes . . .

She was different.

She was not the whimpering girl who'd fallen into his arms for comfort. No, this was a dragon-slayer standing before him. A proven warrior. And a phoenix-blasted good shot of a warrior, too.

Aranya's eyes flew wide, her hands already flying to reload. "Kai!" she screamed.

Kai evanesced, Yong's knife hitting the wall where he'd been a moment ago. His brother gasped, grimacing and bowing over against the stairs, hand clutching his stomach.

"I hate you both," he snarled.

He vanished. The air changed in a flash. It was no longer the expectant hovering when Yong waited to reappear, no longer pregnant with the disembodied soul of another. It was clear. Brighter, cleaner. If a dungeon could ever be called *clean*.

Across the room, Aranya's eyes met his. They swam with far too much emotion to name, and there, hiding behind her strength, was a wisp of the fear that had haunted her these last few weeks. But she blinked, and that wisp was gone.

"He could reappear at any minute," she said, breaking into a run toward the stairs. "I don't know how badly he's injured. I didn't want to kill him if you didn't want me to, but I was afraid he'd hurt you, so I shot—"

Kai sheathed his sword and evanesced in a flash. He reappeared in front of her, cutting off her escape. Before she could do or say anything else, he knocked aside her *jiaun,* grabbed her armored shoulders, pushed her against the wall, and kissed her.

For the first heartbeat, she seemed too surprised to react. Then she softened, even as the metal of their armor clanged together. But almost as quickly, she growled and shoved her fist against his chest.

Seven valleys, when would she ever just *kiss* him?

"Stop being such a . . ." She trailed off, gesturing vaguely at him. "We have to get out of this fortress, idiot! Besides, girls don't like being kissed in a dungeon. You should know that. And I'm mad at you!" Her voice trembled slightly, just enough to reassure him that she wasn't wholly unappreciative of the kiss.

Kai stared at her, brow wrinkled. "Why are you mad at me? For trying to—"

She grabbed his arm, dragging him behind her up the stairs. "For kissing Jie and telling her that she was beautiful—"

"I have *never* told Jie that she was beautiful."

"For kissing her!"

"Seven valleys! What are you talking about? I've never even kissed her!"

She glared back at him, a look that told him she was unconvinced. But how else was he to respond to these nonsensical charges she was flinging in his face? She spun on her heel to march up the stairs.

"Aranya," he growled, catching up to her short, swift strides. "We might be stuck here and then we might die, and I'm not sure why you're mad at me, but can't we talk it thr—"

"*You* can leave whenever you want."

He evanesced in front of her, snatching her face between his hands and tilting it up to look at him. "I'm not leaving you," he said. His voice caught, quavered, and he hated himself for how suddenly the sharp emotion welled up. He swallowed, gritting out fiercely, "I'm *not* leaving you."

He had never meant anything so much in his entire life.

She stared up at him, eyes wide, dark, and rounded on the edges. She seemed to be searching, almost wrestling with herself. What did she fight? Why did she struggle?

Her eyes closed, her eyebrows shuddering, and then little tears ran onto his thumbs.

"I'm not leaving you," he said again, huskier this time. "Aranya, I . . ."

"Yes?" she said. The tone of her voice, the slight faltering, told him she was perhaps afraid of what he was about to say. But there was a desperation lacing those soft timbres. Like she had to know.

"I can't do this with your helmet on," he growled.

She blinked, not moving. So he wrenched his own off, his messy hair flying everywhere, then grabbed hers and removed it much gentler. Her throat bobbed, eyes widening, her mouth parting more with each passing second.

Once those stupid helmets clanked around on the floor, he swallowed every fear rising up in his chest, trying to wrangle control of his words. He would not be undone. They might not come out of this, and he wasn't leaving things unsaid between them.

Crossing the distance between them, he gently—very tentatively—pulled her into his arms. For possibly the first time ever, she didn't resist. Her cheek was wet against his fingers. He used his sleeve to dab the wetness away, then tilted her chin up to him. Her pulse pounded against his touch.

Was this possible? That she . . .? Did she want this as much as he did?

He wanted to tell her through a kiss, but that wouldn't be enough. Not for her. Not when she was rightfully skeptical of him. But *surely* by now she knew. Surely she couldn't deny it further. He'd made it as obvious as the sun at noon.

He rested his forehead against hers, caught her shuddering gasp in response. His hand shook, but he refused to back down. Refused to let this moment go, even if the world was burning around them.

"Sun Aranya," he whispered. His voice broke. "Don't you know I love you with the very beat of my soul?"

CHAPTER 32

ARANYA NEVER THOUGHT those words would ever come out of Kai's mouth.

I love you.

Not that long ago, she'd been trapped in a nightmare where Kai was kissing Jie. But now he held her so tenderly, as though afraid she would spook at the slightest noise, and he said *that*.

"I . . . I don't know what this means," she said. Her breath shuddered out of her mouth, and her whole body trembled. A part of her wanted to spout off about how she *didn't* want to be told that in a rotting dungeon. But . . .

Kai was searching her eyes, his darting back and forth between them, as though trying to catch every thought passing through her mind. "It means I'm not leaving you now, or ever, if we make it out of here. I mean, unless you really want me to, in which case . . . *Aranya*! Will you not say anything else?"

"I love you too," she blurted, without thinking.

The ground rumbled around them, the dungeon shaking beneath their feet. Pebbles and bits of plaster fell to the ground, but Kai was grinning like an idiot.

"We've got to get out of here!" Aranya gasped, trying to twist out of his arms. "Before we die!"

"One kiss?" he asked, grinning sheepishly and looking about ten years younger.

"We're about to die!"

"All the more reason!"

With that, he captured her lips with his. That kiss swept through her, coupled with his declaration, and the weight of it nearly made her break down into tears. She flung one arm around his neck, and for the span of a heartbeat, kissed him back with every fiber of her soul.

I love you, his kiss seemed to say.

Something warm and sweet and *safe* bloomed inside her. *I love you, Kai,* she told him with her own kiss.

Then she broke away, scooped up her helmet, and growled, "We've *got* to get out of here! Where are the prisoners? Where's Renshu?"

"They went to the tunnel," said Kai, retrieving his own helmet. "Hopefully they're through by now."

"I suppose we'll find out."

She was startled when something slid into her hand, and realized with a start that it was Kai's hand. He squeezed hers, smiling grimly down at her.

"Let's do this, Sun Aranya."

She pursed her lips and squeezed his hand in response.

By the time they reached the tunnel, Aranya understood why Kai had said things were bad. The main door to the dungeon was broken off its hinges, hanging limply to the side. Firelight—from torches, phoenixes, or a wild blaze, she didn't know—flooded the main entry to the dungeon. Bodies littered the floor, bodies clearly identified as Zheninghai wielders, brigands, and barbarian soldiers.

But it grew worse the closer they got to the tunnel.

When they reached the chamber, Kai immediately flung Aranya out of the doorway and evanesced. Arrows zoomed past them. They crouched by the doorway, her loading her *jiaun* and Kai unsheathing his sword as boots hammered on the other side of the door.

A barbarian guard poked his head around, aiming his bow straight for Aranya. She squeaked, flinging up hers, but before either of them could shoot, blood sprayed and his head went rolling.

Kai knocked the dead guard down, and then shouted, "Now!"

She leapt to her feet, straight for the doorway. Kai vanished. She raised her weapon, then flung herself into the sights of whoever was in the chamber and looked for a target.

Half a dozen barbarian guards stumbled over bodies of fallen Zheninghai wielders and their own, and Aranya didn't hesitate to shoot. Her arrows landed true. Kai reappeared behind another guard, dispatching him, then evanescing to the next. She ducked behind the doorway, reloading, then leaned around and fired again.

Footsteps behind her made her jerk around.

More guards came pouring down the stairs toward her. Her eyes flew wide, realizing she had no cover. At the same moment, the guards spotted her. They pulled out their bows, some drawing their swords or knives. She shot the one, pulling back his bowstring.

There was no time for thought, no time for loading two *jiaun* arrows. She smashed one into the left slot and fired. The arrow went wide, and she cursed as she reloaded. This time she hit her target, but it wasn't an instant kill. He cried out, stumbling to his knees. His comrades came for her even faster.

"Kai!" she screamed, scrambling with her blocky, trembling fingers. "Kai!"

He reappeared at the top of the stairs, eyes darting from her to the guards charging her. In a flash, he was cutting them down, giving her time to reload and fire again.

More came running down the stairs.

"They're caving in the tunnel!" was the cry of the new guards. "Out of the way!"

Caving in the tunnel?

Across dead bodies, Kai's eyes snapped to Aranya's. He was thinking the same thing she was. *Their only escape.*

Were they the only ones left? Who was caving in the tunnel? Was it their own wielders? Leaving them behind for dead? Or Fang's forces?

It didn't matter.

She stumbled to her feet, reloading as she rounded the edge of the doorway into the other room. But Kai finished the rest of them off, and she raced toward the tunnel. With a garbled cry, she glanced back toward the pursuing guards, jumped, and gripped the stone to hoist herself up into the tunnel.

Kai caught her around the waist and hauled her back.

"We have no time!" she shrieked, pulling away from him. "We have to—"

"It's too late!" he cried. "We can't make it all the way through!"

"Then you get out of here!"

"How many times do I have to tell you that I'm not leaving you?"

She looked up at him, not bothering to hide how distraught she was. "But Kai!"

Just then, the walls of the tunnel started shuddering, trembling. Rocks around them fell, hitting her helmet and her armor. From inside the tunnel, dust started pouring out, filling the chamber they were in.

"We've got to find another way out!" Kai grabbed her hand and yanked her back toward the stairs. Toward the oncoming guards. "Load your *jiaun*!"

"I'm so glad you're an evanescer!"

"What?" he cried over the growing din of the caving tunnel.

"Nothing!"

They faced their opposition head on, and if the guards had possessed magic, Aranya and Kai probably wouldn't have survived the fight up the stairs to the next chamber. But between her *jiaun* and his evanescing, they escaped with their lives, gasping as they raced up through the trembling bowels of the fortress.

They reached the top level of the dungeon, and Aranya wasn't sure if she was relieved or terrified. The night burned outside the open dungeon door, and for a second, she hesitated.

Kai reached out, clasping her hand in his. "Together," he said, his face spattered with blood. "We can make it out." Then, swiftly, he grabbed the back of her helmet, pressed her against his armored chest, and whispered again, "I love you."

It felt like a goodbye.

Kai kicked aside the door, and they faced the world of Fang's fortress. A wall of smoke hit Aranya, and she coughed, stepping backward.

"East wall," Kai was saying. "We've just got to make it over that fallen wall."

Fires burned everywhere, bodies littering the ground. Bodies that were both human and monster. Not far from her, the charred remains of a cursed phoenix lay with a huge bolt through its heart. Aranya shuddered away from it, but didn't have time for pity.

They'd been spotted.

An arrow whizzed and stuck in the ground by her foot. Kai's eyes snapped wide, straight to where the arrow had flown from: the parapets. The sniper pulled back his bow for another shot, but Kai vanished before she could pull out her *jiaun*. She ducked behind the unhinged door as another arrow came thwunking to the ground.

A cry shot into the air, then stopped.

Kai reappeared at her side. "That way!" he called.

They ran—straight into four armed brigands.

It all happened so fast; Aranya could hardly think. Instinct took over. She was shooting, reloading, but then they were in too close range, and one of the brigands smacked his hands together and pulled them apart to reveal a fireball.

That fireball came hurtling toward her. She threw herself to the ground, dodging and rolling up into a crouch. The ground beneath her began shifting, and it wasn't just the rumbling of the tunnel collapsing. One of the other brigands swept her hand in an arc, and the stones Aranya was standing on slid to the side. She stumbled, fell.

Kai attacked the fire brigand. She couldn't watch; she was too preoccupied with trying to get her feet back under her while the ground kept moving. Another brigand snarled, baring her teeth, and before Aranya realized what was happening, she had shifted into a viper.

"I hate snakes!" she screeched, rolling to avoid its bite. But the earth wielder kept shifting the ground beneath her, bringing her closer to the snake. Snarling, she whipped out one of her knives and, gripping the blade between her fingers, flung it straight at the snake.

She missed, but was *really* close.

The snake morphed, growing bigger, bigger, until a bear towered over her.

"I hate bears too!" she shrieked, lifting her *jiaun* in one hand and firing it at the earth wielder. Another miss—arghh! She didn't have time to reload, because huge claws came for her face.

She flipped over backward, onto her feet, but just as she straightened, a voice shouted, "Duck!"

Instinctively, she obeyed. The second after she did, she recognized the voice.

The bear roared.

When Aranya lifted her head, two arrows were lodged straight in the bear's head. It stumbled, then came crashing to the ground.

"Oh dragons!" she cursed, trying to throw herself out of the way. A hand grabbed her wrist and yanked her to safety just in time. "Delan!" Aranya cried, grinning despite her terror from pure relief. "You're here!"

"Watch it!" he said. In a flash, he reloaded and shot his *jiaun* over her shoulder.

Kai reappeared beside them. For a fraction of a second, they stood there, staring at each other, then the collapsed wall on the other side of the fortress, where other wielders were struggling to get out. Delan placed a hand on each of their shoulders.

"Let's do this," said Delan.

And then the three of them leapt into the fray again.

CHAPTER 33

DELAN IN BATTLE was a sight to be seen. Aranya could hardly track his movements. He was so swift, so calculated, so *proficient.* It was like he'd been born fighting. Even against brigands with stronger magic, it was like he knew exactly the best ways to defeat them.

And she *definitely* couldn't keep track of Kai. He was never in the same place for more than a second, but every second was deadly.

Meanwhile, she was furious that *jiauns* didn't load themselves. She was forced to duck behind rubble, or shout for Delan to watch her back, to reload. This time, as she grumbled about how useless her hands were when her adrenaline was exploding in her veins, she was startled when someone dodged around the same bit of rubble as her.

"I hate this," said the newcomer.

Aranya startled, shifting her hands into talons in an instant, but when her eyes met, the startled eyes of the girl next to her, her lips parted. "Lehua?" she said. "Aren't you that siren I arrested?"

The girl's eyes widened with the same recognition. "Hey, you arrested me!"

But she didn't make a move to stab her in the heart or work a siren spell on her, and neither did Aranya lift a finger against her. How was she here?

"You're . . . one of Fang's brigands?"

Lehua winced. "Well, it's complicated. Shh! There he is! Duck!"

"Who? Fang?"

"No! My captor! The person I'm trying to kill. Truce for now?"

"Truce."

"Good. Now shut up!"

Aranya clamped her mouth shut, then peeked out over the edge of the rubble. There, moving haltingly, but still fighting, was Shi Yong.

"I shot him!" Aranya said angrily. "He's supposed to be incapacitated."

Just then, Yong looked up, and his lips twisted back in a snarl. She followed his gaze to where Kai stood, staring back at him from the nearby parapets. Neither moved toward the other. They simply stared.

"This has to end tonight," she whispered.

Kai hadn't told her if he wanted her to kill his brother, if she had the chance. She loaded her *jiaun*, then hesitated. He clearly hated his brother, but did he want him dead? Would he rather spend his future estranged and running, or take his brother's life?

She didn't know. But somehow, she knew one of them was dying tonight.

She wasn't about to let it be Kai.

Carefully, she lifted the weapon and angled the sights on her target. One more arrow, and she should have him. She wouldn't have a clearer shot. Just a pull of the trigger, and the mess with his family could be over.

A cry rent the air. One nearby, and one achingly familiar. She and Lehua whipped around, just in time to see a brigand smash Delan into the ground and lift a downward-pointing spear above his chest.

"NO!" Aranya screamed, just as the spear plunged down.

She ripped her *jiaun* up and fired. Didn't take precise aim—she didn't have time! She let her frantic, flaring instinct guide her hand.

The arrows lodged true in the brigand, and Delan had time to roll out from under the falling spear. His face poured sweat, his mouth hanging open, but he gave a grim nod to Aranya and held up a hand. A silent thanks.

For that bare second, she'd forgotten how to breathe. Oxygen came whooshing back into her lungs, rushing like an overwhelming torrent. She gasped.

"Nice shot," said Lehua.

But when Aranya glanced back to Yong, fingers already busy reloading the weapon, he and Kai were fighting again. They vanished and reappeared, almost as if coordinated. Their fighting was like a dance, a dance to win, to kill. But neither could get the upper hand.

Her gaze was pulled as though by an unseen force. Up, up, *up*. She stopped trying to aim at Yong, but instead let her head tilt back until she saw a tall figure in black standing on the parapets.

He surveyed the destruction, the waging war, below, and she knew she'd seen that stance before. She'd seen it at the *mó guǐ* waterhole.

That—*that* was Fang Zedong.

Aranya's *jiaun* found a new target. Kai could hopefully handle his wounded brother. Carefully, she lined up the sights. He was so far away, but she was good with long shots.

She could do this.

Breathe. In. Out.

She tried to calm herself, relax the tension in her shoulders, and steady her arm.

One shot—that was all she had.

Fang lifted his hands wide. His voice echoed across the destruction between them. "To me! Retreat! Retreat!"

Aranya's finger froze on the trigger. *Retreat?* But wasn't Fang winning? Why were they retreating? She glanced around at the waging war, the Zheninghai wielders fighting with barbarians and brigands alike. Magic flared, weapons sang out, and suddenly, she wasn't so sure Zheninghai was losing.

The enemy forces responded to Fang's call, and they broke away from their fights, running toward the west wall where Fang was.

Determination seized her. *Now or never.* She had to get this shot right. If she took out their leader . . .

Fang turned away from the edge.

No! If he moved—

Was he about to leap over the edge of the wall?

She fired.

Fang disappeared over the wall, the arrow whizzing harmlessly over his head.

The moment Yong broke away from Kai was the moment Kai panicked. Things were going better, improving, and then Fang himself called the retreat. They were winning! But Yong kept fighting, as Kai expected.

They locked swords, dancing around each other. Kai hated that they were so evenly matched. They were wearing themselves out.

But this had to be settled *now.*

They could never go back to the false propriety. Now, it was murderous hostility between them, and if Kai didn't win, Aranya would pay for it.

So when Yong's gaze snagged on something over Kai's shoulder, his heart plummeted to his gut. Yong vanished away from Kai's grip, and his sword sliced through empty air.

Where did he go? It wasn't to keep fighting him. It was to—

He reappeared some twenty paces away, behind a huge chunk of stone wall that had fallen. His gaze fixed downward.

Kai knew without a doubt that was where Aranya must be.

Yong raised his hand, and the knife glinted across the space between them.

She's trained. She's an excellent fighter. She's—the rationale broke off into a frantic pounding of terror. Kai evanesced, but the knife was already descending. It was almost in slow-motion, the world made of syrup. He couldn't move fast enough!

Aranya!

He was just in time to watch Yong plunge the knife into Aranya's gut, right between the plates of her armor. Right where she had shot him.

Aranya stared in shock at Yong, utterly stunned. Had he surprised her? Or had she simply not believed him capable of such a swift blow to end her life? Yong wrenched the knife out of the wound, and blood flowed. Red and thick.

Her head fell backward, her eyes rolling.

Aranya. Aranya. Aranya. Aranya. Aranya. Aranya. Aranya! Aranya—NO.

Kai exploded.

But Yong was expecting him.

"Didn't think I'd actually kill her, did you?" Yong snarled, striking out with his sword fast as a viper even as he held his own wound. "This is your fault, for all your—"

There were no words. Kai stabbed, parried, thrusted the weapon at Yong. For the first time, it was with the full intent to kill. There had always been a part of him that he held back, just a fraction, in the hopes that it wouldn't end this way.

But now, there was no other option.

Except that Yong was crafty, and he vanished, reappeared, and smashed Kai's knees out from under him. Kai buckled beneath his own weight, trying to land so he could roll. But Yong evanesced to the air above him, falling and slamming him into the stone.

"Join her in the grave, little brother!"

Kai stared at the sword coming for his chest, and for a fleeting second, he didn't want to fight it. Not if Aranya . . . He couldn't even think.

"No, it's your turn," came a high-pitched voice from behind Yong.

Then Kai watched, eyes rounded in horror, as the very same siren they had arrested back in Zushui stabbed Yong through the back. He fell forward. Kai evanesced out of the way, just in time to watch his brother hit the ground.

Dead.

A shard of grief, so profound, stabbed into the depths of his soul.

His brother . . . His blood. His entire family now—*gone.*

But then he was in motion, evanescing to Aranya's side. Panic latched onto him fully, but he didn't care. If there was ever a time to panic, now was it.

Her eyes were closed, her mouth wrung in a grimace, her brow scrunched in pain. Her hands pressed against the bloody wound. Was she still alive?

"Aranya! Aranya!" he screamed. He slid to her side, hands trembling violently as he felt for a pulse.

A loud whoop came from nearby.

"We did it!" was Delan's hurrah. "We won! We dragon-blasted won! We—oh fathers."

Delan stopped, frozen for an instant. Then he ran to them, flinging off his helmet and throwing it to the side. "Is she still alive?" he gasped.

"I can't tell!" Kai choked. His hands were trembling so much he couldn't detect her pulse. "There's a healer—one of the missing wielders. If we can get her to the healer, she can save her!"

Delan pried one of her hands away from her side and pressed his thumb into the hollow of her wrist. "She's alive, but we must move quickly. Help me strip off her armor."

Kai began fumbling with the buckles, cursing his wretchedly useless fingers.

Delan glanced up, then, and spotted the siren girl standing over Yong's body. "Friend or foe, girl?" he barked.

"Neither," she said. "I'm *free*. At long last."

"Then get out of here," growled Delan.

Carefully, they removed the breastplate, then the mail, and finally her blood-soaked robes were accessible.

"We've got to staunch the flow as best we can and get her out of here. To a medic."

Kai was already ripping off his own armor, then his tunic. Delan lifted her torso, eliciting a groan from her, and that sound made Kai's heart soar with hope. But then Kai wrapped the cloth around her midsection, and the sheer amount of blood sent his heart plummeting again.

"Careful, there," said Delan as Kai knotted the cloth.

"I *am*," he growled back.

Once they had finished binding the wound as best they could, Kai scooped her up in his arms, and then they were making for the leveled east wall.

"We've got to hurry; the retreat might have been a farce to lower our guard," said Delan, climbing through the rubble.

Kai swallowed, his heart hammering. He glanced to the west wall, where the enemy forces were disappearing, and then around at the other Zheninghai wielders joining their flight for the east wall. At the moment, he didn't care one bit whether they'd won or not.

He held Aranya's limp body closer, trying to avoid jostling her too much as he ran and dodged around debris. Oh, why couldn't he evanesce other people? He could be back at the camp already, they could be saving her—

"Don't let your thoughts spiral," Delan said with a sideways glance at him. "Just keep moving. One step after the other."

Kai bared his teeth, but he redoubled his pace, refusing to glance down again into the pained twist of her features. He had to keep his eyes on where he was going.

By the time they reached the camp, his lungs were on fire, his legs wobbly as wet noodles, and his arms and back ached from carrying her. None of that mattered. Delan cleared the way to the medics, and after an eternity longer of waiting, Kai carried her, half-stumbling, into the tent.

Medics ran to his side, helping him to lay Aranya down on one of the pallets.

"Where's the healer?" Kai demanded. "There's a healer. One of the missing wielders. Where is she? We need her *now*!"

"Move aside! We need to tend her."

"Where is the healer? Where *is* she?"

"The healer is gone! Now leave the tent before—"

Gone? Had she not made it out of the fortress alive? If the healer was gone, then what hope was there for her? Delan hauled Kai to his feet, dragging him out of the tent, away from Aranya. "Don't you dare evanesce back there, boy."

"But she needs—"

"She needs you to give the medics space to work! Now sit down. You're about to collapse."

Kai didn't want to sit. He wanted to be at her side. He wanted to evanesce back into that tent. If he was about to lose her, he didn't want to be out here through it. But Delan grabbed his shoulders and shoved him down in front of a fire. "You've done all you can. Now we just have to wait. Wait and pray."

Kai looked up at him, stricken. Delan's jaw was tight as a *jiaun* string, his face haggard and exhausted, but his eyes flashed with determination.

Suddenly, Kai didn't care about the spats they'd shared, the glares and the irritation. He realized he was looking upon one of the best men he'd ever known, a loyal warrior of the empire, a man with a backbone of steel and a heart as soft as fresh snow. His magic wasn't anything special, but he was dependable, capable, and levelheaded, no matter the disaster that struck.

If not for Delan, they never would have made it through this.

Kai didn't think he'd ever looked at another man that he wanted to emulate, that he wanted to be like. He did now. He might have lost the rest of his family today, but he'd found a truer family.

And all he could do was grip Delan's forearm and choke, "Thank you."

CHAPTER 34

HE HADN'T THOUGHT it possible, but Kai fell asleep sitting up, waiting to hear Aranya's fate. Someone shook him awake, and Kai winced, only able to see a blob of orange fire and a blob of a silhouette he recognized as Delan.

"I have news about Aranya," said Delan.

Kai shot to his feet, a blanket he didn't know he had falling from his shoulders to the ground. "What? Can I go to her? Is she alive? Will she make it?"

"She's lost a lot of blood and there's been some internal complications that pose considerable risk . . . but she's stable."

The torrent of relief sent him back to the ground, reeling. He nearly wept, covering his face with his hands. "She's going to be fine," he whispered to himself.

"Kai, listen. Sit up. The mission was accomplished. All the missing wielders still alive were recovered, every last one. The prisoners from the last failed battle were released. Fang's fortress has been destroyed."

And my brother is dead, he thought. Then, *Renshu must have made it through the tunnel safely with his group.*

"We're going back to Suguan. But the medics are concerned about Aranya traveling in this state. She can't be left here, but going all the way to Suguan, traveling with such a slow party, they're afraid the journey will be too much."

Kai nodded, swallowing, trying to blink away his emotions and master himself. "What do they recommend?"

"They recommend you take her back to Zushui. It's a shorter journey than Suguan, and it would be much swifter than traveling with a group of recovered prisoners. But of course, there is always risk. The journey still may be too much for her, or the countryside may prove too dangerous—"

"I'll do it," said Kai immediately. "Whatever is best for her."

"They said that if she takes a turn for the worse along the way, you need to find the nearest city and get help for her."

"Yes, of course."

"It's simply too dangerous to be this close to Fang's forces. Otherwise the medics would say she shouldn't be moved."

"I understand."

Delan stopped then, drawing in a deep breath and releasing it. "Send updates to me in Suguan—I'll give you the address. I doubt I'll be able to sleep much until I know she's in the clear."

Them both. Kai swallowed and nodded. "When do we leave?"

"Day after tomorrow, if she doesn't get worse. Get some sleep until then."

Kai mounted his horse, the saddlebags full of provisions, medical supplies, and maps for the journey. Delan stood next to him, face tight and grim. They watched as Aranya was carried out of the medic tent in fresh clothes. She was either asleep or unconscious, and every trace of blood and grime had been washed off her.

She will be fine.

He just needed to get her home safely.

They moved carefully, two of the medics lifting her into the saddle in front of Kai. They grimaced, as though they hated this last resort. Kai pursed his lips, wrapping one arm cautiously around her ribcage. Her head lolled back against his shoulder.

He would get her back. She would recover.

With Aranya situated thus, he glanced one last time at the wielders packing up for their own journey. Not far away, Renshu was breaking down a tent, glancing up every few minutes at them. Some of the other rescued prisoners helped prepare for the journey to Suguan, while the rest were in the medic tent.

They'd done it.

Delan reached up and gripped Kai's forearm. "Take good care of her."

Kai only nodded.

"If she recovers . . ." Delan trailed off, shaking his head. His brows furrowed, and he fixed Kai with his fiercest glare. "You know you're never meeting a girl like her again, right? Don't blow your chance with her, idiot."

At that, Kai's mouth twisted. "No need to be worried about that; she's already head over heels for me."

Delan's eyes narrowed. "Get out of here."

With that, he smacked the horse's rump, and the horse lurched into motion. Kai twisted back, angling to get one last glance of him.

Delan stood, arms crossed and stocky legs planted sideways. He didn't wave, didn't shout goodbye. He only watched them go.

Kai turned back in his saddle and faced the road ahead. "Don't worry, Aranya, I'll get you home safely," he whispered into her hair.

The world was foggy, achy, and confusing.

She tried to pry her eyes open, but they remained steadfastly shut. She tried to open her mouth, but her lips were likewise sealed. Slowly, she licked them, and even her tongue was dry. When she moaned, her throat burned.

Then there was something behind her head, gently lifting her up. Something pressed against her lips, and warm liquid spilled into her papery mouth. She swallowed, then coughed, and the latter caused a spasm of pain in her midsection. She groaned again.

"Shh, careful now. Here, eat a little more."

Finally, despite the agony, she peeled her eyes open. Evening light filled the small, familiar space, casting a shadow on the person sitting on the edge of the bed where she lay. His eyes were downcast, focused on the soup bowl he held against her lips. A stray hair fell over his brow.

"Kai?" she croaked.

His eyes snapped up to hers, wide and shimmering with flecks of hazel. "Aranya!" A relieved grin burst across his face, and suddenly those hazel eyes turned glassy. "You're awake!"

"What . . .?"

"Do you want some water? Here, let me get you some water."

He wouldn't let her speak more until she downed several hearty gulps.

"Do you want to sit up more? Or does it hurt too much?"

"Hurt?" she repeated, blankly, then gingerly touched her aching side.

"Forget that, don't sit up. You should stay down. Are you comfortable? Too hot or cold?"

She smiled weakly, wanting to chuckle, but the slightest movement to her abdominals sent shards of pain up her spine. Instead, she managed, "What happened? Where am I?"

Kai seemed to hesitate, his eyes clouding over. "You were . . . stabbed by my brother, Yong. He's dead now, though, so he won't ever hurt you again." There was a tight grimness about his face, as if he were forcing himself to let go of dreamy ideals and face reality. The reality that his family would never be what he wanted them to be.

"I'm sorry," she whispered.

He shook his head. "Don't be. I'm just thankful I wasn't the one to kill him."

"What else happened?"

One of his eyebrows arched, and he looked away. "Well . . . we won. Those wielders who had been vanishing the last twelve years were recovered, plus the other prisoners. I split off from the group to bring you home. The rest of them went back to Suguan."

"Home?" Aranya gasped, lurching upward. Pain shot through her side, and she fell backward with a groan.

"Don't move! Here, you should take your medicine. Better now that you're awake than me trying to pour it down your throat."

Kai got up, walking on long legs to the other side of the room. His back turned to her as the sounds of water pouring and the clinking of a utensil against a cup filled the small space.

"We're in Zushui? You've been taking care of me? For how long? Where are we? Wait!" She gasped, a frantic thought hitting her like a ton of bricks. She forced herself up, a cry escaping her lips at the movement.

"Stay down!" Kai demanded, evanescing to her side and preventing her from swinging her legs over the side of the bed. She bent over her core, one arm wrapped around herself as she gritted her teeth. "You'll aggravate the wound. Here, take your medicine. It will help with the pain."

"Ye Ye!" Aranya gasped. "Is he alright? Is he alive?"

Kai blinked, then knocked aside her flailing hands and sat on the bed again. He caught the back of her head in his palm, bringing a cup to her lips. "Of course. He's in your tenement. I told Na she didn't have to take care of him anymore. Forgive any presumption, but I gave her some money for her trouble. Just as an extra thank you. I've been taking care of him since we got back. We're in my tenement right now. I didn't want to put you back in your tenement because I wasn't sure how sensitive your grandfather was, and I thought it might be distressing for him to see you . . . in your state. So I brought you here."

"He's alright?" she said again, her eyes filling with relieved tears.

"Of course. I don't think I've heard a cat purr so loudly. As soon as you're ready, I can bring him to you. Now stop fussing and take your medicine."

She obediently took her medicine, grimacing at the taste and its grittiness against her parched throat. He watched every sip and swallow as his fingers threaded through her hair. "Delan?" she croaked.

"I've informed him of your progress, that we made it back to Zushui, and I'm sure he will reply once he returns to Suguan. Speaking of which, a missive came for you . . ."

She waited as he got up again, the mattress shifting in the absence of his weight, and she clutched the cup of medicine he'd given her in both hands. He shuffled through a pile of paper on a low table on the other side of the room. The evening sun through the window caught the strands of his hair, making the dark edges turn gold, and illuminating the focused creases on his brow.

He was so handsome.

"Ah, here it is!" He presented it with a dramatic bow, lifting his eyebrow and twisting his mouth into a smirk. "From the Secret Services, themselves."

"What?"

"Read it!"

She did. Kai took the cup from her, freeing her fingers to clutch the white parchment. "Oh! Payment for completing the assignment is to be issued soon. I forgot all about that."

"Keep reading."

"Why? Did you read it?" she demanded.

"No, I got one too."

She eyed him suspiciously, but he only prodded her to keep reading.

"We are pleased to offer you . . ." she read aloud, blinking and staring at the page again. "Wait, they're offering me a position? With the Secret Services? In lieu of my wardenship here in Zushui?"

Her mouth fell open.

Kai was smiling. "It's quite the distinguished offer. Apparently on Delan's recommendation, no less."

"And you got one too?"

His smile turned cocky. "Of course."

"Are you . . ." She hesitated, biting her lip. "Shall you accept it?"

He sighed, then sat back down beside her on the bed. His legs spread wide, his forearms braced against his thighs as he stared at the opposite wall. She stared at his profile, trying to read it.

"I'd like to," he said finally. "For the first time, I'm truly free to do what I want. Yong's gone. My mother is gone. My inheritance is gone—commandeered by Fang Zedong as his personal force of brigands. I don't . . ." He stopped. Swallowed. Then he closed his eyes. "I don't have to hide anymore."

Aranya wished she could lean down and lay her hand on his arm, but she couldn't move that far.

"But I'm not . . . What I told you in the dungeon—I meant every word, Aranya." Color crept up his neck, his ears. "I'm not going to leave you. Well, of course, not unless you want me to. I'd leave then. I mean, I'm not going to force—" He seemed to realize he was babbling. He stopped, stared down at his hands.

"I think you should accept it," she said. "If it's what you want, then that's what I want for you."

"Does that mean . . . you're *not* going to accept yours?"

She shook her head, setting the parchment down on the bed beside her. "I cannot uproot Ye Ye again. Besides, I've always wanted to be a warden. The secret mission was . . . an adventure. One I'm alright forgoing for the time being. Maybe later, I'll reconsider. But right now, these last few years . . . I want to spend them with Ye Ye. I'm sorry if that complicates things for you."

He was silent. Then, he said, "Maybe I will just decline too. I'm sure someone nearby has need for an evanescer. I could find work—"

"No, no. You can't throw this opportunity away for me, Kai. You're an evanescer. This is a perfect fit for you and your magic. And I want you to be free to do what you want."

"But I want to be with *you*, even if—"

"Shi Kai."

He glanced up, and she saw the mingled frustration and vulnerability on his face. She reached out a hand, unable to extend far enough to him. He glanced from her proffered hand to her, then interlaced his fingers with hers and squeezed.

"It's just temporary," she said. "We can write and visit each other. And then, when the time's right . . ."

He twisted, planting his knee on the bed beside her as he leaned over her. She swallowed, staring up at him, and then closed her eyes as he bent down and kissed her.

"I love you," he whispered.

She had never meant words more when she replied, "I love you too, Kai."

He pulled back enough to arch an eyebrow at her. "And if we're going to be a thing, then I get to kiss you—as much—as—I—want."

Kisses punctuated the words, leaving her dazed. But she had the presence of mind to retort, "As much as *we* want, Shi Kai, not just you."

He flashed a devilish grin. "Semantics." Then he climbed onto the bed beside her.

Aranya grabbed the sheets, clutching them to her chest as a blush flooded her cheeks. "What are you doing? This is *highly* inappropriate!"

He wrapped his arms around her, pulling her tightly against his chest—ignoring the blankets she was wrapped up in—and nuzzled his face into her neck.

"Kai!" she gasped, trying to sit up.

"It's only for a minute. You almost died," he groaned. "I was so terrified that I'd lost you. Bringing you back was almost more terrifying—with those long days of travel, those long nights of watching you sleep and checking your pulse every hour. *Please.* I just want to hold you."

With that, he held her tighter, pressed a kiss to her throat, and closed his eyes, letting out a deep sigh. Aranya laid there, momentarily stunned. He'd been that worried about her? As worried for her as she'd been for Ye Ye?

Something settled into her soul, and it was as though she'd spent her life running aimlessly through a vast forest, but at long last, she'd found what she'd always been looking for.

Home.

Aranya was forever home.

She let her eyes drift shut as her body relaxed in Kai's arms. Peace was Kai's scent that filled her nostrils, his thumb as it traced the back of her neck and the curve of her ear. Home was the way he pressed his lips to her jaw and sighed, whispering, "I'm so happy. I've missed you, love."

She held onto him a little tighter. She wasn't ever letting him go.

It must have been shortly after that when she fell asleep because when she woke again, it was almost dark. Kai bent over her, another cup in his hand.

"Medicine time," he said.

She wrinkled her nose. "I just had medicine. It tastes gross."

"This is different medicine. You have a lot of medicines. I'd say this one will taste better, but it'll probably be worse. But once you've taken your medicine, I'll kiss you and make it better." He winked at her.

She flushed despite herself, but accepted the draught and drained it in one horrid gulp. "There," she gasped, setting into a painful fit of coughing. "Now where's my kiss?"

He grinned, and with the way he kissed her then, she'd have drunk a thousand cups of medicine. He pulled back, nuzzling her nose. "Would you like to see your grandfather now?"

CHAPTER 35

KAI RETURNED A few minutes later with a fluffy white bundle. Aranya sat up a little straighter, gritting her teeth to hide her grimace. Her heart pounded, nearly bursting with anticipation.

"Ye Ye!" she cried.

Kai smiled, then gently set the cat in her lap. Ye Ye began purring uproariously, sticking his wet little nose against her skin. He nuzzled into her chin, then her cheek, and she laughed as she scratched along his whiskers. He butted his head against her arm, her shoulder, curling his tail around her wrist and chirping.

"I'm not sure I've *ever* seen you so happy!" Aranya said, laughing. "I'm back now, and I'm not leaving again. Oh, I'm so happy to see you again!" She swept him up into her arms, ignoring the pain, and hugged him as tightly as she could.

Kai was on the opposite side of the room, quietly watching and smiling. She glanced from her grandfather to Kai, and she couldn't help the tears that began coursing down her cheek.

"Thank you," she mouthed to him.

He made a kissy face with his lips in response, making her want to roll her eyes and blush. But in the wake of the cockiness, he gave her a sweet smile that threatened to bring more tears.

After stretching and sticking his backside into the air, Ye Ye hopped down from the bed and shapeshifted into his human form. Kai evanesced to his side, caught him behind the back and gripped his hand.

"Here, you can sit here," he said, helping Ye Ye down where he'd sat only a minute before. "I'll be back after I get more firewood. Then I'm going to make you the best bowl of noodles you've ever had, and it will be just like old times."

With that, Kai's eyes flicked up to meet hers, and then, with the silent promise to return soon in his hazel irises, he slipped out of the room.

Aranya turned her attention to the hunched, grinning old man before her. His white hair and beard had grown long, but his eyes sparkled just as much as ever.

"That boy—oh, what was his name?"

"Kai."

"Oh, well, that boy Yuhan—"

"Kai."

"Yes, yes, girl, so Yuhan was telling me that you shot at a qilin alpha while you were gone!"

She laughed. "I shot at quite a lot of things while I was gone. I should tell you about the phoenix I took down!"

"Well now, that's mighty impressive. Hehe."

Aranya stared at him, realizing only now that she gripped his leathery hand. She lived for that smile lighting up his face.

"I'm glad you're back, little sunflower," he said.

"I'm glad to be back, too."

EPILOGUE

"HE SAID THAT? To *Qigang*?" Aranya gasped, hanging her *jiaun* on the wall of the wardpost armory. Months had slipped by in a constant stream of busyness since she'd recovered from her stab wound, though its scar would remain forever. She'd finally had time to organize the armory—with Qigang's permission—and it gave her great pleasure to see the weapons properly stored and cared for as they ought to be.

"He did indeed," Na replied, chuckling. "That poor new kid reminds me of you when you first showed up here."

Aranya winced. "I don't want to think about the decisions I made back then."

They made their way out of the armory as the sun dipped toward the horizon, casting the flagstone courtyard in shadow. One of the best things about these past few months had been working with Na and becoming good friends with her.

"When is Kai coming to visit?" asked Na. "Hasn't it been over two months since his last visit?"

"It won't be for another month. Secret Services has been keeping him occupied, and it's several days' journey from Suguan. But he writes to me multiple times a week."

"Does he? I wouldn't have labeled him the type to write love letters."

Aranya gave a dry snort. "You'd be surprised. Most of the things he writes are ridiculous nonsense and his recent obsession is extravagantly silly pet names. I'm not sure if he just hates my name so much that he must call me by anything else. But even if I'm certainly not any wiser after reading his letters, they always brighten my day."

That was an understatement. She *lived* for his letters, for his dramatic proclamations of love, until the day the grass turned blue and the sky turned green, for each new horrendous nickname. Most days, she rolled her eyes. Some days, she laughed. And other days, she cried. Every day, she missed him.

The letters and his promises to visit and his sweet kisses when he *did* finally visit were the only things that made the pain of this temporary separation bearable. She was due for a letter today and she could hardly wait.

"I'm glad to hear it," Na said with a smile. "Are we still having noodles at your place tomorrow, like usual?"

"Always!"

As Aranya went to open the door leading back into the wardpost, it swung open and nearly hit her in the face. She jumped back just in time, and was met with Chen's expression that reminded her of a frazzled squirrel. She grinned.

"Don't invite him," muttered Na under her breath.

"Chen! You're coming over for noodles tomorrow, right?" chirped Aranya. "And where is the new guy? He knows he's invited too, right?"

"Ju-long is talking to Qigang," said Chen, wincing.

"Ahh," said Aranya and Na together. They shared a meaningful look.

"You should probably go rescue him. If you can," said Na. "I'm heading out. See you tomorrow."

"One rescue, coming right up," muttered Aranya, waving to her fellow wardens and stepping into the wardpost. No matter how much things had improved since she'd come back from her mission, Qigang's office remained her least favorite part of all Zushui.

She reached the sliding door and couldn't help her grimace when Qigang's irate tone drifted through the wood. A sigh slipped through her lips. Nevertheless, she lifted her hand and gave a hearty knock.

Qigang's berating stopped. Then, a short, "Who is it?"

"It's Aranya, sir!" she called.

"Come in."

Aranya slid open the door, stepped inside as the wood beneath her boots gave a loud creak. Qigang chewed his sugar grass between his fat lips, twirling his empty dragon teacup on the surface of his low desk.

Before him stood a short, skinny young man, his shoulders shrunken as he took Qigang's rebuke. Aranya stepped to the new graduate's side and gave him a quick pat on the back. He glanced up at her, clearly relieved to see her.

"Just who I needed," said Qigang irritably, spitting out his grass and eyeing Aranya. "You can go, boy. Don't be late again tomorrow."

"Noodles. Tomorrow. My place," Aranya whispered to the new warden.

His countenance lifted, and he scurried out of Qigang's office, leaving Aranya standing before Qigang. She couldn't help but widen her stance as she faced her supervisor, clasping her hands behind her back as she waited with more trepidation than she wanted to admit. Why had he wanted to see her?

Once the door closed, Qigang waved his hand vaguely after the boy. "That Ju-long needs help. I tell you, these Academy graduates get worse each year. The fate of our empire rests on the shoulders of idiots. I don't think I'll be comfortable dying and leaving one of them in charge."

Aranya only nodded, not speaking a word.

"I'll need you to take him on some of your routes. I need to make sure he's with someone I trust, someone who knows what they're doing or else who knows what manner of disaster he'll get himself into. So, if you could just take him under your wing for the next few months until he's adjusted, that would spare me a few gray hairs."

She couldn't help the way her lips quirked. "It would be my pleasure. And you're coming to my place for noodles tomorrow night, right?"

"You need to stop inviting him," Na had said, *"or one day he'll actually come."*

Apparently, that day was not today. "If I've told you once, I've told you a thousand times, I hate noodles. Besides, I spend all day with the lot of you. Evenings are my reprieve, for the fathers' sakes."

"Of course. Forgive me. Anything else, Master Qigang?"

He grunted and waved his hand in dismissal, leaving Aranya to spin on her heel and march out of his office. The moment the door was closed, she breathed a sigh of relief. That had actually . . . gone well, if she dared say so! He wanted *her* to train the new warden.

She left the wardpost, letting the door swing shut behind her as her eyes adjusted to the glare of the sun. It was a little later than she'd hoped to get off, but thankfully Peng—a local boy with aspirations to apprentice himself to the apothecary—would be sitting with Ye Ye until she got home.

As nice as her full warden's salary was, the stipend she received from the Secret Services proved to be just what they needed as Ye Ye required more care with each passing month and couldn't be left alone. Without it, she would have had to quit her job to be with him all day, which didn't bode well for keeping food on the table.

She took a deep breath right as a cart rolled by, kicking up dust and giving her a lungful of grit. She coughed, then squinted against the sun to find the steps so she didn't tumble into the street.

That was when she noticed the tall figure lounging against one of the porch's posts, arms and ankles crossed like he had all the time in the world. Grinning teeth caught the sunlight.

"Miss me yet, love?"

Her heart gave a throbbing jolt. No—it couldn't be! He wasn't coming for another month! But she knew that voice, that stance. She would recognize him anywhere. Tears welled up. "Kai!"

She broke into a run—only for him to vanish. The next instant, warmth flooded her back as a pair of strong arms encircled her waist from behind, and Kai's face nuzzled into her hair.

"You need a bath," he whispered into her ear.

As fast as they'd come, her tears disappeared. "Hey!" She struggled against his grip. "You haven't seen me in two months and *that* is what you say first? If I stink so much, then let me go."

Kai grinned, only tightening his arms around her, and pressed a kiss to her neck. "Not a chance."

His kiss made the fight go out of her. She slumped in his arms, then twisted around so she could embrace him back. He squeezed her so tightly she could hardly breathe, and all she could think was: *Home. Home. I'm home.*

He leaned down and kissed her—long, lingering, and full of hope. "I missed you, Partial."

"You can't call me that and expect me to say sweet things back to you."

He grinned and flicked her nose, earning a scowl. "See? Life is so much better when I can insult you to your face instead of via missive."

"Don't make me wish you'd stayed away."

"Don't be ridiculous, love. *That* is impossible."

Aranya huffed, but couldn't resist standing on her toes to give him one more kiss. That one kiss turned into another until she almost forgot she still stood on the wardpost porch. Then a familiar voice drawled: "Look, this is a beautiful reunion, but I have been patiently waiting my turn, and at this point, Kai is just being selfish."

Aranya's jaw dropped as Kai pulled away, lips twisted in a smirk. "So, my coming early might not be the only surprise."

But Aranya was already stumbling out of Kai's arms and barreling straight toward the stocky, bearded wielder. "Delan! Seven valleys, you have no idea how much I've missed you!"

She nearly knocked him over with the force of her hug, and he had to reach out and grab the porch railing to keep from falling. Then he was hugging her back, and that was when Aranya learned Delan gave surprisingly good hugs.

"Glad to see you back to causing trouble," said Delan with a chuckle. "I could hardly sleep a full night until Kai's letter arrived saying you were getting better."

He'd been that worried about her? She gave him one more squeeze before stepping back. Then she just stood there, looking between them like they might vanish into thin air if she looked away for too long.

Perhaps Kai saw something in her expression, because he stepped to her side and wrapped an arm around her shoulder. "So. Are you going to ask why we're here?"

Aranya couldn't help her smile as Kai dragged her down the street with Delan toward her tenement. They kept to the side of the road, letting carts and people pass. "Why, pray, are you here in Zushui, Kai and Delan?"

"Can't tell you." Kai winked at her. "It's top secret."

"In case you're wondering, *yes*, being on a mission with a lovelorn evanescer is just as trying as it sounds," said Delan. "And despite what lies he fills your head with, our mission is *not* top secret and is, in fact, of hardly any importance at all. It's a routine surveillance of communication between cities and Suguan. Quite boring, actually. I take it that Kai didn't tell you that one of the cities we were assigned was Zushui."

"No, he didn't." Aranya shot him a glare.

He only grinned. "I wanted it to be a surprise."

"Stop grinning so much, Kai. You look like an idiot."

"Can't a man be happy to see his wife?"

"She's not your wife, boy," said Delan at the same moment Aranya blurted, "I'm not your wife!"

"She *will* be. Same difference."

Aranya rolled her eyes even as her cheeks heated. They turned onto her street, and her tenement with its wicker gate came into view. "How long will you stay then? Don't answer that, Kai. I don't trust anything you say right now."

"At least a week," said Delan. "Though I'm a little skeptical of how *productive* certain members of our party might be."

"A week! This is like a dream come true! You both will *have* to come over every night. And tomorrow night, I'm making noodles for the wardens, so you'll have to come and meet everyone, Delan. Kai, I'm sure the rest would love to see you again."

"Have they had your noodles before?" Kai asked in alarm.

"Of course! We do this every week."

"Every week? Those poor wardens."

"You are just still sour because Ye Ye said mine were better than yours."

"Your grandcat can't taste the difference between noodles and foot."

"Shi Kai—"

"Enough, enough!" cried Delan, coming between them and shoving them apart. "Aranya, take us to your tenement. Kai, if you're so determined to prove your cooking skills, then *you* make us dinner tonight. I, on the other hand, would like to meet this Ye Ye."

"I'll warn you that his mind isn't what it was a few months ago," said Aranya. "So don't be alarmed if he tells you he spent the day shopping or went to a wedding or if he's missing his boat. Just ask him questions about his career or childhood and he'll probably have comprehensible answers."

It was hard, watching Ye Ye slip away day by day. It was far more difficult than maintaining a long-distance relationship with Kai. And though the grief would never fully leave her—she didn't really want it to, truth be told—she was no longer afraid of the inevitable.

Finding a family, one that extended beyond blood ties, made her stronger. When the day came for her to say her final goodbye to Ye Ye, her sorrow would be great, but she wouldn't face it alone.

That would make all the difference. It already had.

Delan squeezed her shoulder. "Well, good, because I want to see if his account of Butagin aligns with mine. And, to be clear, Kai and I will be staying at the local inn for the week, so we won't need a place to stay."

"Oh good, because if you wanted to stay with us, you'd have to sleep on the floor."

"The floor sounds fine," said Kai.

"You are *not* staying with her, boy," growled Delan. "Fathers spare me. I'm not looking forward to chaperoning an evanescer this week."

"I promise to be on my best behavior," said Kai.

"Don't lie to me. Nothing you say will make me lower my watch."

Kai evanesced from the opposite side of Delan back to Aranya's side, bending down to whisper in Aranya's ear, "He's just jealous." Then he planted another kiss on the side of her face. She couldn't help but grin as warmth swelled in her chest.

Home.

Home was Kai's kisses. Home was Delan snapping, "Jealous of *what*, boy? I'll remind you that I've been *very* happily married for many years now." Home was the sound of the gate creaking open to her tenement, the groan of wood as the three of them walked down the hallway until they reached her familiar door. Home was the slow smile that spread across Ye Ye's face when she entered and went to his bedside as Peng packed up for the day.

Ye Ye's voice was rough and weak, but still discernable as he squeezed Aranya's hand. "Oh, you've brought Yuhan again!"

Kai quirked a grin. "*Yuhan* is about to make you some delicious noodles. And this time, you're going to agree that they're better than Aranya's, understood? Delan will back me up."

Home was here. Home was now. And Aranya intended to savor every minute of it.

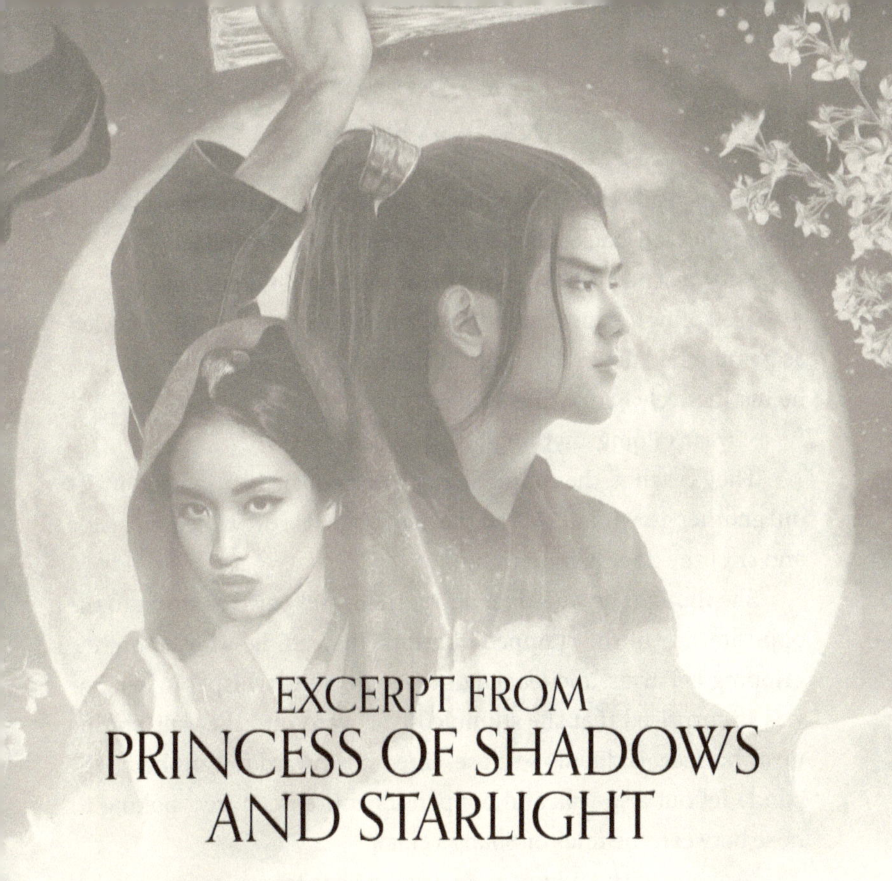

EXCERPT FROM
PRINCESS OF SHADOWS AND STARLIGHT

RIGHT BEFORE THEY reached the stairs, a hand reached out and snatched one of hers. Meiling started so hard she elbowed Shang's stomach in her attempt to pull back. Behind her, his sharp intake of breath mingled with a grunt. She found herself staring at a bearded man, seated between two women wearing more face paint than even her mother during the festivals. His thin eyes crinkled. He held her hand, turning it upward and tracing a finger down the length of her palm. She shuddered, trying to yank away.

"Get your filthy hands off my wife," Shang snarled.

The bearded man released her. He grinned, and cunning sparked in his eyes. "Soft hands," he said quietly, meeting Meiling's terrified gaze with a cool confidence that sent chills racing down her spine.

Shang immediately drew her away, all but dragging her with him up the stairs. As if she wanted to linger any more than he did! She was just as ready to be free of these frightening men as he was—and the way her low back ached with the strain of the panda.

They reached the top, both breathless for different reasons.

"You draw too much attention," he half-whispered, half-growled as he marched down the dimly lit hallway. The ceilings were so low, he instinctively bent while walking.

"I wasn't doing anything!"

They reached the room. Shang inserted the key, jangled it, let out another growl, and shoved the door open. He drew Meiling inside and shut the door behind them.

She thought he would let her go then, and perhaps storm to the opposite side of the cramped quarters. Instead, he whirled on her, gripping her arms, and leaned down so he could whisper to her. She was so surprised that she stumbled backward into the wall, staring up at his face, suddenly so close, tilted downward toward hers. The panda let out a squeak and popped its entire head free, poking its nose between the folds of Shang's cloak.

"Anyone with an ounce of sense in that tavern could see that you're high born. Anyone could—"

"What? *How?* I'm wearing commoner's clothes and I'm pregnant with a panda!"

"Because you *glide* everywhere. Disguise is more than clothes, Highness. You can't carry yourself like an elegant princess if we're to have any hope of getting you to Liafugan alive."

Her lips parted; eyes locked on his. Glide? Elegant princess? Was the way she walked that obvious? She'd never thought . . .

Then his hands began running up and down her arms, her hands, her waist, and her panda as though checking for injuries. His voice was low when he spoke again. "Did any of them hurt you?"

For a second, she was too stunned to respond. She shook her head wordlessly.

His eyes returned to hers, held her gaze for several long seconds, then he dropped his hands and turned away, clenching them into fists. She dragged her attention from him to note the sparse, cramped quarters, which included only one bed.

The panda sniffed. Did it care about mustiness?

"Why would we not be able to make it to Liafugan? If they knew who I was, they would just avoid us more," Meiling said, her voice a tad high-pitched and squeaky as she struggled to untie the knot to release the panda.

Shang had crossed the room toward the window and was fiddling with the latch. At her words, however, he paused. Tilted his head half back toward her. Then he returned his attention to the window. It sprung open.

Why was he opening the window? It was starting to rain.

"Because," he said, keeping his tone quiet, "royal blood is still royal, even without magic, and people find many uses for it."

Her cold fingers struggled with the knot, and the panda squirmed. "Just be patient. I'm trying," she mumbled to it, going to pat its head to make it stop moving so much.

It bit her.

Meiling yelped, more from surprise than pain. Shang spun toward her.

"It bit me, naughty thing," she said, glancing at the side of her hand to make sure it wasn't bleeding. "It won't be patient while I untie this, and it'll hurt itself if it keeps struggling!"

As if on cue, the panda let out a shriek and flailed its one free paw, gnawing on its sling and drooling on Meiling's clothes. Shang's glower only darkened, as if to say, *See? This is why we can't bring the stupid panda along.*

He crossed the distance between them. With a flick of his fingers, he unclasped the cloak and pulled the trailing garment from her shoulders. Her heart skipped a beat when his arms went around her, his deft fingers working the knot at her low back. She tried not to register that the only thing separating them was this squealing panda, that Shang's mouth hovered only a few inches above her shoulder as he worked. Tried not to think as the smell of a clear winter day washed over her, wrapping around her like a quilt.

Apparently, the knot gave him trouble too, because when she stole a glance at him, his brow furrowed, and his fingers kept working at her back. Sensing her gaze, his eyes slid to hers. His hands stopped moving.

"What?" he growled.

Was she staring? Were her eyes too wide? Was she even breathing?

"Nothing?" she squeaked.

The knot gave, and Shang caught the panda before it fell, easing away from Meiling. She sucked in a greedy lungful of air, suddenly desperate. Then she remembered her robes gaped open and hurried to retie her sash before her face colored too deeply.

Flapping sounded outside of the window. A hawk flew through the opening and immediately transformed into a livid Fen.

"One room? You only got one room?"

MORE FROM ANASTASIS BLYTHE

THE ZHENINGHAI CHRONICLES

Maiden of Candlelight and Lotuses

Guardian of Talons and Snares

Warrior of Blade and Dusk

Princess of Shadows and Starlight

Captive of Twilight and Treachery

Daughter of Darkness and Dreams

ABOUT THE AUTHOR

Anastasis Blythe makes her home in central Texas with her husband and their two adorable but rather whiny cats. When she's not writing, she is reading an unhealthy amount of fantasy novels, daydreaming about future books, and trying to keep up with the laundry.

If you would like free novels, regular behind-the-scenes updates on her writing, and an early peek at new book covers, join her community at Patreon.com/AnastasisBlythe.

CONNECT WITH ANASTASIS ONLINE AT:

Website - AnastasisBlythe.com

Instagram - @AnastasisBlythe

Facebook - Anastasis Blythe

Goodreads - Anastasis Blythe

www.ingramcontent.com/pod-product-compliance
Lightning Source LLC
Chambersburg PA
CBHW020241030826
48979CB00030B/2392/J

9781960606020